AN UNEXPECTED ENEMY

Stepping from the privy room, Dahl broke open the shotgun on his way to the hole in the front wall where the balcony doors had been. Keeping watch on the street below for Big Chicago, he pulled out the two spent loads and replaced them with two fresh rounds from his duster pocket. Catching a glimpse of Big Chicago moving across the street in a crouch, gun in hand, Dahl snapped the shotgun shut quickly and cocked both hammers.

But as he raised the weapon and took a step forward onto the balcony, behind him he heard Geneva Darrows scream, "You son of a bitch!"

He turned in time to see her raise Curly Joe's Colt with both hands and fire. . . .

FIGHTING MEN

Ralph Cotton

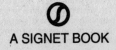

A SIGNET BOOK

SIGNET
Published by New American Library, a division of
Penguin Group (USA) Inc., 375 Hudson Street,
New York, New York 10014, USA
Penguin Group (Canada), 90 Eglinton Avenue East, Suite 700, Toronto,
Ontario M4P 2Y3, Canada (a division of Pearson Penguin Canada Inc.)
Penguin Books Ltd., 80 Strand, London WC2R 0RL, England
Penguin Ireland, 25 St. Stephen's Green, Dublin 2,
Ireland (a division of Penguin Books Ltd.)
Penguin Group (Australia), 250 Camberwell Road, Camberwell, Victoria 3124,
Australia (a division of Pearson Australia Group Pty. Ltd.)
Penguin Books India Pvt. Ltd., 11 Community Centre, Panchsheel Park,
New Delhi - 110 017, India
Penguin Group (NZ), 67 Apollo Drive, Rosedale, North Shore 0632,
New Zealand (a division of Pearson New Zealand Ltd.)
Penguin Books (South Africa) (Pty.) Ltd., 24 Sturdee Avenue,
Rosebank, Johannesburg 2196, South Africa

Penguin Books Ltd., Registered Offices:
80 Strand, London WC2R 0RL, England

First published by Signet, an imprint of New American Library,
a division of Penguin Group (USA) Inc.

First Printing, May 2010
10 9 8 7 6 5 4 3 2 1

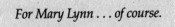

For Mary Lynn . . . of course.

PART 1

Chapter 1

Arizona Territory

Sherman Dahl looked down from atop the high trail at the small cabin standing perched on a rocky turn twenty yards above the braided waters of Panther Creek. He'd observed the cabin and its occupants for the past few minutes, hearing the harsh talk and laughter of drinking men, and a woman's worried voice rising from within the midst of it.

Dahl had already slipped his rifle from its saddle boot and laid it across his lap. But when he heard the woman's voice turn into a plea, followed by a short scream that ended with a resounding slap, he cocked the rifle's hammer and nudged his big chestnut bay forward on a downward winding path through a tangle of bracken and scrub cedar.

"You dirty sons of bitches!" Dahl heard the woman cry out as the cabin door burst open. "I hope you all rot in hell!"

Dahl stopped his horse again and sat still as stone, watching the woman run staggering from the rickety front porch down to the creek's edge, naked, holding a flimsy wadded-up blouse to the middle of her chest. From the open door, he watched Arliss Sattler step out onto the porch, bare chested, a bottle of rye hanging from his fingertips.

"That's right, whore—you wash yourself up some and get back in here," Sattler called out to the woman. "The night ain't even started yet." He laughed heartily; a gold Mexican half-moon ear ornament jiggled on his earlobe.

Dahl stepped the big chestnut bay sideways enough to conceal both the animal and himself from clear view. Yet, even as he quietly did so, he saw Sattler's face turn up toward him and move slowly back and forth, scanning the shadowy evening trail.

From inside the cabin a drunken gunman named Pete Duvall called out, "Don't let her get away, Arliss. I ain't had my turn at her."

"Don't worry, Pete. She can't get away from here until we let her go," said Sattler as he continued to scan the trail in the grainy evening light.

"What are you looking at up there, Arliss?" asked a gunman named Lou Jecker.

"Nothing to concern you, Lou," said Sattler. "I'm just looking, is all." He spat, ran his hand across his mouth and finally turned his eyes away from the trail where Dahl sat watching, having eased his Winchester stock up against his shoulder in case Sattler spotted him.

"Hell," said Duvall to Jecker, "pay Arliss no mind. He's been edgy as a damn cat ever since we turned Birksdale on its ear and that rancher's little gal got shot." He eyed Sattler as the bare-chested gunman turned away from them to watch the woman splash cold water all over herself and dry herself on the wadded-up blouse. "I think Curly Joe needs to come up with some jobs that require less killing. I'm of a notion that Arliss, here, doesn't like dirtying his hands with it."

"Don't you concern yourself with what I like or don't like, Pete," Sattler said over his shoulder. "I'll kill anybody that gets in my way, same as any other man in this line of work." He paused, then added, "Killing that little girl was something that never should have happened. It didn't make me a dime richer. Did it you?"

When Sattler's head turned back toward the open door, on the trail above Dahl took the opportunity to nudge the big bay farther out of sight and down along the trail toward the cabin.

"No," said Duvall. He stood up and walked closer to the open door, stuffing his shirt back into his open trousers. "But Curly Joe likes for us to drop one now and then just to keep folks on their toes. Once word gets around, it shows the next town we ride into that everybody best steer clear and let us alone, else we *will* put somebody in the dirt." He grinned crookedly.

"That's not what it showed me," said Sattler. "What it showed me was that from now on, we can forget about ever giving ourselves up and going to prison. All that's waiting for us is a rope." Then he shouted out to the woman, "Hurry up down there. We're all waiting to get back to it."

"I'm coming—keep your drawers on!" the woman shouted in reply. But as she dipped water in her hand and washed her forearm, she kept her head lowered and searched the rugged, sloping hillside behind the cabin, looking for her best escape route.

"Let Curly Joe hear you talking about giving yourself up and you'll wish somebody would hang you," Jecker said to Sattler.

Sattler turned enough to give Jecker a dark stare and say in a threatening manner, "I never said a damn thing about giving myself up, and I'll burn down any sumbitch who tells Curly Joe that I did."

"We're just talking here," Jecker said, backing away from the matter. He gave a shrug, with a show of his broad, empty hands. "Alls I'm saying is that Curly Joe figures we're in this until they ride us down. There's no giving ourselves up. You should have known that when we joined up."

Sattler let it go. He shook his head and took a long swig of whiskey. When he lowered the bottle and let out a hiss, he wiped his mouth and said, "Killing innocent bystanders is bad business. The whore says that little girl's pa is J. Fenwick Hatton."

"Do you mean James Fenwick Hatton of the Western Pacific Rail Lines?" Jecker asked, his expression turning to one of dread.

"Yep, one and the same," said Sattler. "He also owns one of the biggest cattle operations in this whole territory. His girl was in town shopping with the family's housemaid. Hatton was off somewhere. But he's back by now, I expect, to bury his daughter—knowing it's Curly Joe's gang who killed her in the street."

"So that means . . ." Duvall let his words trail as he contemplated what Sattler had said.

"It means this time Curly Joe has gone and killed the wrong innocent bystander," Sattler said, finishing his words for him. "Hatton has a bunch of his men on our trail right now. You can count on it."

"A bunch of men?" Pete Duvall ventured a nervous laugh. "What, you mean a posse of range hands? I believe we can fight our way through them, no trouble at all." He looked around at Jecker and at a silent Chicago gunman named Chester Goines, also known as Big Chicago, for support. Jecker gave him only a worried look. Goines, who had sat quietly listening, continued to do so with a stonelike stare, his black derby hat cocked jauntily on his forehead. Finally he offered, "I wasn't with you on that job, men, so I'm not worried about it."

"But you're with us now," said Jecker. "If somebody comes looking for our blood, you won't run out on us, will you?"

Big Chicago gave him a look. "I've never run out on a pard in my life. I don't care if Hatton or anybody else sends an army of saddle bums and ranch hands. I'll stick."

"If you think a powerful man like J. Fenwick Hatton only has a few saddle bums and ranch hands working for him, you're not long for this earth, Chicago," said Sattler. He turned toward the creek in the evening gloom and called out, "Get on back up here, whore, before I come drag you back by the hair." He looked back and forth along the darkening creek bank. "Where the hell is she?"

"A man like Hatton gets whatever kind of help he's willing to pay for," Jecker put in, looking around at the faces of Duvall and Goines. "In a case like this, his daughter and all, I'd say he'd hire the devil in hell to ride us down, if the devil's for hire."

"Damn it, the whore's gone!" said Sattler. He reached inside the open door, snatched his gun belt from a wall peg and slung it over his bare shoulder. "Come on—help me find her!" Seeing the other three rising too slowly to suit him, he cursed, turned and bounded down off the porch and out across the rocky yard.

A hundred yards from the cabin, the woman heard them coming, running fast. "Oh God!" They were onto her now, she knew, gasping for breath as she pulled herself upward. They would catch her and they would kill her—

"Stop, whore," Arliss Sattler demanded, "or I'll cut your damn throat!"

She clawed and dragged and kicked her way farther up the steep, rocky hillside, making little headway, like someone trying to run in the midst of a bad dream. She wore no shoes and no clothes, save for the wet, flimsy blouse she'd managed to pull over her head on her way. The whiskey, some of which she'd drunk willingly and some of which had been forced upon her, had her struggling to clear her mind.

Yet, in what seemed as if only a second later, she

heard boots pounding right up behind her through the loose, shifting gravel. "Where do you think you're going, whore?" said Sattler, grabbing her from behind by her blouse.

"Turn me loose," she pleaded drunkenly as the blouse ripped up the back and became a tangle of torn cloth around her neck and under her arm.

Being larger, more powerful, more sober and more able to run across the rocky ground because of his boots, Sattler had overtaken her easily. He held her firmly as the two slid down a few feet through the sharp, loose gravel. "Yeah, I'll turn you loose," he said roughly. He threw her over onto her back and slapped her hard across her face. The world seemed to explode inside her head.

Behind them, halfway across the yard, Jecker called out, "Give it to her right there, Arliss. Damn her deceitful ass."

"Break her damned neck," Duvall shouted drunkenly, the three men stopping only a few feet apart, their guns drawn and cocked.

"Step aside," Jecker called out to Sattler. "I'll put a bullet in her leg—see how she runs then."

"Uh-uh," said Sattler, dragging the woman to her feet. "She agreed to come out here and spend the night. That's what she's getting paid for and that's what she's going to do." He gave her a hard shove down the few remaining feet of rocky hillside and back across the boulder-strewn yard.

"We always get what's coming to us, woman," Jecker

said as she staggered past him. He slapped a hard open palm on her bare buttocks.

"I say we all do her right here, right now," said Duvall. He swung an open palm at her behind in the same manner, but missed and almost fell before catching and righting himself.

"No," said Sattler, "get her inside and keep her there." As he spoke he looked around warily at the high ridges above them. "There's something out here that gives me the willies." He pulled his Colt from its holster and gave the woman a rough jab forward with the hard steel barrel. But as she staggered toward the cabin, he kept the gun out as if he needed the security of it in hand.

Inside the cabin, Sattler gave the woman another hard shove that sent her tripping to the edge of a low-standing cot topped with a thin, dirty blanket. "Get started, whore," he said coldly.

"Plea-please, Arliss," the woman stammered, gesturing a hand up and down her scratched, scraped and battered body. "Look at me. I'm all dirty. I'm bleeding. Let me get cleaned up some."

"Naw, we already tried that. Remember?" said Sattler. "Now hit that cot and get your heels up," he demanded. Without turning to the others behind him, he said, "Goines, get over here. It's your turn."

But the Chicago gunman neither stepped forward nor replied. Jecker and Duvall both looked back at the wide-open doorway, seeing no sign of Goines, but hearing the sound of hooves pounding away in the growing darkness.

"Where the hell is Big Chicago?" Sattler asked, turning himself toward the waning sound of the hoofbeats.

The three froze in place as the door swung shut with a loud screech. From behind the door a tall figure in a long black riding duster stood against the cabin wall, a Winchester rifle in his left hand. He held it at belly level on the three stunned gunmen. In his right hand he held a black-handled Colt cocked and aimed in the same manner.

"What the . . . ?" said Sattler, his Colt still in his hand. Jecker and Duvall both still held their guns cocked and ready.

"Hey . . . ," Sattler managed to say in a calm, even tone of voice, "I bet you're one of the men Hatton sent to take us down." To Duvall he said, "See, Pete? What'd I just tell you? This is what comes from killing bystanders."

"Yeah," Duvall said, "I expect you were right about that."

Beside Duvall, Jecker took a slow, measured step sideways, noting how the barrel of the stranger's Winchester followed right along with him. "Yeah, but he only sent one man to take us in? That doesn't strike me as too smart on Hatton's part."

"He didn't send me to take you in," Dahl offered softly. He knew that having their guns in their hands would give them confidence, make them think they had an edge. That was all right. He'd anticipated it. He wasn't here to talk them down and capture them. He was here only to kill them—nothing more.

"You sure enough picked a tight place for a fight

here," said Sattler, gesturing with his dark eyes about the small, confined cabin. "Like as not, none of us is going to live through this."

"Nothing's perfect," Dahl said in a calm, almost soothing tone.

"This woman will die too," said Jecker, getting worried, looking down the Winchester barrel from only a few feet away. He felt his whiskey wear off quickly.

"Maybe," Dahl said softly. "We'll have to see how it goes."

Duvall started to speak, but before he could form a word, a streak of blue-orange flame exploded from the barrel of the Winchester. There was nothing to talk about, Dahl knew. His bullet lifted Jecker backward and slammed him against the wall above the cot. The woman screamed and tried to roll away as the dead outlaw's blood sprayed her and his body fell limply on top of her.

Sattler and Duvall instantly acted as one, their Colts coming up fast and firing. From beneath Jecker's body, the woman saw a streak of fire reach out from Sattler's Colt and seem to explode on the stranger's chest. But the stranger wasn't the least put off. He fired the black-handled Colt twice, thumbing the hammer back for each shot, taking quick but accurate aim as Duvall fanned three wild shots straight at him, kicking up pine splinters on the wall beside his head.

Dahl's first shot hit Sattler in the heart and sent him backward onto the foot of the cot, causing the woman to scream and kick wildly, as two dead men were now on top of her. As the cot broke under the weight, Dahl's second shot, deliberate and well aimed, hit Duval squarely in his forehead as the black outlaw wildly fanned his fourth and final shot, and sprawled dead on the dirt floor.

Chapter 2

In the ringing silence, amid the strong smell of burnt gunpowder and spilled whiskey, the woman struggled with the heavy bodies atop her until she flung a bloody gunman's arm from her face and looked out from the broken cot beneath the tangle of arms and legs, like a raccoon checking outside its lair before venturing out.

"Hey, over there," she said in a raspy voice, "can I get a hand here? I'm being crushed."

Sherman Dahl stood leaning back against the bullet-scarred wall, his rifle and Colt hanging loosely from his hands. As the woman stared at him and started to say something more to get his attention, she saw him slide down the wall and sit, staring blankly back at her.

"My God, mister," she said, "you're hit bad, aren't you?"

Dahl let both guns fall to the dirt on either side of him. A string of saliva spilled from his lower lip. He gripped his chest with his right hand. His face had grown so red that it had begun to turn purple as he struggled and strained to catch his breath.

"Wait, hold on, mister—don't die! I'm coming!" the woman said, struggling more fiercely with the weight of the two dead men until she somehow wriggled from beneath them and crawled toward him. Then, just as she reached him, she saw his breath come back to him sudden and strong. He took it in with a hard, painful-sounding gasp.

"Here, let me see!" she said, moving his hand and throwing his duster open, looking for the bloody hole she knew she would find in his chest.

"I'm . . . all right," Dahl said in a weak, halting voice, trying to look into her face.

"Yeah, sure you are, mister," the woman said skeptically, still searching for the bullet hole. "I'm surprised you're not dead already. You will be if I can't get you to Pine Ridge. There's a doctor there, a sheriff too. We can tell him what happened here, how you acted to save my life—"

"No doctor," Dahl said, cutting her off. "No sheriff." He managed to wrap his fingers around her wrist, stopping her quest for the invisible chest wound. "I'm all right." He sounded better already.

She watched him stiffly pick up his Colt, slip it down into its holster and push himself up the wall to his feet. Seeing him try to get his shoulder out of his black duster, she said, "Here, let me help you. You came in here and saved my life, you."

Saved her life . . . ? Dahl stopped struggling with his

duster for a moment and stared into her eyes. "I came here to kill Curly Joe Hobbs and his men, ma'am. You happened to be here when I arrived." His voice sounded stronger but still pained.

"Well, you saved my life all the same," the woman said, undaunted by his words. She peeled the duster from his back and watched him unbutton his shirt with his left hand, having difficulty with the simple task. "At least let me help you out of your coat."

"Obliged," Dahl said, letting her take over, dropping his arms to his sides.

Still looking for a bleeding wound, she stopped in surprise when she opened his shirt and saw the quilted padding on his chest. "What's this?" She pulled her fingers back as if they had come upon something she shouldn't touch.

"A bulletproof vest," said Dahl. He looked down at the bullet-sized hole in the thick quilted padding. "The French military call it a *bouclier de balle*—a bullet shield."

The woman looked at him closely, unaccustomed to the mild, soft-spoken aura of the man. In spite of the deadly action she'd seen him take without hesitancy, she understood right away that this was no ordinary range hand or frontier drifter. "Trust the French for the latest in fashion, eh?"

Dahl ignored her attempt at wit. Looking away from her, he said, "Maybe you need to put on some clothes."

"Oh, sure," she said, as if she'd forgotten that she stood naked except for the ragged remnants of the blouse Sattler had all but ripped from her back. She looked up and down her blood-splattered body and instinctively covered as much of her breasts as she could with the ragged blouse. "I have some boots and riding clothes here somewhere."

Dahl reached up, unhooked a corner of the quilted vest and eased it to the side, revealing a large dark circle of swollen flesh already turning the color of fruit going bad. He sighed from the strain of lifting his arm against the pain in his deeply bruised chest. Then he slumped and let his arm fall.

"My Lord, look at you, mister!" the woman said, her attention back to him now as his legs went weak and he slid almost a foot down along the wall before he caught himself. "Is this the best it can do?"

"I don't know. I've never used it before," Dahl said, the hard impact of the bullet still affecting his voice.

"If it is, you ought to find the French sumbitch who sold it to you and beat the hell out of him." She steadied him for a moment.

Dahl moved his forearm from under her hand and said quietly, "There's no cause for that kind of language with me, ma'am. I'm not impressed by it."

"What kind of language?" the woman asked.

"The cursing, the blackguarding," Dahl said. "It's coarse and vulgar—it doesn't bode well for you in my regard."

She saw his eyes turn distant and detached, a man on the verge of passing out.

"Well, I'll be," she said, as if taken aback by his words. "Pardon me from now on." She hooked a hand onto her naked hip. In spite of his moving his forearm

from her hand, she stood prepared to steady him, knowing it was only a matter of seconds before he went down.
"There are men who pay me sizable sums of money to
say worse things than that to them."

"Like . . . those men?" Dahl said, fighting hard against
his dimming senses. He gestured a nod toward the men
lying dead on the floor.

"This had just turned ugly," the woman said in her
defense. "It didn't start out this way."

Dahl didn't seem to hear her. He stared at her, fading fast. "Aren't you . . . a who—"

He couldn't finish his words before a blackness drew
around him and pressed him back down the wall to the
dirt floor. "A whore?" the woman said, finishing for
him, taking his arms, sinking down with him, helping
to lighten his fall as much as she could. "Yes, ordinarily
that would be the case," she said as if he could still
hear her. His broad-brimmed hat tipped off his head.
She brushed a long strand of yellow hair from his face
and looked at him closely. "Tonight, I started out whoring, but it looks like I'm going to be in the nursemaid
business."

No matter how bad Sherman Dahl felt immediately
after the bullet had slammed into his chest, when he
awakened more than an hour later, the pain had grown
worse. He could barely lift his right arm—his gun hand.
His left arm was not much better, although he could lift
his hand enough to place it on his throbbing, swollen
chest and feel the heavy beat of his heart. He did so
carefully.

"Coarse language aside," said the woman, "I meant what I said about whoever sold you the bullet vest." She sat on the floor beside him, her legs folded under her, dressed now, her hair pulled back and pinned in place. She had spread a blanket on the floor and dragged him over onto it, nearer to the stone hearth. Dahl noted she had built a fire in the hearth. The heat felt good down deep in his bones, in his sore and tender chest.

"It did what it's supposed to do. I'm alive," he replied. He closed his eyes for a moment, then opened them and said, "I meant no offense, ma'am, what I said earlier. I was not myself."

"No offense taken," the woman said. "I saw the shape you were in."

"That doesn't excuse my rudeness," Dahl said, "and I hope you will accept my apology."

The woman managed to smile through a bruised lip that bore a half circle of teeth marks left there by one of the drunken outlaws. "You still saved my life, whether you meant to or not." She nodded toward a small dark room off to the side of the cabin. "I found a skeleton wrapped in a woman's shawl and shoved into a corner in there, earlier. That's one reason I decided to make a break for it. I figure she's what's left of the last dove they hired to come make a party with them."

Dahl only stared at her. She knew the kind of men they were, yet she had accompanied them there anyway.

Uncomfortable with his silence, she shrugged as if knowing what went through his mind. "It's a tough business. I know I should have been more careful. I'm only working out of the Eubanks Fair and Square Saloon until I can stake myself and get out of the lousy shi—" She caught herself and stopped. "I mean, this lousy *pig wallow*."

Dahl winced slightly, the pain in his chest still throbbing, but lessening some.

"I'm Lilly Jones," the woman said. "Most of the folks around here call me Knee-high."

"I'm Sherman Dahl. Pleased to meet you, ma'am," he said with an honest air of formality. "Is Knee-high a name of your choosing, or someone else's?"

"I don't have a pimp, if that's what you're asking me," the young woman replied matter-of-factly. "I did acquire the name because a miner from Riley once said he thought I'd been whoring since I was knee high to a short pony."

"I'll call you Miss Lilly, ma'am," said Dahl, "if it is all the same with you."

Dahl saw her actually blush. "Well, it suits me, if it suits you, Sherman Dahl. But just plain Lilly is more to my liking, if I get my say-so on the matter."

"Then Lilly it is," Dahl said in his quiet tone. By the look on his face, the pain in his chest appeared to have subsided. She saw the drawn look around his eyes had cleared some. He'd even managed to show a trace of cropped smile beneath a drooping mustache.

"Thank you, Sherman Dahl," she said, liking the pleasant, courteous nature he summoned from her. "I'll be honored to have you call me Lilly."

"Good evening, Lilly." He nodded stiffly, keeping up the polite banter between them.

"Good evening, Sherman Dahl," she replied. She liked his smile. It was closed and cautious; it came more from his eyes than it did from his lips. And while smiling did not appear to come easily to him, once there his smile lingered long enough to show that it was real. There was a peacefulness to him, she thought. But as soon as she thought it, she had to remind herself that she had watched him mercilessly kill three men within the confines of this small shack.

This soft-spoken man had given no regard for either her life or his own when the shooting had started. Yet now, she could see nothing harsh or violent in him. He was not at all the kind of man she had grown accustomed to in her line of work.

At first she had almost considered him a bit of a dandy. But no dandy could have done what she'd seen him do—could he? she wondered. But not for long. No, she told herself, this man was not a dandy. He was simply quiet and courteous. Was that so bad? No, it was not bad at all, not after all she'd witnessed from men, the miners, drovers, drifters and ne'er-do-wells she had come across in this rugged, merciless land.

Dahl looked at her, noticing that she seemed preoccupied in her thoughts. "Lilly," he said, his voice still courteous, still quiet, yet seeming to have taken on a more somber tone, "where is Curly Joe Hobbs? Why is he not here with the rest of his gang?"

"Oh . . ." She seemed to snap back from somewhere far away. "Curly Joe keeps a woman all of his own, Geneva Darrows, at the Eubanks Fair and Square, back in Pine Ridge," she said. "Leastwise, she makes Joe think she's all his alone, if you know what I mean. She's never turned down a poke for a poke. You know, a poke of gold for a poke in her bed."

"I understand," said Dahl.

"Henry Eubanks, the owner of the Eubanks Fair and Square, slips some customers her way any time Curly Joe's not around." She shrugged. "I suspect Joe even knows about it. But some men like Joe think so highly of themselves they fool themselves into believing they own a gal's heart—" She gave a mischievous smile. "So why not let them? Especially when it's a man like Curly Joe. He goes killing crazy when he sees anybody even standing too close to Geneva Darrows."

Dahl let her finish speaking, even though she had gone far beyond telling him what he'd wanted to hear. "I've got to get up and get going," he said, struggling to push himself upright in spite of the pain in his sore, purple chest.

"Why? What's your hurry?" Lilly asked, even as she stood up with him and steadied him a bit with a hand on his arm. "Curly Joe's not going anywhere."

"He will when Big Chicago gets to Pine Ridge and tells him he heard gunshots when he made his getaway," Dahl replied quietly.

"You know Chester Goines? Big Chicago?" Lilly asked.

"I saw his wanted poster," said Dahl. "He's the one I followed here from up along the trail. He was the last one to arrive here, and the first one to leave. Living on the run must've taught him to make an early getaway.

It doesn't matter, though. I'm not after him, unless he makes a stand against me."

"You saw his wanted poster? Are you a—a bounty hunter, Sherman Dahl?" she asked delicately.

"No, Lilly," Dahl replied, "I'm not a bounty hunter. I'm employed by a man whose daughter these men killed in a bank robbery a while back, right before Big Chicago joined up with them."

A paid killer . . . ? She had searched his eyes closely. She had judged his ways, his mannerism, his demeanor, none of which had given her any sign of him being such a man. "Oh, I see," she said. "So now you're going to go to Pine Ridge and kill Curly Joe Hobbs?" she asked in a conversational manner, as if it were the sort of question that came up frequently.

Dahl stared at her for a moment, then said, "Yes, I leave before first light, as soon as my horse is rested and I have collected proof that these men are dead."

"You're taking their bodies to town with you?" Lilly asked.

"Only enough to satisfy my employer," Dahl replied. He tried rounding his right arm to get it working. The pain in his chest caused him to wince and clench his teeth.

"But won't Curly Joe see you coming from a mile away?" she asked, misunderstanding his words. "Big Chicago has already warned him. All he needs now is to see you leading these three bodies into town."

"I'm not taking their bodies—only enough of them to show proof of kill," Dahl said, trying to keep his words as gentle as possible.

"Proof of kill?" Lilly asked.

Dahl only stared at her knowingly.

After a moment, her face took on a look of dread and horror. "Oh no!" She covered her ears with both hands. "I don't want to hear any more!"

"You're welcome to ride into Pine Ridge with me," Dahl said. He looked all around at the bodies, wondering where to start. Then he looked back at her. "But you best clean yourself up and get some sleep. Like I said, I'll be leaving before daylight."

Chapter 3

In the midst of a troubled sleep, she had half awakened to the feel of him nestled against her back. Lying in the heat of the open hearth fire, she had felt his arm move over her from behind and she had tucked it to her bosom and gone back to sleep, less troubled somehow. Yet when she'd awakened again, before dawn, he was not lying there and it came to her that he never had been.

"Sherman Dahl . . . ?" she whispered. She waited as sleep drifted away from her. She sighed and lay still for a moment, staring into the pale glowing embers. Her hand still pressed his arm to her bosom, but his arm had vanished and with it had gone the warmth of him, as she realized it had only been a dream.

She rose and pulled on her boots, then walked outside, wearing a large wool shirt Dahl had rummaged for her from one of the dead outlaws' saddlebags. She found him seated on a short stool, hunched slightly over a small, licking fire. In the soft glow of light, she saw a large sewing needle rise between his fingertips and tug on its thick thread, then go back down out of sight.

"Good morning, Lilly," he said without looking around from his work. "I hope you managed to rest well."

"Morning, Sherman Dahl," she replied, seeing his fingertips repeat their rise, tug and fall uninterrupted by her. She liked the way he did things, the way he brought a fresh mannerism out of her . . . a niceness of sorts, she thought. "Yes, well enough, thank you. And yourself?"

Dahl's answer was only a courteous nod as his sewing continued. If any pain lingered in his chest or his arms, he refused to let it show.

"There's coffee beans inside," Lilly said. "I can break some and boil us a pot?"

"I found them, thank you. I have a fresh pot waiting for you here." Dahl gestured a nod toward the small fire. It was not until he mentioned it that she smelled the aroma of fresh coffee. "I even have a clean cup waiting for you. Let me first put aside my work so you can get to it." He began the first motion of rising sidelong with a small bundle of cloth in hand.

"That's most considerate of you," Lilly said with a smile. But instead of waiting for him to move aside with his sewing, she said, "Don't get up," and stepped forward beside him, seeing the pot sitting in the edge of the glowing coals. "I can get to it."

"No, please—" Dahl said. He tried to turn away in time to keep her from seeing his handiwork, but he was too late.

She caught a glimpse of the bundle of canvas in his hand. "Are you repairing your vest?" But even as she asked, her words ended in a gasp as the flicker of firelight revealed his bloodstained fingertips and the wet crimson cloth.

"No," Dahl said. His hands fumbled, trying to hide their contents from her sight, but it was of no use. Four of the dead outlaws' ears twisted and turned on a thin rawhide string dangling from his hand. Another ear fell from the cloth and landed on the ground at her feet. She let out a short scream and jumped back as if he'd dropped a rattlesnake.

"I tried to hide them—" Dahl's words were cut short as she stopped him with a raised hand. Her mouth agape, she backed away, turned and ran back inside the cabin.

Dahl let out a breath, picked up the loose ear, sat back down and resumed his work. He wiped dirt from the ear that had landed on the rocky ground and strung it on the thin length of rawhide with the others. He did the same with the last ear. Then he held the string up and inspected it. Of the six ears, two were black— Pete Duvall's. Two were small and a bit pointed, one with a deep, jagged scar halfway down it—Lou Jecker's. The last two were Sattler's, one still wearing the gold Mexican half-moon.

Lilly . . . , he thought. He needed to go inside and say something to her, something to calm her down. He regretted her having seen this. His work was not something he took pride in. Killing was grim, dark and ugly, and yet killing was what he did. He did it, and he did not try in any way to justify it. What purpose would justifying it serve? He knew what he'd become, what his life had brought him to. He needn't delude himself.

A killer of men . . .

Yes, he needed to say something to her—to *Lilly*, he thought, liking the sound of her name in his mind.

He jiggled Sattler's half-moon ear ornament with his bloody fingertip. Then he tied the rawhide strip end to end, forming a circle, and laid the gruesome proof of kills onto the bloody canvas. He wrapped them and put the bundle down inside his saddlebags sitting on the ground beside his chair.

Inside the cabin, Lilly watched Dahl's black silhouette walk straight and steadily toward the open doorway in the first gray light of encroaching dawn. All right, she had been wrong about him, she told herself. It wasn't the first time she'd been wrong about a man. But it had been a long time since she had allowed herself to even think of one as anything more than a customer, a *client*, a means of her making her living.

Whatever goodness, kindness she thought she'd seen in this man was now gone. She'd managed to put it away, to get rid of any feelings she might have begun to have for him. He had saved her life. She had to give him that. But nothing more. If a round or two in bed would pay him in kind, she would give it up free of charge. But that was all she'd give—no more soft dreams of the two of them lying together in the heat of a warm hearth.

A string of ears, for God's sake . . . Be tough about this, she told herself. Her jawline tightened as she heard his boots step onto the porch and walk across it. But when he stepped inside and stopped, as if first seeking her permission, she sighed to herself and felt her toughness leave as hastily as it had been summoned up. Then he took off his hat.

Took off his hat . . . ? For her . . . ? What kind of man was this?

"I—I brought you some coffee, Miss Lilly," he said in a quiet tone. "May I come in?"

She stalled for a moment, wanting to object, searching her mind for a reason, but finding none. "Are your hands clean?" she asked, but even in asking she realized that she was past the shock of his bloodstained fingertips. She had seen worse, much worse, both last night and throughout her life.

"Yes," said Dahl, "they're clean—" He stopped himself and said, "That is, I washed them when I was finished. See?" He held both hands forward for her inspection, one holding the steaming cup of coffee, the aroma filling the small cabin.

"Yes," she said, and she looked away and put a hand to a loose strand of hair and looked embarrassed. "I didn't mean to ask you that. I wasn't prepared for what I saw you doing."

Dahl set the coffee on a battered table. "I'm sorry you had to see that—"

"No, please," she said, cutting him off. "It was just a shock. I'm over it now." She paused, then offered a short, nervous laugh. "I should be glad it wasn't their heads. Last night I thought that was what you meant . . . when I said 'don't tell me'?" She fidgeted and stepped forward toward the table. "I know some manhunters do—don't they?—take the heads back to prove they've done the job."

"Yes, they do." Dahl nodded and looked away himself, offering nothing more on the matter.

"It was silly of me," Lilly offered. She picked up the cup of coffee, blew on it and sipped it. "You told me what you do for a living. I should not have been so shocked."

Dahl dismissed the matter and went on to say, "I found your buggy under the lean-to. Someone took off the front wheels."

Lilly's face turned ashen for a moment above the coffee cup in her hand. "So I really wasn't leaving here alive. . . ." She let her words trail, considering what the grim outcome of the previous night could have been had this man not shown up when he had.

"But you are now," said Dahl. "I picked out the best horse for you, and set the others free. They'll fare well on the grass plains north of here." He said it as if he assumed that she might be concerned with the horses' well-being.

"That's good," she replied with a nod. She sipped the coffee and once again caught herself staring at him. His build was medium to slight, but *range hardened*, she thought, coining an old drover's phrase she'd heard countless times. His face and hands were seasoned and burned to the color of copper. His hair and mustache were the color of pale new wheat, his beard stubble darker, not yet exposed to the scorching sunlight.

"How long have you . . . you know"—she shrugged, uncertain of how to ask—"been doing this kind of work?"

"It seems like forever," Dahl said. Weariness showed in his pale blue eyes as he spoke. "I fought with a forward group of Northern cavalry in the war. I had a hard time settling into normal life afterward. I'd been a schoolmaster before that."

"Yes . . . ?" Lilly sipped the coffee and stared at him, wanting more.

"So I came back and taught school for a while," Dahl said, "but it didn't last." He reflected with a slight shrug; a veiled look of regret moved over him.

"Oh? You quit?" Lilly asked.

"Not exactly," said Dahl, "but there were circumstances . . ." He paused, then said, "A gang of rebels attacked the town and burned my school to the ground. I rode off with a posse searching for the men who did it. . . . I never managed to find my way back."

"Did you find the men?" Lilly asked, experienced in knowing how long to keep a man talking and knowing when to shut him up. Sherman Dahl hadn't talked this much in a long time, she decided.

"Yes, we found them," he said, and he elaborated no further on what became of those men. Instead he continued, saying, "Of course, catching them did not rebuild the school, or repair the damage they did to the town. Nothing ever repairs the damage such men as these do."

"I know," said Lilly. She watched his eyes. He would stop any moment now. This was as much as he would share about himself at this point, perhaps as much as he would ever share period.

But surprisingly he went on to say, "Instead of going

back to that small town, to my old teaching job awaiting me, I traveled all the way to Minnesota, visited
family, tried my hand at a few things. I sold farm im-
plements, brokered cattle, horses for the army." He
paused. "Eventually I found myself once again carrying a gun for a living."

Dahl sighed, almost as if the exasperated sound sum-
marized his entire life. "So here I am, stringing ears for
a living. Doing what I seem to be most suited to . . .
killing men like these, before they kill me."

Lilly thought about it. "You're an assassin, then?"

"There are those would say I am," Dahl replied. "But
I think of myself as a fighting man. My hope is that I
keep myself fighting for the right side. Fighting men
can go wrong so quickly they hardly notice it until it's
too late."

"A fighting man . . ." She pondered the title. A silence set in as a morning breeze swept past the front of
the cabin and moved on across the rocky yard. Finally
she asked hesitantly, as if fearing the disappointment
his answer would bring, "Are you—spoken for, Sherman
Dahl?"

He gave her a curious look.

Spoken for . . . ? As soon as she'd asked, she'd regretted it. *You're a whore, Knee-high Jones!* Good Lord! What
on earth had she meant asking a man such a thing as
that? She shook her head as if to regain her senses.
"What I meant is, are you—"

"Am I married. Betrothed. I understood what you
meant, Lilly," he answered in a way that made her ask-

ing seem all right. "No, I am neither. There is no woman in my life. I was once married, but it ended shortly before the war. My young wife died in childbirth, as did our child."

"I'm sorry," Lilly said gently. She set her cup on the table and took his hand. "I fear I'm prying too deeply where I have no right. . . ."

"It's all right." He shook his head slowly, his eyes closed for a second. "You're not prying. I offered. It's been a long time since I spoke to anyone on matters of this nature." He paused in contemplation. "A very long time." He paused again, then said, "At any rate, I never remarried. I never found anyone, I never tried. Now, as things are, I would not inflict this life of mine on a woman I care for." He managed to summon up a trace of his cropped smile. "It's hard enough on me."

She continued holding his hand, feeling its warmth against hers. There were things about him she wanted to know. There were injured places inside him. She wanted to help him heal those places. There were flaws and fractures within his nature and his life that she wanted to tell him with authority would be all right, things that she could *make* all right, somehow, given the time, the place, the two of them.

Here you go . . . , she told herself, studying his hand in hers. You saw the shooting, the men dying, the string of ears. Yet here you are, thinking about—

"Lilly?" Dahl asked her quietly.

"Yes?" she said, as if just returning from some distant place.

"May I have my hand back?" Dahl asked gently, giving her an expectant look. "It will be daylight soon. . . . Time to ride on."

"Oh! Yes," she said, turning loose of his hand quickly. "I'm sorry."

"Don't apologize, I enjoyed it," said Dahl. "But for now we have to go."

"Yes, I understand." She pulled herself together. "So you can ride in and kill Curly Joe Hobbs," she said.

Dahl turned and picked up his Winchester from where he'd leaned it against the wall in the night. "Yes, exactly," he said in a resolved tone, "so I can kill Curly Joe Hobbs."

Chapter 4

Big Chicago arrived late in the night at Pine Ridge. As soon as his horse's hooves touched the town limits, the tired animal tried instinctively to slow down to a walk. Instead, Chicago booted the animal on, straight to the Eubanks Fair and Square Saloon, a huge, garish red and yellow building standing at the end of a wide, empty dirt street.

Along either side of the street, flames from oil fire-pots still flickered on the fronts of buildings with a ghostly glow, even though most of the inhabitants of Pine Ridge had long since retired to their beds, cots and blankets. From the dark shadows of an alleyway, only a scrawny cat watched the gunman's arrival with any noticeable interest.

At an iron hitch rail, Big Chicago stopped the horse, stepped down from his saddle and spun the animal's reins around the rail. From a darkened room above the saloon, Curly Joe Hobbs stood naked, gun in hand, and looked down at the street as Big Chicago shook the sleeves of his riding duster and disappeared beneath the saloon's overhang.

From the big feather bed behind him, Geneva Darrows rose onto one elbow. "Who is it, Joe?"

"It's Goines," said Curly Joe, disgruntled to see the gunman in town. He knew that Chicago's presence at this hour meant something was wrong.

"Who's Goines?" Geneva asked.

"It's Big Chicago. Chester Goines is *Big Chicago*'s real name," said Curly Joe. "Damn it," he cursed under his breath. "This better be something awfully important."

"I didn't know that was his name . . . Goines," she said, as if trying the name out.

"You know it now," Curly Joe said gruffly. "Go on back to sleep. I'll see what he wants." He walked to where his clothes and gun belt lay over a chair back beside the bed. He hurried into his trousers and reached for his battered boots standing at the edge of the bed. "If they got out there with that whore and got drunk and burned my cabin down, I'll kill them. . . ."

At the bar, Henry Eubanks stood counting the night's take. But he instinctively circled his forearms around stacks of paper money, loose coins and small pouches of gold dust when Big Chicago burst through the batwings doors and stomped across the floor toward him, a grim, hard look on his dust-streaked face. "Whoa! What is this?" Eubanks said. Across the bar a stocky, bald bartender swung a sawed-off shotgun into sight.

Big Chicago came to a sudden halt and spread his hands in a show of peace. "Where's Curly Joe?" he said. "I've got to talk to him."

"That's no way to walk into a man's saloon this late at night," Eubanks commented.

"Where's Curly Joe?" the gunman repeated in a stronger tone. "I told you, I've got to talk to him." He stood firm, his derby cocked to the side, low over one eye.

Eubanks scrutinized him closely, then gave the bartender a look. The bartender's shotgun sank out of sight. Easing his forearms from around the money, Eubanks said to Big Chicago, "Joe can't be disturbed just now." He gestured a nod toward the stairs leading to the bedrooms on the second floor. "He's *busy*."

"The hell you say," said Big Chicago. "I'm talking to him." He started toward the stairs; the shotgun came back from under the bar; Eubanks stepped over quickly, blocking his way. The two met chest to chest. Chicago's hand squeezed around the handle of a Walker Colt tucked behind a black sash at his waist. Eubanks' fists clenched at his sides.

"It's all right, Henry. I'm coming," said Curly Joe from atop the landing rail above them. With his gun belt looped over his shoulder and his shirttails out, he started down the stairs.

Eubanks stepped aside, but with a hand raised, as if to hold Chicago in check until Curly Joe had descended the squeaking stairs and walked over toward them. "Ever get in my way again, barkeep, I'll shoot holes in your belly," Big Chicago growled just between himself and the saloon owner.

"I'll remember you saying that," Eubanks growled in reply, not backing an inch.

"Back here, Goines," Curly Joe said, jerking his head toward a table in a rear corner. To the bartender he said, "Stan, bring Chicago a bottle. . . . Bring two glasses."

"I didn't like having to wake you up, Joe," said Big Chicago. "But I figured I needed to."

Curly Joe slung his gun belt from his shoulder and sat down at the table. He kicked a chair out across from him. "Sit down."

Chicago sat as the bartender hurried over with a bottle and two glasses, which he stood on the table in front of Curly Joe, then disappeared. Curly Joe poured two shots of rye whiskey and slid one in front of Big Chicago with his left hand. His right hand rested on the tabletop near the butt of his holstered Colt. "All right, Goines, you've got about five seconds to make me understand why I'm down here listening to you while Geneva is up there." He gestured upward toward the bedrooms.

"There was shooting out at the cabin," Chicago said quickly. "I knew you'd want to hear about it." He snatched up the shot glass and emptied it in one gulp.

"Yeah, what kind of shooting?" Joe asked warily. "Was it drunken gunfire or something more serious?"

"This was no drunken gunfire," Chicago said, making up his own version as he went. "This had the makings of a posse to it—an ambush, I'm thinking."

"An ambush . . . ?" Joe considered it as he sipped his whiskey. "Where the hell were you when all this shooting started? Why weren't you in there with Sattler and the rest of them?"

"I was on my way here, Joe," said Chicago. "I was

all finished with the whore. I was riding back for more whiskey, you know, for the rest of them."

"You were going to ride all the way back here for whiskey?" Joe asked skeptically. "Then ride all the way back there?"

"Hell, I've ridden farther than this for whiskey, Curly Joe," said Chicago. "Like I said, I was through with the whore. I was ready to come back to town for a while anyway." He shrugged. "I thought you'd be damn glad I rode straight here to tell you."

But Curly Joe glared at him. "Why'd you ride straight here when the rest of them could have used your help at the cabin?"

"To warn you, Curly Joe," Chicago said in his own defense. "Look, for all I know, Sattler and them might have killed whoever it was came to ambush them. But if it didn't turn out that way, it wouldn't do you much good if I got myself shot down too. I thought I'd best let you know what's going on, in case whoever it is rode on in here after you. Tell me if I did wrong by coming here. I'll ride back out there."

"Naw," said Curly Joe, "forget about it." His right hand eased away from his gun butt atop the table. "You did right, coming here. If Sattler and the boys got ambushed, I expect it is best I be ready for whoever it is." He stood up and tossed back his whiskey. "Go round up Russell and Thatch. We'll make a street fight for whoever comes riding into Pine Ridge."

At midmorning, Dahl and the woman stopped their horses at a fork in the rocky trail. To the left lay Pine

Ridge; to the right lay a ten-mile stretch of grown-over stage trail that ran through a maze of buttes and tall rock ledges before swinging back to a newer trail on the far side of town.

At the fork, Dahl stood in his stirrups and looked all around, squinting in the harsh sun's glare. "I'm not riding into town just yet, Lilly," he said as he scanned the rugged terrain stretched out before them.

"If I had any say, you would ride away from here altogether," she replied. "If Big Chicago rode in and warned him the way you said he'd do, there's no telling how many guns Curly Joe will have waiting for you."

"I've considered that," Dahl said quietly. "But his gunmen have been waiting since before daylight. By now they'll be ready to let down their guard a little."

"Maybe," said Lilly, "but I wouldn't stake my life on it if I were you."

Dahl didn't answer. Instead he said, "I plan to ride around and get above town and rest awhile. Would you care to join me?"

"Yes, I'd like that," said Lilly. "Curly Joe is going to be all over me as soon as I ride in, and so will Eubanks. I'd just as soon put it off as long as I can. I don't want to slip up and say something that could get you hurt." She paused for a moment and considered her next words before saying them. "Besides . . . I like being with you, Sherman Dahl."

"And I with you, Lilly," Dahl said as he eased back down into his saddle and looked her in the eye. He kept a gentle gaze directed at her for a moment, then kept the mood of conversation from straying any further by pointing out across the sky to a higher ridgeline above the far side of town. "Is there a good trail leading up there?" he asked.

"Depends on what you call *good*," said Lilly, changing the mood right along with him. "I know some miners used to use it when they worked the passes on the other sides. Now they come in on the main trail." She eyed him curiously. "You want to go up there and look down on Pine Ridge?"

"Yes, that's where we'll wait out the day," Dahl said. "I'd like to get above town and watch the comings and goings—get a feel for the place." He nudged his chestnut bay forward.

Lilly rode along beside him. On their way from the cabin, he had told her why he was in pursuit of Curly Joe and his entire gang. Now that she'd had time to think things over, she asked, "What if you only killed Sattler, Duvall and Jecker? What if Curly Joe heard someone was coming for him and he managed to get away?"

"Then I would not have completed the job I set out to do, would I?" Dahl replied.

"You mean you wouldn't get paid?" she asked.

"It is not for pay alone that a man does this sort of work," Dahl said. "It only starts once a price is agreed to. But from there the money becomes, by far, the lesser issue."

"So I would be wasting my breath trying to talk you out of riding into Pine Ridge and facing whoever Curly Joe has lined up against you?"

"Reasoning is never a waste of breath, Lilly," Dahl said. "There is always something to be said for honest discourse, whether its content be taken to heart or rejected out of hand."

"Is there an answer there somewhere?" Lilly asked, uncertain of what he'd just said.

"No," said Dahl. He looked at her with his cropped smile. "It's only an attempt to keep you talking. I enjoy the sound of your voice."

She returned his smile. "Yet you're paying no regard to what I asked?"

"I've considered every word," said Dahl. "But your question is the one I had to resolve for myself long ago, before I considered carrying a gun for hire."

They rode on.

"Once resolved, you can never change your mind?" she asked. "Even if doing so might save your life?"

"I can't only carry out a job when it's safe and convenient to do so," he continued. "It's when the work gets dangerous and difficult that my principles come into play. Therein lies the difference between common thugs and fighting men. When I go on a job, the person who pays me knows that if I don't come back it will be because I'm dead, not because I have given up." He looked her up and down, then faced the trail ahead.

"Fighting men . . . ," she murmured under her breath, as if having difficulty accepting the kind of life he had revealed to her.

Midmorning had turned to early afternoon by the time they reached the high ridgeline on the far side of Pine Ridge and rode upward on a narrow trail overlooking the town. At a place where the trail widened and flattened behind a low rim of rock, they stepped their horses into the thin shade of a ledge overhang and rested out of the high, scorching sunlight.

She watched Dahl stand at the edge of the shade and stare down at the trail in and out of Pine Ridge through a long, battered army field lens. "What if Curly Joe isn't even there? What if he left before daylight and you've missed your chance altogether?" she asked, knowing he was watching for any sign of Curly Joe riding out of Pine Ridge.

Without turning to face her, he said, "Curly Joe's still there. If he has a woman there, he won't want to leave unless he has a better idea what happened out at the cabin. He has his place in town marked, like a pack leader. He'd look foolish riding out on Chicago's word alone and finding out later there was nothing to be worried about."

Lilly shook her head slowly, considering his words. "I don't know if all this waiting is making Curly Joe edgy, but it sure is working well on me." She sipped water from a canteen. "When will you ride in? I see that I can't say anything that will talk you out of it."

"Soon," said Dahl, still gazing through the field lens, watching an old man walk into town alongside a two-wheel donkey cart. Moments earlier he'd watched another old man walk in from the south trail, also accompanied by a two-wheel cart. "As soon as I'm certain his gunmen have stopped expecting me."

"What makes you so certain they *will* stop expecting you?" she asked.

"They won't stop expecting me altogether," Dahl replied. "But they'll tire of waiting for me, especially since they have no idea what to expect." He put her question aside and asked, "Tell me about these old men with their donkey carts?"

Lilly stood and put a hand above her eyes as a visor and looked down at the trail, the old man and his donkey cart looking as small as insects to her naked eyes. "They are what's left of the only independent miners left around here. Most everybody has sold out to the big companies. These old men dig for gold, silver, tin, anything that has a scale value on it. There's an assayer office in town who buys their diggings from them."

"So everyone here is used to seeing them come and go?" Dahl asked.

"Yes, you could say so," Lilly replied. "Why do you ask?"

He didn't answer right away. Instead he lowered the battered army telescope, closed it between his palms and held it down at his side. He continued to stare down at the town through the wavering sunlight.

Chapter 5

Across the street from Eubanks Fair and Square Saloon, a burly gunman named Bart Russell said to a smaller, thinner gunman standing bedside him, "Don't look over there now, Thatch, but Curly Joe is watching us from up on Geneva's step-out."

"Aw yeah . . . ?" said Morris Thatcher. He managed a quick glance up at the small balcony on the upper side of the Fair and Square. "Must be making sure we're doing our job." He grinned and jiggled the shotgun cradled in the crook of his left arm.

"Which I'll admit I'm a little puzzled as to just *what* that job is right about now," said Russell, also cradling a shotgun. "I don't know if we're watching for two damn men or two damn thousand. Chicago said 'posse.'" Russell grinned. "So it has to be more than three or four."

"That's my thinking too," said Thatcher. "But at daylight this morning, I expected we'd be dusting somebody's hide before breakfast. Now it's getting on toward sundown, and we ain't killed nothing but time. So I ain't sure what to expect."

"Me neither," said Russell. "I don't mind killing time either, so long as Curly Joe's paying for it. I can kill more time than you ever saw, if the price is right."

"Yeah, me too," said Thatcher. "And for Big Chicago or Curly Joe, either one, I can swing hell out of this shotgun if I'm put to the task."

"So can I," said Thatcher, "just so's we understand one another. Whoever rides in after Curly Joe will take a double load of scrap iron from me." He patted the shotgun affectionately.

On the balcony above the saloon, Curly Joe Hobbs stood barefoot and shirtless, rolling a black cigar in his mouth. He stared at one of the independent miners leading his donkey cart onto the main street. The miner slowed and seemed to return his stare for a moment, then lowered his face and walked on. Inside the open doors from the balcony, Geneva Darrows lay on the bed wearing a flimsy nightgown, having not bothered to dress with Curly Joe in town.

"Why can't you keep your nose inside this room, Joe?" she asked in exasperation. "You have men paid to keep watch. Let them *keep watch*."

Curly Joe didn't answer. But under his breath he said to himself, "If Chester Goines has lied to me, I'll feed him his own liver." He looked again at the approaching miner, then down at the two men with shotguns standing across the street in the shade, then at Big Chicago, who'd just stepped out of the barbershop with a fresh shave and haircut, his derby under his arm. "*Sonsabitches . . . !*" Joe growled. Giving Big Chicago a dark look, he snatched the cigar from between his teeth, turned and stomped back inside.

"Joe, stop it," Geneva demanded when he stepped inside. She looked up at him and spread open the top of her gown. Her large breasts spilled forward. "Come down here, hold these for me. It'll settle your nerves. . . ."

On the street, Chicago had stopped and said, "What the hell?" seeing the angry stare Joe had directed at him from all the way up on the balcony. Now that Joe was out of sight, he looked all around as if searching for what was wrong. Spotting Thatcher and Russell standing across the dirt street from the Fair and Square Saloon, he walked straight to them and said, "Hey, what are you two doing over here? You're supposed to be keeping watch out front of the saloon."

"We can't see nothing from there but the sun," said Russell. "We figured this time of day we best get over here in the shade, give ourselves an advantage."

"You *figured*, eh?" said Big Chicago angrily.

"Yeah," said Thatcher. "We can't keep watch if we can't see."

But Big Chicago wouldn't listen to reason. "Let me tell you both something," he said, pointing a thick finger at their chests. "Neither one of yas is paid to figure anything. I do the figuring, you do the watching. Now get back over there before Curly Joe jumps down my shirt."

Looking past the angry outlaw, Russell noted the man walking toward them with his donkey cart. "Hey, Chicago, take a look at this. It's one of the miners. . . ."

Big Chicago turned and saw the man walking toward them, his head lowered, his hat brim hiding his face. The man had broken from the usual path to the assayer's office and led the donkey cart across the dirt street, coming straight toward them. Seeing the ragged striped serape covering the man from his shoulder to his knees, Chicago called, "Hey you, Mexican, hold it right there."

The man didn't speak, but he stopped in the middle of the street and spread his hands.

"Watch for a trick, men," said Chicago, looking all around warily as he stepped out of the shade toward the man and his donkey cart.

"Watch for a trick . . . ?" Thatcher said under his breath to Russell as Big Chicago walked out onto the otherwise empty street. "What kind of trick have you ever seen out of one of these old geezers?"

Russell spat and stepped forward. "First time for everything, Thatch," he said, also taking on a wariness toward the man with the lowered head and empty hands. "It's what you don't expect that gets you every time."

In Geneva's bedroom, Curly Joe stood up from the edge of the bed, still barefoot and shirtless, when he and Geneva heard the knock on the door. "Jesus," Geneva said in disgust. Her gown lay spread open all the way down the front. She pulled it closed in a huff. "Just when I was starting to feel tingly all over."

"Who the hell is it?" Curly Joe growled, raising his Colt from his gun belt slung over a chair back.

"Joe, it's Chicago. I've got something you've got to hear for yourself," said the outlaw.

Curly Joe swung the door open, Colt in hand, and said in no pleasant voice, "You're starting to really aggravate me, Chicago. What is it?"

"One of the miners is downstairs," said Chicago. "He says he has something to tell you—a message from out at the cabin."

"From the cabin? All right, what's the message?" Joe asked, impatiently. He shot Geneva a look as she turned over on the bed with a show of interest.

"He wouldn't tell me," said Chicago. "He's scared half out of his wits. He says he'll only talk to the boss, meaning you."

"I don't like this," said Joe. "Who is this man? A Mexican? A Yank?"

"I can't say," said Chicago. "He's too afraid to even lift his face. He's standing down there right now, shaking in his boots."

"You mean in his sandals?" Geneva asked warily.

"Boots, sandals, either way he's shaking over being here," said Chicago.

"Don't go down there, Joe," Geneva said quickly. "I smell a trap bigger than hell."

"A trap?" Joe let his pride step out and take over. "If it's a trap, Geneva darling, let's get it sprung. I'm not worried about any sumbitch who shows up leading a donkey cart."

"You needn't worry, Miss Geneva," Chicago offered.

"I've got him covered. So does Russell and Thatch. If anything starts to look—"

"Hey!" Curly Joe said, cutting Chicago off in a sharp tone of voice. "She doesn't need to hear a damn thing from you."

Chicago backed off quickly. "No offense intended, Joe," he said. "Hell, if this is all about J. Fenwick Hatton's girl getting killed, I wasn't even there. I don't even have a dog in this fight. I'm only here to do whatever you want done."

"Then shut up and get behind me," Joe snapped. "Let's go see what this miner has to say." Carrying his Colt, he left his gun belt over the chair back and stomped barefoot out the door and down the side stairs to the street.

At the corner of an alley where the stairs met the dirt street, Russell and Thatcher stood with their shotguns ready in hand, the hammers already cocked and waiting. "Keep him covered, boys," Chicago said under his breath as he stepped past them.

"What have you got to say to me, old man?" Curly Joe demanded as soon as he approached the stranger, who stood beside his donkey cart, his head bowed beneath a ragged flop hat. "Look up so I can see your face." Joe stopped less than eight feet away, his Colt cocked and poised.

"Plea-please, Mr. Hobbs," said a nervous voice, "I don't want any trouble. I was told to say these words to you, from a man I don't even know."

"You know me, old man?" Curly Joe asked.

"I've seen you many times," the old miner said. "I've been digging in these hills and coming to this town for many years."

"And now you've become a messenger," said Curly Joe. "So, messenger, what have you got to tell me, from this man you *do not* know?"

The old miner raised his head slowly and glanced quickly and cautiously into Joe's face, then lowered his frightened eyes back to the ground. "He told me to tell you that he has killed your three friends, and now he's waiting to kill you, outside of town at the fork in the high trail. He said come alone."

"One man is waiting for us?" Curly Joe looked all around the wide dirt street with a sly grin.

"He said *come alone*, Mr. Hobbs," the old miner repeated.

"Yeah, right, I heard you," said Curly Joe. His sly grin widened. "Only one man, you say?"

"One is all I saw," said the miner. His expression said he wanted to be done with this and get on his way.

Curly Joe turned to Goines. "What do you say, Big Chicago? Was it only one man out there? Could one man kill those three?"

"I heard lots of shooting for only one man," said the gunman, staring hard and skeptically at the old miner as he spoke. "As drunk as they were, I can see how one man might do it if he caught them off guard."

"Yeah, maybe," said Curly Joe. He stared off in the direction of the fork in the trail south of town for a moment, then said, "But we're not drunk, and we're not off guard." He turned back to the old miner. "What does this man look like?"

"He's young," said the miner, "long yellow hair, a mustache. About as tall as I am."

Observing from the balcony above, Geneva called down, "Watch him, Joe. How do you know that's not *him* you're talking to?"

"Say! You're not him, are you?" Curly Joe said in a harsh tone. His Colt came up quickly, the tip of the barrel jammed against the miner's cheek.

"That's real damn funny, Joe," Geneva said with disgust. She turned in a huff and walked back inside her bedroom.

The old miner's knees buckled slightly. He almost fell. "Please, Mr. Hobbs, I don't want no troub—"

"Yeah, I know you don't want no trouble," said Hobbs, cutting him off again. "You already told me that." He laughed gruffly and gave the miner a push with his gun barrel. "You've delivered your message. Get out of my sight." As the miner turned to flee, Curly Joe gave him a rough kick in his behind. "Stick to mining, old man. Delivering messages ain't your strong suit."

Russell, Thatcher and Chicago joined Joe in laughter as the miner hurriedly gathered his donkey and cart and scrambled away, one hand on his sore rear. Along the dirt street the donkey brayed wildly and struggled against its lead rope.

"What do you say, Joe?" Chicago asked. "Are we going out there?" As soon as he'd asked, he glanced up to see if Geneva was still on the balcony, listening.

"What are you looking up there for?" Curly Joe

asked sharply. "It's not up to her to say where we're going. I'm the boss here. Keep your eyes on me."

"Sorry, Joe," said Chicago, having noted that Geneva had gone back inside. "Are we going out there?"

"Hell yes, we're going," said Curly Joe. "I want to know what the hell really happened out at that cabin." He cut Big Chicago a narrowed stare. "Looks like the only way I'll know for sure is if I ride out there myself and see if my men are dead or alive." He looked at Russell and Thatcher and added, "If we happen upon some lone sumbitch at the fork in the trail, and have to kill him, I suppose we can all handle that, can't we?"

"He's dead, soon as we get ourselves into scattergun range," said Thatcher, patting his shotgun. Beside him, Russell nodded in agreement.

"Good! Get our horses while I grab my boots and gun belt," Joe commanded. He turned and hurried back up the side stairs into Geneva's bedroom, slamming the balcony doors behind himself. Beside the bed, he pulled on his boots, grabbed his gun belt and threw it around his waist. Buckling the belt, he looked at the privacy curtain, beyond which were a chamber pot and wash pan. "Hurry up in there. I'm leaving," he said.

When Geneva gave no reply, he holstered his Colt quickly, stepped over and threw back the curtain. "Damn it, woman, I said—" His words stopped short.

Sherman Dahl stood facing him, his feet shoulder width apart beneath the long black riding duster buttoned up to his collar. In Dahl's hand was a sawed-off shotgun no different than the ones Russell and Thatcher carried on the street below. Against the wall of the small room stood Geneva, spread-eagle, her eyes wide in fright, a bandana tied tight around her mouth.

Seeing the look of stark, puzzled terror come over Curly Joe's face, Dahl said, "This is from James Fenwick Hatton." Then he pulled the trigger; the first hammer dropped.

"No!" said Curly Joe. He'd managed to snatch up his Colt, but it flew from his hand as the first blast picked him up and drove him backward across the room to the closed balcony doors. The second hammer fell. The blast picked him up from there and hurled him through the balcony doors, ripping out the doors, frames, curtains and all.

"Lord God!" shouted Russell on the street below. All three men ducked and looked up from the hitch rail toward the double explosions. Above them, Curly Joe, his body entangled in ripped white lace curtains, jolted through the balcony handrail and flew out in a red mist as if launched from the barrel of a cannon. Along with splinters of wood, strips of white lace and shards of glass, Joe's airborne body sailed out past a low overhang and dropped dead onto the street.

Stepping from the privy room, Dahl broke open the shotgun on his way to the open hole in the front wall where the balcony doors had been. Keeping watch on the street below for Big Chicago, he pulled out the two spent loads and replaced them with two fresh rounds from his duster pocket. Catching a glimpse of Big Chicago moving across the street in a crouch, gun in hand, Dahl snapped the shotgun shut quickly and cocked both hammers.

But as he raised the weapon and took a step forward onto the balcony, behind him he heard Geneva Darrows scream, "You son of a bitch!"

He turned in time to see her raise Curly Joe's Colt with both hands and fire repeatedly, the bandana off her mouth and hanging around her neck. The shots hit him hard, moving him steadily backward. The cocked shotgun slipped out of his hands as he stumbled off the edge of the balcony and plunged toward the ground below.

"I got this son of a—!" Geneva shouted loudly. But her words were also cut short when Dahl's dropped shotgun hit the floor butt first, angled straight toward her, and both hammers fell as one.

The double explosion picked her up and blew her through the wooden door out into the hall. Splinters, flesh, brain matter and blood painted a wide streak along the wallpaper as her body hit the top of the stairs and slid down five feet, backward, before stopping, her wide dead eyes seeming to stare at the saloon below.

Chapter 6

In the alley behind the saloon, Lilly Jones sat atop her horse, holding the reins to Dahl's big chestnut bay. Dahl himself had ridden in under a pile of blankets and supplies aboard the old miner's cart. He'd slipped off the cart and into an alley as the cart rolled along the street toward the saloon. He'd told Lilly to hitch his bay in the alley and get away from there, lest she get tangled up in his trouble. Lilly had arrived unnoticed, a woman leading a spare horse along the back alleyways of town.

But she had not followed Dahl's instructions to the letter. Instead of leaving his horse, she'd waited for him, holding her ground with the animals even as she heard the shots explode from the street. From her spot in the alley, she'd heard Geneva's voice call out loudly from around the side of the building. She continued to sit for a moment longer, until the double blasts of the shotgun roared again, followed by return pistol and shotgun fire, which finally unnerved her.

"That's it, I can't sit here doing nothing!" she said aloud to herself, gigging her horse forward, leading Dahl's bay by its reins.

At the front corner of the alley, she stopped for a second and saw Big Chicago and the other two men backing away from the middle of the street, their emptied shotguns smoking in their hands. Dahl lay half atop Curly Joe's mangled body. The dead gunman had served to break Dahl's fall. Unlike Curly Joe, whom the impact of the shotgun had launched out past the low overhang, Dahl had fallen first onto the sloped roof, then rolled off, down onto Joe's dead, bloody back.

"That's enough, men," Big Chicago said to Russell and Thatcher. "He's dead."

Oh no.... Lilly closed her eyes for a second, then nudged her horse forward.

As she drew close, Russell's eyes narrowed and he asked, "Who the hell is this?" Then, recognizing the woman on the horse, he exclaimed, "Hell, it's that whore, Knee-high. Wasn't she with the lot of yas out there at the cabin?"

"Yeah, she was there," said Chicago, giving Lilly a hard stare.

"Now we'll hear what happened," said Thatcher.

"Like hell we will," said Big Chicago. He threw his Colt up at arm's length, aimed it straight at Lilly's chest and pulled the trigger.

Seeing the gun aimed at her, too late to get away, Lilly winced and braced herself for the impact. Then she let out a tense breath as she heard the hollow click of the gun hammer fall on a spent round.

"Damn it to hell," said Chicago to Russell and Thatcher, "shoot her! My gun's empty!"

"So are ours," said Thatcher.

"Then load up, damn it!" Chicago bellowed. "Before she cuts and runs!"

"I'm not going anywhere," Lilly said, staring past the three at Sherman Dahl lying limp atop Curly Joe. "I saw what happened out at the cabin . . . this man shot all three of them, straight up. But it doesn't matter now. All I want to do is take him away from here."

Chicago watched impatiently as Russell and Thatcher reloaded their shotguns. "Are you two jakes going to shoot this whore or not?"

The two raised their reloaded shotguns toward Lilly at the same time. But this time before they could fire, Henry Eubanks and Stan the bartender stepped out through the batwing doors with raised shotguns of their own. "Hold it, gawdang it!" said Eubanks. "Nobody is shooting this whore. Knee-high is my *em*-ployee. Lower them scatterguns!"

Chicago raised his hands chest high. "Easy, Henry, she rode in with this sumbitch," he said. "I'll wager that's even his horse she's leading."

"So?" said Eubanks. "I don't give a damn if she was with him. It means nothing now." His hands tightened angrily around the shotgun stock. "If you go and take a look, you'll see Geneva Darrows is splattered out, bone to gut, all over the upstairs hall! Ain't nothing you can say that'll make me feel any better about it."

"It wasn't us who killed Geneva," said Chicago. "It

was this lunatic." He gestured toward Dahl, lying bloody and still on the ground. "He come here bent on killing Curly Joe. Geneva must've got in his way."

"I know he killed her," said Eubanks, his shotgun still up. "But I've lost one good whore already. I'm not about to lose another one today, unless you're prepared to take her place."

"Don't talk like an ass, Henry," said Big Chicago. He cooled down quickly and considered things. With Curly Joe dead, as well as the man who'd killed him, it made little difference what Lilly Jones had to say about anything. "All right, men, lower the meat choppers," he said at length.

"Are you sure, Chicago?" asked Russell. "You are the boss now, far as we're concerned."

As the gunmen, saloon owner and bartender stood facing one another, their weapons held at the ready, townsfolk began to venture forward from storefronts, tents and adobes.

Noting the bystanders approaching, Big Chicago said, "Yeah, go on, lower them. It's time we get into the wind anyway, before somebody else shows up with our names in their mouths."

Lilly stepped down from her saddle and led both horses over to Dahl, lying broken and still on top of Curly Joe. Eubanks and the bartender stood watching as Chicago, Russell and Thatcher gathered the horses, mounted and rode away at a trot. "You all right, Knee-high?" the bartender called out.

"I'm good, Stan. Obliged," Lilly said.

"You ain't coming back here, are you?" he called out, lowering his voice as if to keep Eubanks from hearing him.

Lilly only shook her head in reply.

"I thought not," said Stan. He sounded disappointed.

"Can you square it for me with Henry?" she asked.

"He's going to raise all kinds of hell," Stan said.

"Will you square it for me?" she repeated.

Stan shrugged. "It's squared," he said, and he waved her away with his hand as he turned and stepped back inside the saloon.

Stooping down over Dahl, Lilly laid a hand on the back of his bloodstained riding duster. "Are you all right, Sherman Dahl?" she whispered.

After a pause, she heard a single tight, dry cough; then his rasping voice said, "I've . . . been better."

"Are you bleeding anywhere?" she asked.

"I'm bleeding . . . *everywhere*," he said. "Except where I'm wearing . . . my vest."

"At least you're alive," she whispered.

"Yes . . . at least," Dahl rasped, not sounding overjoyed by his good fortune.

She breathed a sigh of relief and closed her eyes as if in a short prayer. She patted his back gently and whispered, "You lie still until I can get somebody to help carry you over to the doctor's office."

"I've . . . got to . . . get up. . . ." He tried to rise, but Lilly pressed him back down firmly.

"Lie still," she said. "You're in no shape to be getting up right now. You rest. I'm going to take care of you."

"No . . . there are things . . . I've got to do," Dahl whispered as gathering townsmen drew closer around them in the dirt street.

"What do you need to do that I can't do for you until you're back on your feet?" Lilly said. She kept him gently pinned down atop the dead outlaw.

"I need . . . Curly Joe's head," he rasped, "for . . . proof of kill."

"Oh . . . I see," she replied with a look of dread coming over her face. "Well, Curly Joe's head will just have to keep for the time being."

As the townsfolk drew in closer, surrounding her and the two bodies on the ground, Lilly said to a familiar face, "Arnold, have someone help you carry this man over to Doc Shelby's office. He's in bad shape."

"Bad shape?" said the broad-shouldered townsman. "Hell, I don't know how he can even be alive. I saw the men with shotguns both shoot him. . . . Chester Goines shot him too."

"Well, he is alive, and he's losing blood," Lilly said, not bothering to mention Dahl's bullet vest. "Now help me get him over to Doc's. See if Doc can keep him from bleeding to death."

The gray-haired doctor, Martin Shelby, had quickly taken Dahl in, and he immediately set about removing glass and splinters from the man's wounds. He stopped the bleeding from almost a dozen open cuts, none of which were life threatening.

Three hours later, he plucked another tiny piece of

scrap metal from Dahl's exposed upper arm and dropped it into a tin pan sitting on Dahl's chest. By now, the pan held a fistful of broken scrap iron and misshapen buckshot, all of which were covered by a thin coat of Dahl's blood.

"Improvement or not, this thing likely saved your life, young man," Dr. Shelby said, gesturing with bloody fingertips toward the bullet-riddled, buckshot-chewed vest piled in a ragged heap on a wooden chair beside the gurney where Dahl lay. "Everything that's happened to that vest would have happened to your body had you not been wearing it." He shook his head, a pair of long tweezers in his hand, and went back to probing the small bloody holes in Dahl's arm for more bits of iron.

"How did you ever keep from getting shot down before you owned one of these?" Lilly asked Dahl, standing back out of the doctor's way. She eyed the torn, chewed-up bullet vest.

"I'd say he *didn't* keep from it very often," the doctor put in, giving her a look over his shoulder. "From the looks of these old scars on his chest, he's been on the ground more than he's been on his feet." He bowed back into his work with the tweezers. "What'd you say you used to do for a living?" he asked.

"I taught school," Dahl replied.

"Go back to it," Shelby said bluntly. "You've got too many holes in you. This work will kill you if you let it."

"I don't plan on letting it," said Dahl, his voice only slightly strained by all the physical abuse he'd been through. "That's why I bought the vest."

"But now that your vest is torn to shreds, what'll you do?" the old doctor asked.

Dahl gave Lilly a look and replied, "Buy myself another one, first chance I get."

"I'd advise you to buy several, and keep them on hand," Shelby said. "As long as Chester Goines is still running loose, you'll never know when you're going to need one."

"I wasn't here looking for Big Chicago," said Dahl. "He just happened to be with Curly Joe's men when I got here. I spotted him first and followed him up to the cabin."

"I shouldn't say this," said Shelby, "being a man of medicine, such as I am. But you should have killed Chester Goines while you had him in your sights. If he even thinks you are after him, he'll not stop until one of you is dead."

"It's not as if I had him in my sights, Doctor," said Dahl. "I saw him taking a position across the street right before I fell from the saloon balcony. After that, there wasn't much I could do to stop him and his two men."

"I see, then." Shelby nodded, leaning in closer to Dahl's flesh, examining it for more bits of embedded scrap iron. "All the same," he said, "if you come across Goines, *Big Chicago* as you call him, like as not he'll try to kill you." Finding a likely spot on the tip of Dahl's shoulder, the doctor probed into it as Dahl winced from the pain.

When the doctor had finished, he washed the blood from his hands and said, "There, that's about the best I can do for you. No bones are broken, thanks to Curly

Joe breaking your fall for you." He gave a slight, dark chuckle and shook his head at the folly of what his years in medicine had shown him about the species of man. From his cabinet he took a hypodermic needle and spent several minutes readying it.

"What is that?" Dahl asked, eying the needle.

"It's hydrochloride morphine sulfate," Shelby answered. "Just a little something to make you sleep good for a while." With his thumb on the syringe, he plunged the liquid into Dahl's arm with authority.

"I need to be awake, Doctor," Dahl protested. "I don't like not having my wits about me."

"Then I'm afraid you're in for a disappointing couple of hours, young man. Because without a doubt, you are going to sleep."

Lilly stepped in as Dr. Shelby patted Dahl's shoulder and stepped back from him. She stood at Dahl's side as the doctor began rolling his shirtsleeves down and buttoning them at his wrists. "Don't worry, Sherman Dahl," she said. "I'll be right here the whole time. Nobody will come or go without my seeing them." She turned her head and looked at the doctor in anticipation.

"You're welcome to stay right here with him, of course, Lilly," the doctor said. He straightened his string tie and reached for his derby hat hanging on a wall peg. As Dahl drifted away on the powerful drug, Shelby said to Lilly, "I don't know what this man has done to deserve you, but he is a fortunate man indeed."

Lilly reached out a hand and brushed a strand of blond hair from Dahl's forehead. "No, Doc, I'm the one who's fortunate. . . ." Her words trailed as she looked down at Dahl's dozing face.

"I'm glad to hear you feel that way for a change, Lilly," the doctor said quietly. He wasn't sure she'd even heard him as he backed away, turned and walked out the door.

Part 2

Chapter 7

———

Santa Fe, New Mexico Territory

Six weeks had passed before a two-horse buggy pulled up in the circling path out in front of the J. Fenwick Hatton hacienda outside town. Assisted by Mexican house servants, Sherman Dahl and Lilly Jones stepped down from the rig. Owing to several deep scrap-iron wounds still healing in his upper left arm, Dahl's left forearm rested in a black cloth sling looped around his neck.

In Dahl's right hand he carried a wooden crate by its top brass handle. The crate held a large wire-sealed glass apothecary jar. From inside the jar, the head of Curly Joe Hobbs stared out at the world through a pickling saline solution, a dull but scornful expression etched upon his face for all eternity.

No sooner had Dahl and Lilly set their feet on the grounds than a silver-haired gentleman in a black swallow-tailed coat appeared as if from out of nowhere and bowed slightly at the waist. "Mr. Dahl, sir," the man said. "Madam," he said to Lilly.

"Lilly," said Dahl, "let me introduce you to Farris, Mr. J. Fenwick Hatton's personal assistant."

"Pleased," Lilly said.

The man acknowledged her with a curt nod, then directed his attention to Dahl and said, "Mr. Hatton awaits you in the summer house, Mr. Dahl." When he'd spoken, he centered an expectant gaze back on Lilly.

"This is Miss Lilly Jones," Dahl said easily. "She accompanies me."

"Yes, of course," said the houseman. "If you will both follow me, please." He turned and swept an arm toward a stone walkway leading around the side of the hacienda and toward a smaller adobe structure standing amid a garden of cactus, exotic plants and blooming flowers. Inside the entrance foyer of the summer house, Farris excused himself to go announce the two to Mr. Hatton.

As Dahl and Lilly stood waiting for a set of large polished wooden doors to open before them, Lilly whispered sideways to Dahl, "You seem right at home here, Sherman Dahl."

"Then I have fooled you, Lilly," Dahl said. "This is my second trip here. The first was when I took the job. I believe Farris knew why I was here. I don't think he ever expected me back."

"Yet here you are," Lilly whispered. She patted his forearm proudly. Then she took his flat-crowned black hat from his head and helped him hold it cradled against the sling.

Dahl gave a slight smile and whispered in reply, "And you right beside me."

In a moment the polished wooden doors opened in front of them, and Farris led them across ornate Mexican tiles to an open office where J. Fenwick Hatton stood up to greet them from behind a dark, gleaming desk. "Welcome back, Mr. Dahl. I understand you have brought me some good news." He gave a gesture to Farris and added, "Along with some *other items*, of course."

As Hatton spoke, Farris stepped over to Dahl and stood waiting while Dahl took a leather pouch from inside his linen suit coat and handed it to him. With the leather pouch in hand, Farris took the crate from Dahl by its brass handle, walked over and set both items on the edge of Hatton's desk.

Hatton's eyes had followed the pouch and the crate with a strange indiscernible look on his face. "So, here are the dastardly men who killed my beloved daughter," he murmured.

"To the man, sir," Dahl said respectfully. He and Lilly stood quietly and watched while Farris unsnapped the strong wire catches of the wooden crate and lifted its long top and set it aside.

"Yes, to the man . . . You did it, sir," Hatton said as if awestruck, staring at the stark, pale face looking out at him from within the small, briny world Dahl's hand had committed it to. Beside the desk Farris unrolled a wanted poster of Curly Joe and stared at it in comparison to the dead, pickled flesh, Curly Joe's namesake dark hair afloat in the saline.

With a confirming nod, Farris rolled the poster back

up and laid it down. On the desktop, he spread out the
string of partially dried ears from the leather pouch.
"Sir?" he said to Hatton, holding out a silver letter opener
for him to take.

"Thank you, Farris, I will," said Hatton in a grim yet
rapt tone of voice, his eyes now fixed on the grizzly
string of human ears.

"Yes, sir," Farris said quietly.

Hatton took the letter opener and picked the string
up on its shiny silver tip. He examined the ears closely,
as the string turned back and forth on the point of
the letter opener. Looking even closer at Duvall's ears,
blacker than the others even though all of them had
darkened in six weeks of drying, he said to his assistant, "Mr. Dahl had no idea Pete Duvall was a Negro?"

"No, sir, I never mentioned it to him," said Farris.

But Dahl cut in almost before Farris had finished
answering. "Begging both your pardons," he said. "In
fact I *did* know Pete Duval was a black man. I found an
old poster of him before I went tracking the gang." He
paused, then said, "But I had no idea that Sattler wore
a Mexican ear bob."

"I'm quite certain that only you and I knew that,
sir," Farris whispered between him and Hatton.

Hatton reached and lightly flipped the half-moon
ear ornament still dangling from Sattler's shriveling
ear. He watched in contemplation for a moment, then
stared at Dahl and said, "I see. . . ."

Dahl said, "If these weren't Hobbs' men, they
wouldn't be here, Mr. Hatton. That's not the way I do
business."

Hatton stared at him for a moment longer until a look of appreciation came to his stern businessman's face. He nodded, saying to Dahl, "Most commendable, Mr. Dahl—or should I now call you *Teacher*, as I understand many do across the Western frontier?"

"Whichever you prefer, sir," said Dahl. "My former profession was an honorable one. I take no offense at being called *Teacher*."

"As well you should not," said Hatton, clearly impressed at what this mild-mannered young man had accomplished for him. "I use the name with the utmost respect and admiration." He gave a tired smile and gestured toward Farris. "I daresay you have taught my man Farris to never underestimate you, sir."

"My congratulations, Mr. Dahl." Farris bowed slightly, in respect and concession. He lifted the top of the wooden crate and lowered it over the glass jar, closing Curly Joe into his dark, watery tomb. Then he picked up a leather travel case standing out of sight around the corner of the desk. He brought the bulging case to Dahl and set it at his feet.

Dahl and Lilly watched Hatton lay the ears, letter opener and all atop his desk and turn to them with a dismissing look on his stern face. "I know you'll want to be getting on your way . . . ," Hatton said. As if in afterthought he added, "You'll find I've included a substantial bonus in there . . . for the remarkable work you've done."

"Obliged," said Dahl. He put his hat atop his head as Lilly stooped and picked up the leather case by its strap handles. The two turned to follow Farris to the doors. But Hatton said, "Tell me, Mr. Dahl, if this *Big Chicago* brings any further trouble to me, may I count on your services once again?"

"Of course, you have my word on it," said Dahl. "And should that become the case, I must consider myself paid for such services in advance."

"Splendid," Hatton said with admiration in his eyes.

Dahl stood for a moment longer and said in a quiet and sympathetic voice, "I know what I've done doesn't help you as much as you thought it would, sir. I wish it did."

Hatton only nodded his thanks and turned to the wide window behind his desk. "Good fortune to you, Mr. Dahl," he murmured over his shoulder.

Only when the two were back in the buggy—Lilly handling the team of horses—and well on the trail back into Santa Fe did Dahl reach down, open the leather travel bag and look at the bound paper money lying neatly stacked inside. After a moment, he said, "Stop, Lilly, we've got to go back."

"What's wrong?" Lilly asked, already pulling back on the buggy reins as she veered the buggy to the side of the trail.

"Hatton's made a mistake," said Dahl. "He's given me too much money."

"Too much money?" Lilly asked skeptically. She looked down at the cash as the buggy rocked to a halt. "How much was he supposed to have paid you?"

"Ten thousand for the lot of them," Dahl said. "But there must be twice that." He rummaged through the stacks of money.

Lilly stared down, awestruck. But then she swallowed a knot in her throat and said, "He did tell you he'd included a bonus."

"A bonus, yes," said Dahl, "but this is too much. . . ." He paused as his hand came up with a folded note. "Wait, here's something," he said. He opened the note and read it aloud to Lilly. "Mr. Dahl. May this additional *ten thousand* dollars serve to express my deepest gratitude for what you have done for me. Sincerely, J. Fenwick Hatton."

"So he *didn't* make a mistake," Lilly said with a breath of relief. "It is the bonus he was talking about. He knew that without the note telling you, you'd think it was a mistake and take the money back to him." She paused, then said, "And he was right, you were going to."

"Yes, I was," said Dahl.

Lilly shook her head and smiled. "I swear, Sherman Dahl," she said, looking him up and down, his arm in a sling, his coat covering the countless other flesh wounds in his arms, his thighs, his lower back where it had been exposed beneath his bullet vest. "I'm starting to think you're too honest for your own good."

Dahl folded the note, put it inside his coat and said quietly, "Honesty isn't meant for *my own good*. It's meant to serve the good of others."

"Yes, I know that, Sherman Dahl," she said quietly. She jiggled the buggy reins and sent the horses forward onto the trail ahead. She smiled and closed her eyes, feeling a cool breeze blow down from the Sangre de Cristo mountain range. "There was a time I forgot it. But now I've started knowing it again . . . like it's something all brand-new."

"Yes, it all feels brand-new to me too, Lilly," he said, his injured arm resting in its sling against his stomach. He looked at her and squeezed her forearm gently with his good hand. The horses trotted along in the sunlight, their manes lifting on the cool, gusting breeze.

In a six-week run up along the upper edge of Arizona Territory, Chester Goines had celebrated his recent and bold step up the ladder of crime. He, Russell and Thatcher had robbed a bank in the town of Cottonwood and killed its manager.

A week later, running ahead of a Cottonwood posse, the three robbed, pillaged and burned to the ground Mama Chase's Hotel and Bordello in the town of Rocking, on the stretch of badlands along the northwest border. From Rocking they had traveled east past a large bordering canyon, on toward Rimrock, fighting a town posse the entire way. When Big Chicago had put a well-aimed bullet from his Winchester into the posse leader's chest, the robbers had gained some time while the posse stopped to attend to their wounded sheriff.

Big Chicago led his two-man gang into the small supply town of Rimrock in search of food, whiskey and ammunition. Later in the night, in a dimly lit tent saloon, he stood at a plank-and-beer-barrel bar, drinking whiskey from a dusty bottle. When he and his two men heard someone call out, "Big Chicago" from the front fly of the big ragged tent, in the blink of an eye they spun toward the voice as one. Their side guns came out, up, cocked and pointed at the same time.

"Whoa, men!" a tall, thin gunman said with a fearless chuckle. "If you shoot me, who's going to buy the next round?"

Recognizing the grinning man, Chicago said to the other two, "Relax, men, it's only a rat." Then he said to the gunman, "Bobby Candles, what you doing running loose when so many, including myself, would love to see you bleeding to death?"

"What an ugly thing to say, Chicago," said Candles, stepping inside, still grinning, keeping his gun hand away from the big Lemat pistol on his hip. "Here I came all this way just to catch up to you and tell you the posse from Cottonwood is no longer on your asses." He shook his head. "It disheartens me to count you as a friend."

"Then don't," Chicago said bluntly. "What's that about the posse?"

"It's gone," said Candles. "I got rid of them for you. Don't bother thanking me." He lowered his gun hand back to his side, walked forward, stopped and rapped his knuckles on the plank bar top. "Whiskey, pronto," he said to the sleepy-eyed bartender. "I rode with them as far as I could. They sent me and another fellow ahead to scout. I shot him in the head by accident. He fell over a cliff and under some rocks, as strange as it sounds. Anyway, here I am."

"Wait a minute," Russell cut in. "You were riding with that damned posse, hunting us down?" His and

Thatcher's guns were still up and cocked even though Chicago's Walker Colt had gone back down behind his waist sash.

"Put your damn guns down," Chicago said with irritation. "Beat him to death with sticks if you have to kill him. But don't let word get out that you wasted a bullet on him."

"Yes, think of your reputations," said Candles. He raised a bottle the bartender had stood before him. When he'd finished a long swig, he said to Chicago, "The posse was the only way I saw of ever catching you long enough to join up with you."

"Well, I'm honored as hell you'd want to join up with me, Candles," said Chicago. "But Russell, Thatcher and me all three piss in the sand. . . . We've no need for somebody to empty chamber pots for us."

"Should I check back later?" Candles asked with sarcasm.

"Suit yourself, but I see no need in it," Chicago said. "Me and these two are rolling fast and bold. We've got no time to slow down and show you what to do."

"Yeah, you're feeling cocky over killing the man who killed Curly Joe, I can see it," said Candles.

"Yeah? You really think so?" Chicago said with a short, tight grin. "Can you see *cocky* just oozing in my eyes?"

"Sure enough, I can," said Candles, "except the thing is, you didn't kill him. You left the sumbitch alive on the main street." He shook his head. "It's the kind of stupidity that'll be talked about for years to come."

"The hell are you talking about, Candles?" Chicago

demanded. "I emptied my Walker into him. These men put a total of four shotgun loads in him. Geneva Darrows shot him a bunch of times. You can only shoot a man so much, and then your arm gets tired."

"He's alive," Candles insisted. "We heard it from more than one person in Pine Ridge. The man was wearing a bulletproof vest. Ever heard of them?"

"Yeah," said Chicago, "I've heard of them. But I never heard of one in this part of the country."

"You have now," said Candles. "Sherman Dahl, the Teacher, was wearing one. You didn't kill him."

"The Teacher?" said Chicago. "Damn, I've heard of him. He's gotten himself quite a reputation in the Territories."

"Well," said Candles, "from now on he can be known as the man you *didn't* kill."

"Not after I see him again, he can't," Chicago said with a dark stare.

To change the subject, Thatcher said to Candles, "Say, whatever happened to those idiots you used to ride with—Oak, Milo and Garr? What a bunch of turds, them three."

"They're standing outside the tent listening, keeping their rifles on you three, in case things don't go well in here."

Chapter 8

In the light of a flickering campfire, Sheriff Lewis Morgan lay coughing up bloody bits of his shattered lung. The posse men surrounding him looked at one another gravely, each sure that the seasoned old lawman would not live to see another sunrise.

"Sure to God there's something more we can do for him," whispered Owen Nichols, the blacksmith from the town of Cottonwood. "I can't stand sitting here doing nothing. He deserves better than to die like this." He turned a look toward the young deputy and said, "Eddie, do you suppose our two front trail scouts really did cut out on us?"

"You saw the hoofprints, Mr. Nichols," said Deputy Sheriff Eddie Lane. "They're gone." The young deputy sat with the dying sheriff's head propped on his lap, to keep the blood from choking him when it surged up from his chest.

"But I've know Stewart Wiser for years," the blacksmith said. "He'd never run out on us when we need him."

"I expect you're right," said Lane. "I won't be surprised if we find Mr. Wiser lying dead somewhere down there." He nodded out into the darkness to where the trail edge dropped off into a rocky canyon two hundred feet below. "I suspect Newton—if that's really his name—and these other three killed Mr. Wiser." He gestured toward the sets of hoofprints they had followed up the high trail.

"Don't even think something like that, Deputy," said a townsman named Curtis Shepard. "I fear you are rushing to judgment against Mr. Newton. I drank with him and three other gentlemen at the saloon only two nights ago. I found all four of them most affable."

"I hope I'm wrong," said Lane. He added with grim resolve, "But I'm not."

On Lane's lap, the sheriff gasped for another breath and said in a wet, wheezing voice, "You men . . . listen to my deputy. He knows . . ." His words fell away into a spasm of racking pain. Lane held him firmly as if to still his convulsions.

The posse men exchanged looks in the flicker of firelight. "Knows what?" one of them whispered under his breath.

Lane looked at them in turn and said, "All right, here's what it looks like." As he spoke, he slipped the sheriff over to another man's lap and stood in a crouch and moved along the hoofprints, boot scrapings and large circle of dried blood that they had found on the ground when they'd arrived. "This fellow Newton rode this far with Stewart Wiser. Once he figured the robbers were holed up in Rimrock, he called in these other three riders who'd been following close behind. They killed Wiser, and then they rode on."

"Jesus," said a townsman named Art Fuller. "What have we gotten into here?"

"We're after these sonsabitches who robbed our bank, Art," said a townsman named Wilson Densmier.

"Yeah, and shot our sheriff, don't forget," said Nichols the blacksmith.

"Don't you go getting soft on us, Fuller," said Densmier. "None of us wanted to be out here, getting shot at. But it had to be done, and it has to be finished."

"Keep running your mouth, Densmier," Fuller said, anger rising in his eyes. "I'll show you who's getting soft!"

"You're not showing anybody anything!" Nichols said to Fuller, his rifle gripped tightly in his hand. The three men each took a step forward toward one another.

"That's enough," said Eddie Lane, moving forward and taking a stand amid them. "All three of you stand down." His voice was controlled, strong and level. His hand was not on his gun butt, but it didn't have to be in order for the three townsmen to see he meant business.

Densmier, Fuller and Nichols backed away grudgingly. The young deputy looked from one to another until the three showed signs of cooling down. "It's time we get some rest and keep moving. I'm going to figure now that we're looking for seven gunmen instead of the three we started out chasing."

"He's motioning for you, Eddie," said the townsman holding the sheriff's head in his lap.

Lane hurried over and stooped down beside the wounded sheriff. "What is it, Sheriff Morgan?"

The weakening sheriff placed a trembling hand around the deputy's forearm and drew him closer. "Send them home," he whispered in a failing voice near Lane's ear.

"Sheriff, you take it easy," said Lane. "We're going to ride into Rimrock. There could be a doctor there. If there is, we'll—"

"Send . . . them home," the sheriff repeated in a rasping whisper as the others drew closer around him in the campfire light.

Leaning down to keep their conversation between them, Deputy Lane said, "But, Sheriff, we're getting close. The robbers are in Rimrock, I'm almost certain."

"Send . . . them . . . home . . . ," the sheriff repeated, this time with much more effort, but much less strength.

"What'd he say?" asked Fuller, from a few feet away.

"Sounded like he said for us to go home," said Densmier.

Lane said into the sheriff's dying face, "But what about these robbers who killed you?"

"Go . . . after them," said the sheriff, gripping Lane's forearm with determination.

"Alone?" said Lane. "Sheriff, I want to do what you ask me to, but I can't bring these men in *alone*. I'll need help."

"Don't . . . bring . . . them in," the sheriff gasped. His

eyes took on a wild, pleading look of desperation for a moment, then went blank. He sank back onto the townsman's lap.

"Sheriff Morgan . . . ?" said Lane, feeling the grip loosen from his forearm and slip away.

"He's dead, Deputy," the townsman said gently. He tucked the blanket around the dead sheriff's body, closed the blank, open eyes and pulled the corner of the blanket up over Sheriff Morgan's face.

"Oh no . . . ," Lane murmured. He straightened up from beside the sheriff's body, dusted his knees and looked around at the others. "You all heard him," he said to the townsmen. "He said for me to send all of you home."

"Amen to that, Deputy," said Art Fuller. "I know when I'm licked. I'll be ready to ride back as soon as you say the word."

"Hell, so will I," said Densmier with disappointment in his voice.

"Me too," said Nichols. "You both done the best you could. It's time to draw in our horns and get back to decent normal life."

"I'm not going back with you," Lane said.

The men all looked at him. "Where do you think you're going, Eddie?" said Densmier, not even using his title of office.

"I told the sheriff I'd go on after them," said Lane, overlooking the disrespect Densmier had shown toward him.

"So what?" said Densmier. "The sheriff is dead. Nobody is holding you to your word to a dead man." He gave a troubled, bemused grin. "What's the matter with you anyway?"

"Besides," Fuller cut in, "like as not, the sheriff didn't know what he was saying anyway."

"He knew what he was saying. So did I," Lane said stubbornly.

"Now, hold it," said Nichols. "Did you give your word or just tell him that you would go on after them?"

"What's the difference?" said Lane, not giving an inch.

"Well, there's a hell of a lot of difference," said Nichols. "A man gives his word, that's one thing. But anybody might say they'll do something. It doesn't mean they have to do it." He gave a nervous chuckle and looked to the others for support. "Does it, fellows?"

"Naw, not really," said Densmier. "It's just talk. It's not a man's word."

"A man's word is given in everything he says and everything he does," said Lane. He looked from one silent face to the next. "If a man doesn't hold to his word in everything he says and does, he ain't a man— he's shit out of a chicken."

"Hey, boy," Densmier said in a challenging tone. "You're starting to talk like you're some kind of fighting man or something. I've got news for you—you're not. So get back down to earth here, before you ride out and get yourself killed."

"How do you know I'm not?" said Lane in a strong, even voice. "You've never seen me in a fight. I've never been in a fight."

"Well, there now, that says it all," said Densmier, as if having proved his point.

"But I'm going to be. I gave my word," Lane said as if he hadn't heard him.

"Again with that *word* business," said Densmier. He shook his head.

"Now, you hold it right there, Deputy," said Nichols, seeing Lane step toward his horse. "I don't like how you looked at us when you said that about being shit out of a chicken." He shook a finger at Lane.

"Christ, Nichols, it was just a figure of speech, is all," said Fuller. "Can't you see he's just broken up over the sheriff dying?"

"That's another thing, Deputy," said Nichols. "If you act responsibly, maybe you can wear Sheriff Morgan's badge until his term runs out. We're still going to need a sheriff, don't forget."

Lane stared past the townsmen toward the darkness ahead, the high trail leading to Rimrock. "Keep the badge. Take the sheriff's body back to town. I'm done killing," he said.

In Rimrock, as the three riflemen filed in through the rear tent fly, Big Chicago gave Thatcher a bemused look and said, "Damn, I bet you're embarrassed!" But before Thatcher could reply, Chicago laughed and said to Bobby Candles, "I always said you're a sneaking sumbitch, Candles. That's about the only thing I ever liked about you." He turned toward the three gunmen and said to the tired bartender, "Give these boys what they want. It's on me."

"Does this mean we're going to ride together after all?" Candles asked.

"How can I say no?" Big Chicago grinned. "You slipped three men in on us while my pards here were fingering their peckers. That bodes favorably in my book. We'll make room for yas." He gave Russell and Thatcher a hard look.

"How are we going to make room for four more at the trough?" Russell asked bluntly. "There's not enough cash to go around as it is."

"We'll rob bigger banks," Chicago said. "Never mind how we'll do it. I'm the boss. I'll say who rides with us and who doesn't." He turned and raised his filled shot glass in a toast toward the three new men lined along the plank bar. "Drink up, men. Welcome to my gang. I should say, the former Curly Joe Hobbs Gang."

The riflemen nodded and drank in reply. As they lowered their shot glasses, one of them said to Thatcher with a cold stare, "We heard you call us idiots from out there."

"Come on, now, Milo," said Chicago with a grin, giving the man a slap on his back. "No harm done, eh? Consider it an act of camaraderie."

"*Camaraderie*, eh?" Milo said grudgingly, keeping his cold stare on Thatcher.

With the same hard stare, Thatcher said, "Yeah, you know, like *pal, idiot, pederast.* That sort of thing."

"Oh, I get it," Milo said, his eyes glaring, his knuckles white, "like *turd, poltroon, catamite—*"

"Yeah, that's the spirit," said Chicago, cutting him off, his hand close to the big Walker Colt in his black waist sash. "All of it in fun," he added.

"Whoopee," Thatcher said in a dull, flat tone.

Once the two men stopped glaring at each other, Chicago turned to Bobby Candles and said, "I like that kind of fighting spirit in a man, don't you?"

"Yeah," Candles replied. Staring at Thatcher, he said in warning, "But the next time you call a man a *turd, poltroon or catamite*, you best be ready to kill him, *camaraderie* be damned."

"No problem. I will be," said Thatcher coolly, holding his stare.

Candles finally eased down and sipped his whiskey, seeing Thatcher wasn't going to give an inch. Letting his own hand fall away from his gun butt now that a storm seemed to have passed, he said, "I realize it's not always easy, men like us having to come together under new leadership."

"New leadership?" Chicago said, his face turning serious.

"You know," said Candles, "you and me sort of acting as one, now that Curly Joe is up there dancing with the angels." He gave an upward toss of his eyes.

Chicago didn't like it but he let it go for the time being. "It ain't angels he's dancing with, but I get your meaning all the same," he said. Changing the subject, he said, "Bobby, ol' pal, you're going to have to tell me more about the Teacher. It looks like I'll have to kill him all over again, first chance I get."

"He's nothing," said Candles. "I saw him back when he rode with a posse led by Abner Webb and Will Summers. He made a big stir for a while. He's been shot more times than any man I ever saw. But he's overdue for a bullet in his head. You should have killed him while you had him pinned to the dirt." He shook his head at Chicago's mistake.

Chicago took a deep breath and let it out in exasperation. "You're not going to let up about that, are you, Candles?" he said darkly.

Candles chuckled and dismissed the matter. "Soon as I heard you'd taken over Curly Joe's business, I set out to find you. I wanted to stop by the Fair and Square and put the ol' stiff leg on Geneva Darrows first, but I'd heard the Teacher had shot her all over the upstairs wall."

"In other words, you're out to lay claim on everything that belonged to Curly Joe."

"Does it sound that way to you?" Candles grinned and raised his glass as if in a toast.

"What about this posse you and your three idio—I mean gunmen—followed here?" Chicago said, catching and correcting himself.

"Follow them? Hell, I told you—I led them," said Candles. "They even made me a trail scout—me and the fool I had to kill. I had my pards here following close behind the posse, though. I wouldn't have led them right to you."

"That's kind of you," Chicago said, not meaning it.

Candles shrugged. "It doesn't matter. I left their sheriff sucking air through his belly. He'll die. They'll go home. That's that. Like I said, you don't have to thank me for it."

"Then I won't," said Chicago. "What makes you so cock-certain they'll all turn back when he dies?"

"They have to turn back. There's no fighting men

among them," said Candles. "Just some townsmen and a slow-witted deputy."

"Slow-witted, huh?" Chicago asked, pondering it.

"Slow as an iron door," said Candles. "Follows that sheriff around like a hound pup."

"You checked him out good?" said Chicago.

"I checked him out *real* good. He's stupid enough to bang his balls against a tree stump if the sheriff told him to."

"Ouch," Chicago said with a chuckle. "I hope you're right. I hate surprises."

"I never miss when it comes to reading a man, knowing what he will or won't do," said Candles. "This one was cleaning stables when the sheriff hired him. I doubt if he was smart enough to do that."

"*Smart* never has nailed a hide to the wall, my friend," said Chicago.

"I know," said Candles with a grin as he raised his glass to his lips, "but neither has *stupid*."

Chapter 9

———

Throughout the night the outlaws drank inside the ragged tent. A rounded glow from a single lantern hanging above the bar marked the tent from the surrounding hillsides and rocky cactus flats. Before dawn, as a few other lanterns, candles and torches began to blink to life from inside shacks, tents and adobe hovels, a scrawny red rooster made his way onto a hitch rail in a single hop and a batting of wings and let out a long broken screech.

Before the luckless bird completed his bid at waking the town, a shotgun blast from the open tent fly swept him away in a flurry of blood and feathers. The explosion resounded across the silent town and echoed off the surrounding hillsides.

"Damn it, Thatcher, that was right in my ear!" said Candles. He rounded his finger inside his right ear and shook his head to get rid of the ringing. The other men only stared, bleary-eyed in their whiskey-induced stupors.

"You'll have to excuse Morris Thatcher," Chicago said to Candles. "I still haven't gotten him all the way housebroken yet."

"I hate a loudmouthed rooster something awful," Thatcher said, breaking open his shotgun and replacing the spent load. "My pa had one like that when I was a little boy. I hated the son of a bitch—his rooster too."

"Hell, we're going to have townsfolk swarming here any minute to see what that shot was all about," said Delbert Garr.

"When did you become so shy about meeting folks, Delbert?" said Dayton Oak, a big Nebraskan outlaw who had ridden for a time with Memphis Beck and The Hole-in-the-wall Gang.

Behind the bar the exhausted bartender had been sitting asleep atop his tall stool. The shotgun blast made him spring onto his feet. Half asleep, he began wiping the bar top wildly, like a man obsessed.

"I'm not shy," said Oak. He gestured toward Thatcher and said, "Your chicken-shooting pard here just woke the whole damn town up, is all. I don't want a damn bunch of nosey sumbitches crowding around me first thing in the morning."

"I didn't mean to upset your delicate nature," Thatcher said. "Next time I'll try to be more considerate."

Oak's eyes flared beneath his angry brow. He started to offer a scorching reply, but before he could, Chicago cut in unexpectedly.

"Let's go find ourselves some breakfast," Chicago said. "I don't know about you, Candles, but this all-night drinking makes me as hungry as a grizzly bear. I could eat my weight in hoecakes."

"I could eat something, for sure," Bobby Candles said, his voice a bit slurred by all the whiskey he'd drunk.

"Then let's do it," said Chicago, "before everybody gathers here." He turned to the bartender, who had gotten a grip on himself and stopped wiping the bar top. "Barkeep, where's a man eat in this town without getting himself poisoned?"

"Up the street, next to the stage office," said the worn-out bartender, thankful to hear the drinkers were getting ready to leave. "There's a restaurant run by a widow woman, Shelly Ann Haspers. She feeds all the en-route stage passengers. . . . She's never poisoned one that I can recall."

"Sounds like my kind of place, then," said Chicago. He picked up his hat from atop the bar and made a sweeping gesture toward the tent fly. "After you fellows," he said to the others.

As Candles, his three riflemen and Thatcher filed out into the grainy morning light, Big Chicago held back and took Russell by his shoulder before he could leave behind them. "Hold on, Russell, I've got something I need to say to you," he said. Turning Russell toward him, he grabbed him by the front of his coat lapels and said in a gruff, lowered voice, "Don't you ever again question me like you did last night, or else I will gut you through to the bone."

"Whoa, what are you talking about?" said Russell, taken aback.

"I'm talking about last night, you questioning me

about taking Bobby Candles and his men in with us," said Chicago, still with his gruff tone of voice lowered just between them.

"All right! Okay!" said Russell, his hands chest high in surrender, in spite of one of them holding his shotgun. "I wasn't thinking straight."

Chicago turned loose of his lapels. He settled down a little, but said, "I'm the one taking over running the gang. I say who joins us or who doesn't. Do you understand me now?"

"Yeah, I understand," said Russell. "Only . . ." He let his words trail.

"Only what?" said Chicago. "Spit it out. They're waiting for us."

"Only, I still can't see why you're bringing Candles and his men in," he said in the same lowered voice as Chicago's. "Bobby Candles is the most sneaking sumbitch in the world—he always has been. I thought you knew that."

"I do know that," said Chicago. He grinned and straightened and adjusted the front of Russell's wrinkled coat as he spoke in a softer tone, using Russell's first name in a fatherly manner. "You see, Bart, the best place to keep a sneaking dog like him is close to the side of my boot. That way, I'll see when he's about to bite, and I'll kick his damn teeth in. Do you get me?"

Russell considered it, nodding slowly. "Yeah, I guess so, since you put it that way."

"See?" Chicago went on to explain. "This smiling asshole just led a posse up from Cottonwood. He took a chance on them finding out what he is, just so he could meet up with us."

"I don't see that as something good he did," said Russell.

"Nor do I," said Chicago. "But there's a message in him doing that. It tells me that he'll do anything to get what he wants. What he wants is to be top dog here. Word has gotten out about Curly Joe being killed. There's going to be more than just Bobby Candles wanting to round up Joe's old pals and take the gang over. Most of them will be damn good and ready to kill whoever they have to to do it. Right?"

"Sure they will," said Russell.

"So why not let Candles think he's taking over, let him have to deal with whoever shows up? Does that make sense to you?"

Russell thought about it and finally grinned, getting the picture of what Chicago had in mind. "Yes, it does. I like that, Chicago," he said.

"I'm so happy you approve, Bart," Chicago said with a trace of sarcasm in his voice. "Now let's go, before Candles gets all edgy and suspicious, thinking we're talking about him."

Outside the tent a few yards away, Bobby Candles looked back over his shoulder and past the other men and said, "Where the hell is he?"

"Who, Chicago?" said Winston Milo, also turning and looking back. No sooner had the two looked around than Chicago and Russell walked out of the tent fly into the changing morning light.

"Here he comes now," said Candles. He stopped and

looked all around, waiting for Russell and Chicago to catch up to him. On either side of the street stood townsfolk, each staring wide-eyed at the gunmen, drunk and surly, filing past them.

"You people go on about your business," Chicago called. "Everything is under control here."

"Are you a lawman?" an elderly bearded man called out from a boardwalk.

"No, I'm no damn lawman," Chicago shouted, yanking his Colt from his waist sash and waving it for all to see. "But you can bet your ass I am the law while I'm here!"

The townsfolk backed a step but continued to stare, not so much in fear as in contempt. A few feet away an old Mexican, hat in hand, gathered what appeared to have once been his rooster. He held a pale yellow rooster's foot in one hand, a limp piece of the rooster's feathered back in his other.

"It'll be a long time before that crowing sumbitch bothers anybody else," Thatcher said proudly, walking on, shotgun in hand.

"Crazy sumbitch, shoots a chicken," said Winston Milo, walking at the head of the gunmen along the empty street.

Farther back along the street, only half hearing Milo, Thatcher called out, "What'd he say to me?"

"He called you a crazy sumbitch," Oak chuckled, his rifle swinging loosely in his hand.

Without looking back, Milo called out to Thatcher in a spirited tone, "If you don't like being called a sumbitch, don't act like one—"

Milo's words stopped abruptly as a bullet ripped through his chest and splattered warm blood all over Oak's face behind him. Following the bullet came the sound of its explosion catching up to it from far up on the hillside south of town. Looking ahead and seeing Milo fly backward, almost into Oak's arms, Russell shouted, "Jesus, Thatcher, he was only joking."

"Damn!" Thatcher looked bewildered. "I didn't shoot him—"

"Posse!" shouted Candles, cutting him off, seeing a thin rise of rifle smoke on the distant hillside.

"Take cover!" shouted Chicago, already running to the shelter of a low, thick adobe wall where a small herd of goats scattered to make way for him. As he leaped to the ground, a chunk of dried adobe was gouged from the top of the wall, followed by another explosion from the hillside.

"Somebody get the horses before they start shooting them!" Candles shouted from behind the cover of a horseless buckboard sitting out in front of a mercantile store.

"What about breakfast?" Russell shouted from a few yards away, pressed against the wall of a small plank shack.

Breakfast . . . ? Chicago stared at him in disbelief from a few yards away, his Walker Colt out, in hand, even though it was useless from such a distance.

"To hell with breakfast," shouted Candles. "Get the damn horses!"

From the cover of the adobe wall, Chicago stared with a slight smile and a look of scrutiny on his face, listening to Candles shout orders like some cavalry officer.

"I'll get them!" shouted Oak. He leaped to his feet and started across the dirt street at a straight, fast run. But his straight run turned into a sidelong stagger as a bullet ripped through his left upper arm, streaked across his chest and thumped into a boardwalk plank fifteen feet away. Again the following explosion resounded from a spot on the hillside where gray smoke had gathered and begun to billow on the morning air.

Chicago chuckled to himself, seeing Candles rise, run out to Oak, help the wounded man take cover, then run on to the horses and hurriedly gather their reins. Turning to where Russell stood pressed against the wall, Chicago said in a guarded tone, "See that, Bart?" He wagged his Walker Colt toward Bobby Candles and grinned. "It's always good to see a *leader* want to get himself involved."

Across the street, Candles fanned the last of the horses into a small adobe through a doorway he kicked open and off its leather hinges. As the horses ran inside in a flurry of dust and hooves, the two elderly inhabitants of the adobe fled out the rear door and disappeared down a narrow alleyway.

While the horses settled, Candles ran back to the front door, rifle in hand, and shouted out to Chicago and the others, "Over here! The horses are safe."

"Obliged," Chicago called out, keeping his voice serious, but giving Russell a grin. "There's only one man up there, Bobby. I've been watching."

"All right," said Candles. "We're going to get ready

to make a move." He levered a round into his rifle chamber and stared up along the hillside. "One man is not going to hold up our show."

"Damn right he's not," Chicago said, liking the way things were going so far. Whoever was up there had killed one of Candles' riflemen, maybe two, he thought, looking over to where Oak lay behind a pile of wooden crates beside a freight office. *It served him right, the son of a bitch, bringing a posse up here . . .* , Chicago said to himself. He called out to Candles, "You and Garr ride up around him and flush him down to us. We'll be waiting to kill him at the bottom of the trail."

Candles thought about that, realizing that Chicago was pushing the hardest part of the job onto him and his last standing rifleman.

From ten yards away Delbert Garr ran in through the open door and threw himself up against the thick adobe wall. "It looked to me like Big Chicago was laughing about Milo and Oak getting shot."

"Oh?" said Candles, gritting his teeth. "Like he thinks it was funny, us out here scrambling with the horses while he's holed up over there safe and sound?"

"It sure looked that way to me," said Garr.

"Can you believe that bastard?" Candles growled under his breath. "He wants *us* to go after whoever that is shooting at us?"

"Yeah, I can believe it," Garr said, giving him a look. "I'll get our horses."

"Get one for Oak," said Candles. "If he's still alive, he's going with us." He looked up along the high ridges and scanned back and forth for any sign of the rifleman. "If it's that damn deputy, I'm going to cut his heart out. . . ."

Beside a large embedded boulder high up on the rocky hillside, Deputy Eddie Lane levered a fresh round into his rifle chamber, raised it to his shoulder and looked down its raised sights onto the wide dirt street running the length of Rimrock. "There's two for you, Sheriff," he said quietly, speaking to the fallen sheriff, his idol, his mentor, as if the man were there beside him.

Good shooting, Deputy . . . , he imagined Sheriff Morgan saying in reply. He pictured Lewis Morgan there somewhere nearby, although he couldn't point out exactly where, he thought, as his eyes moved warily from one spot to the next on the distant street below. *Clearing the street . . . ,* Sheriff Morgan would have called it.

Lane lowered the rifle after seeing that no one was going to step into his gun sights. Now that he'd seen Candles—the man who had called himself John Newton—rush over and get all their horses out of sight, he expected the outlaw's next move would be to get out of town.

That's right—they'll ride out now . . . , he could imagine the old sheriff saying, *but in which direction . . . ?*

He considered it. By now they'd have realized from his rifle smoke that there was only one man up here. They wouldn't run from one man, he decided. Not these murdering thieves. If there was only one man dogging them, their first move would be to ride up here and kill him, if they could get to him without putting themselves in his line of fire.

What do you think, Deputy . . . ? He pictured the sheriff watching him, checking out his decisions, making sure he knew that his next move would be the right one. *There's no second guesses. There's only getting it right. . . .*

Okay. He knew what to do, he thought, stilling the voices inside himself. He looked at the trail leading up in a wide circle from the town below. Then he looked above him, knowing that the trail would circle around up there through a maze of rock, leaving him in a blind spot while they took higher ground above him. *Uh-uh,* he wouldn't let that happen, he told himself.

He backed away, stood up in a crouch and ran over to where he'd left his big smoke-colored barb hitched to a rock spur. "Time to go," he said aloud, unhitching the restless animal. Swinging up into the saddle, rifle in hand, he batted his heels to the horse's sides and sent it bolting off along the rocky trail.

Chapter 10

Bobby Candles, Delbert Garr and the wounded Dayton Oak had ridden halfway up the high switchback trail when a bullet thumped into the dirt only inches from Candles' horse's hooves. The big claybank dun reared, twisted, whinnied and tried to bolt away. But Candles got the animal in check quickly. When the spooked horse's hooves touched the ground, Candles sent the animal racing off the trail. Garr and Oak raced along beside him.

In the cover of rock and scrub juniper, the three leaped down from their saddles. They snatched their rifles, took cover and began firing repeatedly up along the high ridgeline where the sound of the rifle shot had come from. Dayton Oak could only fire one-handed, as his wounded upper left arm was unable to give him assistance in either holding or firing his Winchester.

After the three fired a heavy barrage up along the

ridgeline, Candles called out, "Hold your damn fire! Do you see him up there?"

"I don't see a damn thing up there," Oak said, his face pained, his wounded arm hanging limp at his side. The three continued to search the ridge and hillsides until Carr shouted, "There he goes, Bobby! I see him!" He pointed up toward the trail above them.

Above them, Eddie Lane saw that he'd played out his position. His foot had slipped on the rocky ground and caused him to miss his shot. It was time to move on again. There would be plenty of hiding places along the trail ahead. He'd have to be patient and bide his time, until he killed every one of them.

"It's that damn deputy," said Candles, catching a glimpse of the deputy's tan oversized riding duster and tall Montana-crowned hat as Lane hurried out of sight, his rifle in his hand.

The three gunmen saw that firing now would only be wasting bullets. They stared intently for a moment, and then Garr asked confidently, "Do you want me to ride up and nail him?"

Candles just looked at him for a moment. "No, Delbert. He'll be long gone by the time you can ride up there. These high switchback trails are all to his advantage. He was only going for one of us just then, the one riding in front. He knew he'd be out of sight before we could fire back at him. Lucky for me, something caused him to miss." He looked all around the rocky terrain. "We're wasting our time up here now. He's going to get to the flats ahead of us and pick another spot to hit us from. He's taking his time."

"You have to give him some credit for having patience," Garr said quietly, also surveying the high ridgelines.

"Patience, hell," said Candles. "This boy is just too scared to fight us any other way."

"I don't think he's scared," said Garr. "If he's as slow-witted as you say he is, he's not smart enough to be afraid of us."

Candles just looked at him.

In a pained voice, Oak said to Candles, "Scared or not scared, it looks like this stable boy ain't nearly as slow or stupid as you thought he was."

"How's the arm, Dayton?" Candles asked Oak in an even tone of voice, changing the subject. He looked Oak up and down, noting the fresh wet blood seeping to the surface of the bandana tied around his upper arm.

Instead of answering, Oak repeated, "I said, it looks like that stable boy ain't near as slow or stupi—"

"I heard you, Oak, *damn it*!" Candles shouted, his rage and frustration finally boiling out of control.

"He killed poor Milo," Garr cut in. "Oak here will be lucky if he don't die from the fever, the shape his arm is in—"

"I know all this, Garr!" Candles shouted. "Both of yas let up off me! Maybe I misjudged the son of a bitch a little, all right?" He glared angrily back and forth between them. "I figure the sheriff must've died and this ol' boy has gone wild in his sorrow. Slow-witted fellows do that. They get something like that pressing on their minds and they go wild as a buck for a while."

Seeing Candles reaching his boiling point, Oak withdrew and said, "Hell, you rode up from Cottonwood with him, you know him better than we do."

"That's right, thank you, Oak," said Candles. He let out a tense breath.

"Was him and that sheriff kin or something?" Garr asked.

"Not that I know of," said Candles. "But being kin doesn't matter to folks like this stable hand. He acted like the old sheriff was his pa. Said Sheriff Morgan made him a lawman, and he'd never let him down." He shook his head. "See? That's the kind of mind he's walking around with." He looked back and forth between the two.

"Hmm," said Garr, considering it.

"Just how far do you figure he's willing to take this thing?" Oak asked, his face looking drawn and pained.

"I don't know," Candles said with a troubled look on his face as he scanned along the higher trail, seeing the drift of dust the deputy's horse left in the air. "I never figured he'd be the kind to come riding on alone, that's for sure."

"Hell, don't worry about it, Bobby," said Garr in a consoling tone of voice. "Sooner or later, he'll slip up and we'll get him."

"Yeah, I know we will," Candles said, still scanning the higher trail above them as the dust drifted out of sight. "I'm just hoping we're all alive and kicking by the time he does."

"Yeah, that's the thing of it," said Garr. "Who's going to be the next one in his rifle sights?"

"Enough about this stable hand. What about this lousy prick we've taken up with?" Oak asked. "I was lying there shot, and I swear I saw him grinning—that son of a bitch."

"I saw him doing the same thing," Garr said to the wounded gunman.

"Right now Big Chicago thinks he's the cock of the walk," said Candles. "But I'll take care of him when the time comes."

"Yeah, if he doesn't get us all three killed first," said Garr. "He's down there taking it easy right now, while we're up here getting shot at."

"He'll get his," said Candles. "I give you my word on it. But for now, I'm going along with him."

"I see you going along with him," said Oak, "but what I can't see is why."

"Never mind why," said Candles. "There'll be others joining us before long. When the time comes for me to take over, everybody will know that I'm really the one who's been running things."

Garr and Oak looked at each other. "If that's the way you want to play it, we're both behind you."

"Good," said Candles. He reached for the dangling reins to his horse and said, "Let's get back down there and see what this bastard wants us to do next."

"What about this deputy?" Garr asked. "I can go kill him real quick and get back here."

Candles doubted it. But he didn't say so. Instead he said, "Forget him for now. He got lucky on us while we were drunk and not expecting him. It won't happen again. Next time he pops back up, he's dead." He swung atop his horse and jerked it back toward the trail.

In Rimrock, at the edge of town, from behind a fortress of embedded rock, Chicago and his two men awaited the return of Candles and his men. Chicago was sitting sipping water from a canteen when Russell said, "Riders coming," and the three grabbed their rifles and gazed off along the trail. "It's not Candles and his men," Russell added.

Watching three riders come up into sight along the trail, Chicago said, "Easy, boys. I know who this is. Lower your guns."

"Who is it, then?" Russell asked as he and Thatcher lowered their shotguns and cradled them in their arms.

Chicago gave him a look, remembering how the gunman had harped about taking in newcomers. "It's Buddy Short, his brother Epps and a cross-eyed Texas killer named Baldhead Paul Crane. Satisfied?" he added with a growl.

Russell didn't reply. He only stared at the three riders as they drew closer and stopped when Chicago stepped out of cover and waved them down. "Damn, Buddy," said Chicago. "I figured you'd be the first to come looking for me once word got out."

"You mean I'm *not*?" the tall, broad-shouldered gunman asked, reining his horse to a halt a few feet from Big Chicago. As he spoke he looked all around as if to see who had beaten him in joining Chicago.

"Bobby Candles and his men got here last night,"

said Chicago. "You know Candles. If there's something on the wind, his nose is right in it."

"It's been over a month," said Buddy Short. "I didn't expect we'd be the first ones to find you. Fact is, we were headed down to look for you in Cottonwood. We heard so much shooting from this direction, we thought we best come take a look-see."

Epps and Baldhead Paul nudged their horses up beside Buddy. "And, by damn, here you are," said Baldhead Paul, his crossed eyes making it hard to tell whom he was talking to.

"Howdy, Baldhead, howdy, Epps," said Chicago, touching his derby hat brim respectfully. "You all know Bart Russell and Little Morris Thatcher here?"

"He just added the *Little* part," said Thatcher with a peevish look on his face. "Nobody ever called me that until just now."

"Howdy, Bart. Howdy, Morris," the two gunmen said almost in unison, overlooking Thatcher's complaint. Buddy only touched his hat brim in greeting them.

"It's a good thing we met you before you rode on to Cottonwood," said Chicago. "I'm afraid you would have been met with ill tidings." He grinned. "That whole town has a mad-on at me and anybody who knows me."

"Yeah?" Buddy returned the grin. "How much did you get?"

"Not near enough," Russell cut in.

Chicago shot him a hard stare, then said to Buddy Short, "A little over fourteen hundred."

"Dang," said Baldhead Paul, "he's right, that's not

nearly enough. Did we make an unwise move, coming to join you fellows?" He smiled, his crossed eyes seeming to look in no particular direction.

"Things will start getting better real soon," said Buddy. "To tell the truth, Curly Joe had grown so attached to Geneva Darrows' pudenda, he sort of let this business go to seed on us. Bank tellers have gotten belligerent, local law has gotten sassy as hell. Bobby Candles had to shoot the Cottonwood sheriff."

"Well, good for Bobby," said Buddy Short. He sighed and shook his head. "That's a damn shame about Curly Joe getting so stricken over Geneva Darrows, although I had my thoughts that he might be slipping. That's why brother Epps and I cut away from his gang last fall. He'd gotten awfully sloppy. Then I heard about the Hatton girl getting shot. I figure Curly wasn't long for this world, him or Sattler either."

"Yeah," said Chicago with a sad look, "and poor Pete Duvall."

"And don't forget Lou Jecker," Buddy Short reminded him.

"No, sir. How could I ever?" said Chicago. "I wasn't with them long . . . but they become my pards. I can't help but feel like—"

"Anyway, all that sad stuff is over and done with," Buddy Short cut in, realizing it was all just so much hot air. "And now we're back and ready to do whatever it takes to get this gang together."

"Hear, hear!" rallied Baldhead Paul. He gave a broad grin. "I'm busting to get started."

"We'll get started soon enough," said Chicago. "Right

now we've got the deputy sheriff of Cottonwood hounding us. That's where Candles is, him and a couple of his men. Up there, takin' care of business." He gestured toward the high trail where moments earlier they'd heard rifle fire.

"Damn," said Buddy Short. "He must be tougher than barbwire if it takes that much shooting to kill him."

"I don't care how much shooting it took," said Chicago, "so long as he's dead. We've all got better things to do than to get pinned down here by some half-simple sheriff's deputy."

As the men talked back and forth, from a distant hillside far out of rifle range, Eddie Lane stared down at them through a battered telescope he'd taken out of the dead sheriff's saddlebags and brought along with him. He couldn't shoot any of them from here. *Too far away . . .* , he told himself. But he could watch them, count them, figure out who was who among them. He looked from face to face at the new arrivals. These were men he had no fight with, unless they sided with the sheriff's killers.

As he watched, he saw the three men, one with his arm wrapped in a bloody bandana, ride back down from the higher switchback where he'd fired at them. He followed Candles with the telescope, seeing that the man's usual cocky smile and demeanor were gone now. *That's good*, he told himself, remembering the confident smugness the man had about him all the while he'd ridden with the sheriff's posse.

Making fools of everybody, Lane reminded himself. But not now. Now he was starting to get to him, to all three of them, he thought, collapsing the telescope between his palms and staring down for a moment through his naked eyes. *One dead, three to go, Sheriff . . .* , he said to himself, as if giving a report on his progress. All he had to do was stay alive, be careful and be patient, he could picture the old sheriff telling him.

So far so good. The one who'd called himself Newton would have been dead right now had Lane's foot not slipped in loose dirt and rock when he'd made his shot earlier. But mistakes happened, he reminded himself. He wouldn't make that one again.

The most important thing in winning a fight with these kinds of odds against him was *position*, he told himself, realizing that this too was something he'd learned from the wise old sheriff. Well, he now had position, and he wouldn't give it up. From up here he could pick his chances, swing down like a hawk and kill another one of the sheriff's murderers, until he had them all culled out from among the gunmen gathered below.

Chapter 11

———

Sitting atop their horses on the trail, still partly covered from above by brush and rock, Big Chicago watched as Candles led his two men down off the trail. Chicago saw this as a chance to better himself by lessening Candles in the eyes of the three newly arrived gunmen. As Candles and his men nudged their tired horses toward him and the others at a walk, Chicago smiled to himself.

"We heard all the shooting," he said to Candles. "Where's that deputy's body? Did you leave him lying dead over the edge of the trail the way you did the posse scout?"

"Posse scout? What's he talking about?" Baldhead Paul Crane said under his breath to Epps Short.

"Hush, maybe we'll find out," said Buddy Short in the same lowered tone.

"We didn't get him yet," Candles said, sounding annoyed by the question.

"Yet?" said Chicago. "You mean all that shooting I

heard, and that one man the three of yas were after, flat got away, *unscathed*, as they say?"

"I'll *scathe* his ass the next time I see him," Garr offered.

"Next time, huh?" said Chicago. He looked the three up and down, then said, "Maybe next time I'll send Russell and Thatcher here. No offense, Bobby b'hoy, but you three haven't impressed me much today."

"The man is high above us, and I have one man with a bad arm," Candles offered. "We'll get him next time he sticks his head up."

"I know you will. Right now you look like he's worn you out." Realizing he'd said enough for the time being, Chicago turned a hand toward the Short brothers and Baldhead Paul Crane before Candles could offer anything more in his own defense. "Anyhow. Look who showed up to join us while you three were fooling around up there shooting at shadows." He grinned, knowing he was needling Candles just enough to keep him from being able to make an issue over it.

The wounded Dayton Oak gave Chicago a hard stare and said sharply, "I wouldn't exactly call what we were doing up there fooling around, unless I was prepared to ride up and give an account of myself."

"That's enough, Oak," said Candles, cutting him off, knowing anything Oak said would make it look as though he didn't have control of his men. "Get down and rest some in the shade, get your arm looked after."

The Short brothers and Baldhead Paul gave one another a look, each of them seeing the tension between Chicago, the new gang leader and Bobby Candles, the wannabe who was out to take his place at the drop of a hat.

"Not to step on anybody's toes here," Buddy Short said to Big Chicago and Candles, "but we didn't ride all across the territory to get shot at by some stray-calf deputy whose sheriff got sent to hell."

"Yeah," said Baldhead Paul, his crossed eyes staring in a way that oddly looked as if he were staring individually at every man there. "We're more what you might call *working outlaws*."

Epps cut in, "We're itching to rob something straightaway. If we come at a bad time, you let us know. We could just as well ride on, maybe check back up with you when you're all more settled in with one another."

"Whoa, fellows," said Chicago. "We're ready to rob something first thing in the morning. Don't let this little situation throw you off of us. We're as ready to rob as we were when Curly Joe ran this bunch." He turned a harsh look to Candles for support. "Ain't that the truth, Bobby?"

"Hell yes, it's the truth," Candles said. "You fellows came at the right time."

"Well, that's good to hear," said Buddy. He grinned proudly all around. "Anybody who knows me and brother Epps knows that we're nothing if not workingmen."

"Same goes with me," said Baldhead Paul, the same beaming grin on his broad, hairless face. "So, just what play have you got in mind, Big Chicago?"

Chicago looked back and forth, making it up as he went along. "Call this a hit-or-miss, or even a practice run. But I figured we'd hit the relay station this side of the badlands. If we get in there, keep our heads down and wait for the northbound stage, there's a good chance they'll be carrying money up to the mines."

"A good chance?" Buddy said.

"I told you it's hit-or-miss," said Chicago. "But it you're itching for action, that's what I've got for you today." He stopped talking and looked back and forth between the Short brothers and Baldhead Paul.

After a moment of silence, Buddy Short shrugged and said, "Yeah, sure, why not? Like you said, it's practice. We'll all get to see how well we work together without Curly Joe at the lead."

Russell, who had been sitting quietly while the others spoke, finally said to Chicago, "That relay station is over thirty miles from here, if anybody's interested."

"I know how far it is, Russell," said Chicago. "I figured we'd get there in the night while nobody can see us coming. Come daylight, us and our horses will all be out of sight. No shotgun rider is going to be expecting anything when they roll in for fresh horses."

"Sounds good to me," Baldhead Paul said, his crossed eyes a-glitter at the prospect of robbing something.

"Then we ride in tonight," said Chicago. He jerked his reins and pulled his horse around toward the trail and said over his shoulder to Candles in a voice filled with authority, "Bobby, you and Garr hang back, look after Oak's arm wound. Catch up to us when you're finished."

Candles and Garr seethed as they watched the others ride away. But they kept their mouths shut and rode over to where Oak sat with his open canteen between his knees. Having washed the bandana, he sat ready to wrap it back around his wounded arm. "Help him out," Candles said to Garr. "I'll be over here watching the ridgeline in case that deputy is still sneaking around up there."

Garr just looked at him, knowing as well as he did that the deputy had already moved off along the trail ahead of them.

In the evening light, Eddie Lane watched the procession of gunmen from atop the high trail ahead, keeping in front of them, anticipating them, moving in the same direction. To the unknowing eye it might have looked more like the gunmen were following him instead of the other way around. When darkness fell he realized he would no longer be able to tell if the men had made a camp or kept moving forward in the night.

Rather than risk his horse on the rocky switchbacks, Lane made a dark camp, slept lightly and resumed his tracking as daylight crept above the distant horizon.

At a fork in the trail where he saw the fresh hoofprints had turned north in the night, he turned with them. But instead of staying in sight on the stretch of flatlands ahead of him, he circled wide and rode along the trail in the cover of morning shadows. When he spotted a low-lying log and adobe relay station through his telescope, he realized that was where the gunmen were headed. Where they were headed . . . ? No, he told himself, collapsing the telescope and putting it away. He booted his horse up into a faster gait along the rocky trail. They had ridden all night. They were there already.

Inside the relay station, a teamster named James Earl Coots sat staring down at the body of his pal Norman Beale, the depot manager. Beside Beale's body lay the body of his aging red hound, Oscar. "What kind of son of a bitch kills a poor old half-blind dog?" Coots said, in disgust. He stared coldly at Big Chicago, who had been the one to commit the foul act.

No one answered.

Dried blood had crusted down Coots' forehead, all the way from his hairline to his wiry beard. His hands had been tied behind his back; his lowered eyes shifted back and forth on the gunmen keeping vigil on the trail from inside the shuttered windows.

"You sonsabitches ought to be real proud of yourselves, killing Norman and Oscar," Coots said, not the least intimidated by the many guns brandished inside the small room. "I've know this man damn near all my life. He never harmed a fellow human being in any manner, thought, word or deed. Oscar neither." He spat in contempt. "Then here comes you bunch of turds."

Candles said over his shoulder from the cracked open front door, "Shut up, old man, before I have Garr bend a rifle barrel over your head."

"I'd like to see you untie my hands and try that yourself," Coots said.

Realizing how bad this made him look to the others, Candles turned his rifle toward the old teamster. He didn't intend to shoot Coots, but he hoped to scare him enough to shut him up.

"That's enough, Candles," said Chicago, a little more authority in his voice than was actually needed. "I said no shooting, I meant it." He stared at Candles and went on. "You've been in this game long enough that I shouldn't have to tell you."

Candles just looked at him. Big Chicago knew he wasn't going to pull a trigger and give up their being here. He'd only wanted to call Candles down in front of the men. *This son of a bitch . . .*

At a front window, Buddy and Epps Short each gave Candles a skeptical look, shook their heads and turned their eyes back toward the trail. Baldhead Paul spat, ran a thick hand across his lips and grumbled under his breath. But before another minute had passed, he said with a dark chuckle, "Here comes that fat little piggy, ready to get itself scalded and cooked."

The gunmen watched the big Studebaker stagecoach roll up into sight, stirring dust on the rocky trail.

"If you fellows knew what's good for yas, you'd hightail it out of here now, while you've got a chance. In case you didn't hear, the last men who crossed paths with J. Fenwick Hatton got themselves hunted down and killed like the dogs they were."

"We heard all about it," Chicago said, him and the men giving each other knowing looks. "You mean to tell us that Hatton owns this stagecoach line too?"

"Mr. Hatton owns everything—stagecoaches, railroads, banks, cattle and hotels," said Coots. "If I can think of anything else he owns, I'll tell you, first thing."

"Well, I'll be damned, men," said Chicago. "It seems

no matter which way we turn, we keep bumping heads with J. Fenwick Hatton."

"You won't bump heads with him long," said Coots. "He'll find out who did this. Then you can say hello to his regulator."

"His regulator?" said Chicago, as the big dusty coach rolled closer to the station. "Now, just who might his regulator be?"

"They call him Teacher," said Coots. "Seven weeks ago he killed Curly Joe Hobbs, his gang, whore and all. Just him, all by himself." Coots grinned, with no idea whom he was talking to. "He'll be coming for all you turds, soon as Hatton hears about this."

"They're rolling into the yard, Big Chicago," said Epps Short, reporting on the stagecoach.

"Good," said Chicago. "Nobody makes a move until they walk through the front door. Russell, you and Thatcher get out back, circle around and get that stage under control so they can't make a run for it." He looked over at Garr and said, "Gag the teamster. If he makes any noise, cut his throat."

Hearing the gunman call Big Chicago by name, Coots shut up and stared in silence as Garr walked over to him from the window, a knife handle standing in his boot well. "Don't make me have to clean your belly off my blade, mister," Garr warned. He pulled Coots' faded bandana up around his mouth and drew it tight.

Atop the big stagecoach, the driver, Milton Dona-hue, brought the horses to a halt and sat back on the long brake handle. Beside him, Charlie Stevens, the shot-gun rider, said warily, "Something ain't right here."

"Yeah," said Stevens, picking right up on Donahue's concerns. "Where is old Oscar? He never misses greeting a stagecoach."

As the two looked all around warily, from inside the stagecoach a man called up, "Are we going to disembark from this ship of torture? I fear the young lady here is quite in distress."

"Quiet inside!" the stage driver barked down in reply. He slid a second shotgun from under the driver's seat and said in a lowered voice, "Watch your step, Milton. I've got you covered whilst you look things over."

"It might be nothing, but I'll feel better checking first," said Donahue, swinging down from his seat and walking toward the relay station door.

Inside the stagecoach a businessman named Lawrence Eddington fidgeted impatiently in the seat. "What's taking so long out there?" he said to the man who'd been shouted out by the driver.

"I dare not ask after that last harsh recourse," replied the down-in-the-heels implement peddler named Karl Sanderson. "But apparently they feel there is something amiss here."

"Yeah, something *is* wrong," said Eddington. He drew a small Navy Colt from inside his suit coat and held it poised at his side. "Indians, I'll wager. There's every kind of murdering, bloodthirsty savage in this part of the territory, Apache, Cheyenne—"

"*Ahem.*" The peddler cleared his throat with deliberation and cast a slight nod toward the young woman seated across from them.

"My apologies, ma'am," said Eddington, catching himself. "I didn't mean to frighten you."

The peddler cut in, saying to her, "This is exactly the sort of situation I was alluding to last evening when I said a young lady should not be traveling unescorted in this barbaric wilderness."

Across from the two men, a young woman named Rachel Meadows closed a book she'd been reading and looked out the open coach window and back and forth across the barren land. "Mr. Sanderson," she said, "this is the nineteenth century. A woman has every right to travel alone and not expect to be mistreated or judged unladylike for her action."

"Of course, forgive me," said Sanderson, tipping his frayed-brimmed bowler hat. He and Eddington looked at each other, then cast their interest back toward the front of the relay station as the shotgun driver reached out a hand and shoved the thick plank door open.

Something was wrong here indeed; she felt it in her bones. From the far hills to the left, she saw a tiny black speck riding toward them at the head of a tall rise of dust. *Indians?* She didn't think so. Whatever it was, she had to be ready to fend for herself, if these armed men weren't able to keep the stagecoach safe.

She reached under her linen riding shawl and wrapped her hand around the long, slim penknife she'd secreted there before starting her journey across these untamed badlands.

Chapter 12

When the shotgun rider swung open the relay station door and stepped inside, three rifle shots picked him up and hurled him backward, out across the plank porch and into the dirt. The explosions spooked the stage horses. Atop the stagecoach, the driver swung his shotgun up at Russell and Thatcher as the two men came racing toward him from around the side of the building. The rearing, whinnying horses caused the driver's shotgun blast to go wild. But Russell's and Thatcher's shots were dead on-target.

"Jesus!" cried Eddington. "They're killing us!" He threw open the door and jumped out, Colt in hand, as atop the coach the dead driver landed atop a pile of tied-down luggage and mail sacks. The peddler jerked his hat down snug over his ill-kempt hair and rolled into a ball on the stage floor.

Rachel Meadows jerked the penknife from under her shawl and screamed, then drew it back and stabbed wildly at the air as a shotgun blast sent a spray of the businessman's blood and brain matter all over her. "Grab the horses!" shouted Chicago from the open doorway.

But before he'd even given the order, Thatcher had already begun scrambling up into the empty, bloody driver's seat, grabbed the traces and stood holding the horses firmly in place, helped by the brake handle being firmly set. "Whoa. Whoa," he called out.

"Settle them or shoot them," Chicago shouted, seeing the horses still rearing high.

"Hold on," said Candles, running from inside and leaping up atop the big coach beside Thatcher. "We don't have to kill the horses." He threw the brake off, let the spooked horses bolt only a step forward, then yanked back hard on the traces. This time the frightened horses came down chuffing and blowing. But they stood in place.

"You have to show them what you want from them when they're spooked that bad, Thatcher," he said, knowing it looked good to the others, him taking control of the situation.

Chicago saw what he was trying to do. He played it off with a laugh and said, "All right, hero. Throw down the strongbox and mail sacks while you're up there giving wagon lessons. Let's see what we've got here."

Inside the stagecoach, the peddler looked up at Rachel and whispered, "Get down here and be quiet. They will most certainly kill us!"

But the young woman could see nothing to gain by

lying in a ball on the floor. She fell silent, but climbed over the back of the peddler, opened the coach door on the other side and hit the ground at a hard run. Clutching her dress up above her knees, the penknife in her hand, she ran straightaway from the coach out across the rocky, barren land.

Gathering around the strongbox, the gunmen watched her. "That is one fast, high-stepping woman," said Baldhead Paul, grinning along with the others.

"She is to be sure," said Chicago. As he spoke he raised his revolver from his waist sash and fired a single shot at the fleeing woman. The young woman flew forward with a loud scream and hit the ground. "Now, back to this," Chicago said, gesturing toward the strongbox. He fired another shot and watched the brass lock break and fall in two pieces to the dirt.

"She's back up, Chicago," said Russell.

"Damn it." Chicago was more interested in the contents of the strongbox. "Somebody shoot her, please!" he said.

Russell raised a Colt from his holster. But Epps Short said, "No, wait. I'm going to ride out and get her and bring her back. There's no need in killing her right off. We ain't even had a chance to say howdy." He grinned and ran to the horses.

"Suit yourself," said Russell. He turned back to the strongbox as Chicago reached down and opened it. "My God!" he said at the sight of bound stacks of cash.

In their excitement, the gunmen had not seen Eddie Lane headed their way from the distant hill line. But Lane had drawn closer, hearing the gunshots and seeing what was going on out in front of the relay station. When he'd heard Chicago's gunshot and saw the woman fall to the ground, his rifle had come out of his saddle boot. He'd levered a round into the chamber one-handed, his horse's hooves pounding on beneath him, and raised the rifle butt to his shoulder.

On the flats beyond the station, Rachel Meadows had risen to her feet and tried to run farther away. But on the rocky ground, she only made it a few yards before she tumbled back to the dirt. Behind her she heard the sound of Epps' horse riding down on her. She gripped the penknife to her breast and lay gritting her teeth.

But as Epps Short raced toward her, a silent bullet sliced through his back and blew a hole the size of a large apple in his chest. As the sound of the distant shot caught up to the bullet, Epps had already spilled sidelong from his saddle and fallen dead onto the ground.

"What the hell?" Chicago and the others ducked slightly at the sound of the rifle shot. As they straightened and saw the single rider pounding down on them, Chicago instinctively grabbed the loaded strongbox and dragged it toward the horses around the side of the building. "Shoot that sumbitch!" he shouted.

Seeing the gunmen taking cover, Eddie Lane slid his horse to a halt, leaped down from its back and dropped prone behind a rock. His horse ran a few yards, circled and stopped in the thin shade of a saguaro cactus. "It's that damn deputy you keep telling us is nobody to worry about!" Chicago shouted at Candles.

"Hold it," said Oak, standing at a wooden rail fence, his wounded arm hanging limp at his side. "I want to put the first bullet in this ambushing bastard myself."

"Take cover, damn it," Candles shouted at him as he hurried around the side of the building.

"Not until I cut his spine out," said Oak. He laid his rifle up on the rail fence for support and started to stoop down and take aim. But before he could, a bullet slammed into his chest and hurled him backward. He landed dead on the ground, a spray of dark blood settling over him.

"Damn it, somebody *shoot* him!" repeated Chicago, who had been grabbing bound stacks of paper money from the strongbox and stuffing them inside his duster. From the cover of the side of the building, the gunmen returned rifle fire out across the flats. Yet, even as they fired, a widening drift of rifle smoke was the only sign of anybody being out there.

Firing wildly, the gunmen had gathered closer around the heavy strongbox, stuffing the money into their shirts and riding dusters to make it easier to carry. "He's a long ways off, Chicago," said Thatcher, dropping a stack of money back into the strongbox, knowing he'd be taken care of later. "Want me and Russell to circle wide and ride him down while you keep him pinned from here?"

"Yeah, yeah, you do that," Chicago, sounding detached from the matter and looking more concerned with hoarding the bulk of the cash from the strongbox.

Candles saw his chance and cut in, saying, "I'm rid-

ing with them. This *stable hand* doesn't kill my two
pards and get away with it."

"Go get him, men," said Chicago. "We'll finish cutting up the money and ride the north trail toward
Saverine Pass—on to the Roost. Catch up to us on the
way. Your share will be waiting." He grinned and said
to the others, "To tell you the truth, I wasn't expecting
such a haul as this. We hit the jackpot here."

Baldhead Paul gave a leering, lopsided grin of approval, but Buddy Short said angrily, "My poor brother
is lying out there blown all to hell! I can't think of
money right now!"

"Then ride out there with them and kill the man,"
said Chicago, not being deterred from the large pile of
cash in the strongbox. "I'll see to it you get what's coming to you."

Buddy Short considered it, then replied, "I expect
brother Epps knew the risk when he decided to ride
this outlaw trail."

"Yeah," said Chicago, still stuffing cash inside his
buttoned duster as Delbert Garr and Baldhead Paul
returned fire, "that's the way I always look at it."

Inside the plank and adobe relay station, still tied to his
chair, James Earl Coots tipped himself over onto the
floor to stay down away from any stray bullets. On the
dirt floor beside the bodies of Norman Beale and his
old dog, Oscar, Coots rubbed his face back and forth
on the rocky ground until he got the bandana off his
mouth.

He rolled sidelong until he reached the sharp corner of the stone hearth. There he raised himself high enough to throw himself down and crush the straight-back chair beneath him. Then he hurried out of the loose rope, crawled inside a smaller room off to the side and bolted the thick plank door behind himself.

In moments Coots heard two sets of boots run across the plank porch and into the station. "The bastard's gotten himself loose," Coots heard Garr say angrily.

"Try the other room," Baldhead Paul said. "Chicago wants him dead."

Coots heard Garr shoulder the bolted door. "To hell with this. If Chicago wants him dead, he can pound this door down and kill him. Let's get out of here."

Coots lay as still as stone. He dared not risk standing or moving about until he heard the sound of the gunmen's horses pounding off across the flatland. "Thank you, Lord . . . ," he said on a sigh of relief, finally standing, realizing that whoever was out on the flats had saved his life by keeping the gunmen busy while he'd freed himself and locked himself away.

In the front room he hurried to a window and looked out, seeing Buddy Short heft his dead brother across his saddle and hurry away to catch up with Chicago and the others. Beyond where Buddy had picked up Epps' body, Coots saw the young woman still lying facedown on the ground. Staring for a moment, he saw her raise her face slightly, look back and forth, then lower it, playing it safe, he thought. . . .

Out on the flats, Candles, Russell and Thatcher slid their horses to a slow, cautious walk and looked back and forth in every direction, seeing no sign of the young deputy who had caused all the trouble. "He's disappeared on us like smoke," said Russell, his shotgun in his bedroll now and a rifle standing tall, the butt end against his thigh.

"Yeah, he's vanished," Thatcher said in disgust, sliding his rifle back down into his saddle boot, his shotgun also stuck in his bedroll. Rather than sit empty-handed, he drew a long Remington from his side holster and held it across his lap.

"Damn it! A son of a bitch can't just vanish!" Candles said angrily. He jerked his horse back and forth, seeing the disturbed dirt behind the small rock standing at their horses' hooves, seeing the boot prints leading off to the shade of the tall saguaro cactus where Lane's horse had stood.

Russell and Thatcher gave each other a look. "This one does," Thatcher said flatly. Then in the same voice he went on to say, "You know, the one *you* led to us?"

"Hey, if either one of you've got something to say, get it done now," Candles said.

"I've got something to say," Russell called out, raising his hand as if in a schoolroom. "I believe you're wanting everybody to decide who should run this gang, you or Big Chicago."

Candles gave a short, wise grin. "You mean you figured that out all by yourself?"

Russell let the remark pass. "Thatcher and I talked about it. The sooner we decide who's the boss, the better off we'll all be."

"Yeah?" Candles listened intently.

"Nothing against Big Chicago, but he's not our first pick when it comes to running this kind of business. It just fell to him when Curly Joe got killed."

"All right," said Candles, relaxing a little, his interest piquing, his hands crossed on his saddle horn, "I can go along with that."

Russell said, "So we decided."

"Yes, and . . . ?" said Candles.

Thatcher gave a short, thin smile. "Guess who we decided on, you *turd, poltroon, catamite. . . .*" His big Remington turned only slightly on his lap.

"No, wait!" Candles shouted, his confident grin suddenly gone, replaced by a look of terror.

The Remington bucked on Thatcher's thigh. Candles fell backward from his saddle and hit the ground with a loud grunt. He lay limp and dazed in a cloud of dust. Thatcher and Russell gave each other their same flat expression. "It's called the *democratic process*," Russell said.

"Yeah, I like it," said Thatcher. He stepped his horse over Candles and leveled the big Remington down at his head. But before he could fire a killing round, dirt kicked up at his horse's hooves and caused the animal to rear slightly as the sound of the rifle echoed across the flats from the far side of the relay station.

"Jesus!" shouted Russell. "He's gotten halfway around us."

"Cut out!" cried Thatcher, jerking his horse sideways and batting his heels to the animal's flanks.

North of the station, Eddie Lane stood up from the

ground and dusted his trousers. As the final two gunmen rode away in a long stream of rising dust, he rode
out to where he found Candles crawling across the
dirt, struggling to reach his horse standing a few yards
away.

"Well, well, it's Mr. Newton," he said, stepping down
from his saddle. He picked up Candles' handgun from
the ground where it had fallen from his holster and
shoved it down behind his belt as he walked over to
Candles.

"Don't—don't kill me," Candles pleaded, looking
up, seeing the young deputy stop and stand over him,
rifle in hand, the tip of the barrel only inches from his
face. "You're a lawman, Eddie . . . you can't . . . just shoot
a wounded man."

"Yes, I can," said Lane, cocking the rifle hammer
with determination. "Anyway, you're not wounded.
You're only grazed."

Candles felt of his bloody, throbbing shoulder with a
look of relief, feeling a long cut rather than an open
bullet hole. *Lucky break. . . .* Then he turned his eyes back
up to Lane.

"So long, murderer," said Lane, ready to pull the
trigger before Candles even had time to savor his good
fortune.

"Wait! I—I can help you," Candles said. "I know
things about . . . Chicago and his men!"

"I don't care about them," said Lane. "I only came to
kill you, and the men who killed Sheriff Morgan."

"What about those poor people . . . lying dead back

there?" said Candles. "Don't you . . . owe them anything? What about the others who will die . . . if you don't stop Chicago and his men?"

The young deputy stopped and looked back toward the relay station, considering it. When he turned back to Candles, the wily gunman had come up with a derringer from his boot and pulled the trigger. The shot sliced through the side of Lane's neck as he ducked away and kicked the small gun from Candles' hand.

"Wait—don't shoot," Candles shouted, pleading once again now that his sneak attacked had gone afoul. "I—I didn't mean that. I lost my head."

Lane quickly grabbed his bandana from around his neck and pressed it to the flowing blood. "On your feet, Mr. Newton," he said with contempt. "One more move like that and it won't matter how much you can tell me. I'll kill you dead."

Jesus. . . . Candles couldn't believe it. After all he'd done, this stable hand still wasn't going to kill him? How stupid could this man be? He stared up at him and raised his good arm chest high, the bullet hole in his shoulder keeping him raising the other. "No . . . I'm all through. You don't have to . . . worry about me," he said, giving Lane a whipped-dog look as he struggled up to his feet, the impact of the bullet graze on his shoulder starting to wear off some.

As he righted himself on his feet, Lane jammed the rifle barrel into his side and forced him up into his saddle. "These will keep you honest," the deputy said, taking a pair of three-way handcuffs from behind his back. He snapped an iron cuff onto each of Candles' wrists and tightened the third cuff around his saddle horn.

"I mean it," said Candles, "I won't give you any more trouble—"

"You've seen my rifle shooting," said Lane, cutting him off. "If you try to make a run for it, I'll just figure you want to die." He took the reins to Candles' horse, turned and stepped up into his saddle and led his prisoner back toward the relay station.

Chapter 13

Instead of riding to the relay station, Eddie Lane rode straight past it to where the woman lay trembling on the ground. Jumping down from his saddle, the young deputy hurried forward, his rifle still in his hand, keeping a watchful eye on the dust still looming above the flats. Beneath the dust he knew that the riders were still riding hard toward the distant hill line.

"Ma'am, get up. Let's go," he said as he approached the terrified woman. As he hurriedly stood over her and reached down and took her arm to help her to her feet, he said, "I'm not going to hurt you. I'm here to—"

Before he could finish his words, the woman reeled up and around with a loud scream. She drew back the penknife and plunged the blade deep into his chest. From atop his horse, Bobby Candles winced as he saw what happened. But it took him only a second to realize that this was the break he needed. He gave a bemused smile as he saw Eddie Lane stagger back and forth, his rifle falling to the ground as his hands went instinctively to the knife handle and grasped it firmly.

As soon as the woman saw Lane's face, something told her she had made a bad mistake. "Oh God!" she cried, seeing Lane sink to his knees.

"Bless your heart, ma'am!" Candles chuckled. He batted his horse forward toward the rifle on the ground even though there was no way he could jump down and pick it up with his hands cuffed to the big California-style saddle horn. "Hand me that rifle, lady!" he said, hoping the authority in his voice would cause her to do his bidding without question.

She stared at him in disbelief for a stunned moment, then reached down and picked up the rifle. But instead of handing it to Candles, she raised it and aimed it at him. He watched her fumble with the lever, with no idea how to fire the weapon. Yet. *Uh-oh!* Candles saw the rifle aimed at him. At the same time he heard a rifle shot explode from the front of the relay station and heard a bullet whistle past his head.

"Get away from him, lady!" shouted Coots as he came running with a limp toward them, a smoking rifle in his hands.

"Damn it!" said Candles, his horse chuffing and spinning restlessly beneath him, ready to go. Unable to even grab his horse's reins with the cuffs on, he batted his boots to the animal's sides and took off in an awkward jagged run across the open flatlands, hanging on to the saddle horn with both cuffed hands, his reins waving in the air beside him.

The woman stared wide-eyed and stunned at Eddie Lane as he rocked back and forth on his knees, his face flushed and pale, a patch of seeping blood widening on the front of his shirt. "Help me . . . ," he managed to say in a hoarse, broken voice.

But she could do nothing, except drop the rifle, kneel down in front of him and steady him by both hands until Coots ran to them and dropped to the ground beside her. "Ma'am, you have stabbed the wrong man. This one was here trying to help."

"I—I didn't know," the woman said. She noted the rope and busted pieces of the wooden chair back still dangling from his forearm. "Who are you?"

"I'm James Earl Coots, ma'am," the teamster said to her as he stared at the knife blade in Lane's chest.

"You—you work here?" she asked.

"I teamster freight out of here, ma'am," said Coots. "I was visiting a friend and his dog. Those murderers killed them both."

Coots saw the dark shape of the deputy badge on Lane's otherwise faded shit. "Help me lay him back easylike, so he won't fall and gut himself," he said.

She reached in to help and saw the bloody bandana tied around the side of Lane's neck from the bullet graze. "His throat is bleeding too," she said. Then in a wave of remorse, she cried, "My God, what have I done to him?"

"Hush, and help me out here," Coots said sharply. "You had nothing to do with the wound on his neck. Stabbing him was bad enough." He stared into Lane's eyes as the two eased him back onto the ground. "You hold on, young fellow. I won't let you die. It'd be a shame to lose you after all the good you done here today."

"It's all my fault, it's all my fault," the woman repeated, shaking her lowered head.

Eddie Lane looked up at her and said in a strained and failing voice, "It's not . . . your fault."

"You hush up too," said Coots. "Let's see if we can keep you alive. You can talk about whose fault it is later."

Across the wide stretch of flatlands, Bobby Candles stopped long enough to look back and make certain he wasn't being followed. Seeing nothing but his high drifting dust on the trail from the stage station, he shook his head and chuckled to himself. Man, what a strange piece of luck he'd been handed, he told himself. What were the odds that a woman would stab the man who'd probably just saved her life?

His dark chuckle continued as he pictured Eddie Lane staggering around, the knife handle bobbing on his chest. That had to hurt, he told himself, almost laughing out loud. *That poor, stupid bastard . . .*

He relaxed. Hell, there was no one trailing him, certainly not the stable-hand deputy, not with all that iron stuck in his chest. All right, he had to kill Russell and Thatcher as soon as his path crossed theirs again. For now, though, he'd have to try and avoid all of them. He knew the two would never have tried to kill him without Big Chicago's approval.

Now that Delbert Garr was the only man of his still left alive, he couldn't count on anybody but himself. Garr wouldn't stick his neck out for him. Not with his pocket lined with all the money the gang had just made from the stagecoach robbery. Garr would have changed sides. Hell, he couldn't blame him, Candles thought. Considering the situation for a moment longer, he finally shrugged.

All right, some things had taken a bad turn for him. Other than that, he was free as a bird. He started to lift his canteen by its strap, but the handcuffs on his wrists and his saddle horn stopped him from doing so. "Damn it," he said hoarsely, his throat caked with dust and no way to even reach up to his bandana and raise it across the bridge on his nose. "What kind of sumbitch does something like this to a man?" he shouted back across the flatlands, knowing that no one could hear him.

All right, stay calm, he told himself. He gripped the thick California-style saddle horn with both hands and yanked back and forth with all of his strength, not feeling it give in the slightest. "What the hell is this?" he grumbled. "Damn, lousy saddle-maker. Why'd he have to make something this damned strong?" This was stupid!

In his anger, he shouted and jerked and pulled wildly, but it didn't help. He raised a boot and stomped his heel repeatedly against the saddle horn. Still nothing. "Damn it! Damn it, Damn it *to hell!*"

Finally, his anger spent, he settled himself down and looked closer at the saddle horn and slid the clamped cuff up and down on it. All it needed was a fraction of an inch for the iron cuff to turn over the top flat head of the saddle horn and pop right off. But that fraction of an inch might just as well be a mile, he told himself, his throat getting drier, more caked with dust, his face and eyes starting to itch and burn from dust he could not wipe away.

Son of a bitch . . . He couldn't even guide his horse, he reminded himself. Taking a long, deep, calming breath, he nudged the horse forward, his reins dragging in the dirt behind him. He recalled a water hole at the base of the hills a full twenty miles north into the badlands. With any luck the horse would head there on its own once it caught the smell of water.

In the long shadows of evening, three riders moved up as quietly as ghosts onto a rock shelf overlooking the water hole that Bobby Candles had spent most of the day trying to reach. The three had watched horse and rider meander across rock and sand and through stands of cactus and bracken until finally reaching the water's edge.

"At last, this asshole gets here," said a half-breed desert bandit called Dad Lodi. "What the hell could he have been searching for out there?"

"I do not know. But we have never waited this *long* for this *little* in my life," said a one-eared Mexican widely known as Pie Sucio, or Dirty Foot in English. They looked Candles up and down from fifty yards above him, seeing nothing of much value to him, except the tired, sweat-streaked horse.

"He is not wearing a gun, Dad," Dirty Foot went on. "We should split him open and step all over his insides for keeping us waiting this way."

The third man, a desert–hardened gunman named Frank Dorsey, eyed Candles closely as the cuffed outlaw swung down from his saddle holding the horn and shook the saddle back and forth until he was finally able to pull it down the tired animal's side. "Jesus . . . ," said Dorsey, watching the strange sight. "There's something you don't see every day."

The horse stood in the shallow water, drawing thirstily, paying Candles no regard as the choking, dust-caked outlaw pulled the saddle down the horse's belly, hung from it, twisted his face to one side and lapped at the water like a dog.

"I can't wait to hear this one's story," Dad Lodi said flatly, nudging his horse forward quietly, down toward the water hole.

Hanging under the horse's belly, Candles didn't see the three riders slip up on him until he heard the cock of a rifle hammer and froze for a second, knowing the helplessness of his situation. "Easy, boy," he whispered to the horse, to make sure it didn't spook and take off with him cuffed beneath it.

"Who taught you how to water a horse?" Dad Lodi asked. Beside him the other two sat staring at Candles with rapt interest.

Candles turned his head slowly and looked at the three desert hard cases from his position under the horse. He didn't offer a reply, but none was expected. Instead he watched in silence as the three came forward, their horses at a slow walk, and spread out in a half circle, surrounding him.

"Look," said Frank Dorsey, "he's handcuffed to his saddle horn."

"I bet he had something to do with all that shooting we heard earlier, from the stage stop," said Dad Lodi. He stopped the closest to Candles. He stepped down and picked up the horse's dangling reins from the water. He bowed slightly beside the horse, his hands on his knees, and looked Candles in the face.

"Would I be wrong in thinking there was a stagecoach robbery out there today?" he said.

Candles knew these men were bandits. "Yes, there was," he said, taking his chances.

"It didn't go real well for you, did it?" Lodi said flatly.

"No, it went bad," said Candles, hanging beneath a horse but still trying to look calm and in control of his situation.

"So, now you're headed for Robber's Roost to lick your wounds," Lodi continued.

"You're calling it about right," said Candles. "A lawman ambushed us."

"*Us?*" said Lodi. "How many were with you?"

"Oh, eight, nine maybe," said Candles.

"And *one* lawman ambushed you?" Lodi said. He rose slightly and gave his two companions a bemused look.

"Yeah, one, but with a Winchester repeater and a raised scope," Candles offered. "Anyway, he caught all of us by surprise, killed a couple of our men and captured me. I got away, but as you see—" He jiggled the iron handcuffs. "Not before he cuffed me to this blasted saddle."

Lodi shook his head in contemplation. "Then, just when you thought you had got away clean, damned if you didn't run into us."

Candles caught the threat in Lodi's words, but he ignored it and said, "Running into you men might be the best thing that could have happened to all of us."

"Oh, really?" Lodi looked engrossed in what Candles had to say. But then he grinned and flagged the other two in closer with his dust-caked hand. "Come over here, boys. He's going to tell us how lucky we all are."

"This is no yarn, mister," Candles said, knowing he had only a slim chance of talking his way out of this. "We got more money off of that stagecoach today than I've ever seen come out of a strongbox in my life. That's the honest truth."

"Congratulations, you must be awfully proud," said Lodi. He pointed the tip of the already cocked rifle into Candles' face.

"No, wait! Please!" said Candles. "We can have all that money, the four of us!"

Lodi grinned. "We can? How?"

"I know where they're going," Candles said.

"So do I," said Lodi. "They're going where everybody goes. They'll lie low in Robber's Roost. Emmen and Brady Shay will hide them out there until it's safe for them to leave. Meanwhile, all the whores and gaming tables will be busy taking most of that money away from them." He grinned. "Anything else you want to tell me?"

"Listen to me," said Candles, talking fast to save his life. "If one lawman can ambush them, think what four of us can do. The way you fellows know these desert hill trails, this will be easy pickings."

"Yeah?" Dorsey asked, stepping closer. "Then why is it we need you?"

"Because you three don't know the Shay brothers the way I do." Candles stared at him. "The Shays say you sand bandits don't have enough money in your pockets to hold you steady in a windstorm."

"Sand bandits. Now, that hurts," said Lodi with a thin, tight grin.

"Get me loose," said Candles. "We'll hit them before they get to the Roost. With the kind of money I'm talking about, Robber's Roost will treat you like close kin. I know the Shays. I can do this for yas."

"What do you say, fellows?" asked Lodi. "Want me to shoot this peckerwood, see if it would shut him up? Or you want to take this stage money he's talking about?"

"We can shoot him any time," said Dorsey. He reached in, took Candles by his shoulder and dragged him up, saddle and all, until he stood beside the horse. "I wouldn't mind seeing how our *betters* live. I've heard they've got a bathtub in the Roost you stretch all the way out in."

"Let's do it," said Dirty Foot.

"All right!" said Candles, feeling better by the second. "Has one of you got a saw, an ax, something I can use to get this damn saddle horn—"

As he spoke, Dirty Foot reached out, took the saddle horn with both hands and gave it a hard twist to his left. The saddle horn gave a loud screech and snapped off into his hands. Candles stared at the broken saddle horn in disbelief. "Son of a bitch . . . ," he said in awe.

Chapter 14

———

Inside the hacienda, Lilly Jones did not see a lone rider from Silver City stop at the barn and hand Sherman Dahl a written message. All she saw was the stir of dust drift past the window as the rider touched his hat brim, turned his horse and rode away, not even taking time to water his animal before making his trip back to town.

Odd . . ., she said to herself.

When she stepped out onto the porch and saw Dahl walking toward her, she noted the grim, serious look clouding his brow. As he came toward her, Dahl folded a piece of paper and slid it into his shirt pocket. "What is it? Who was that?" she asked, gazing out as the rider grew smaller along the dusty, winding trail. "Is everything all right?"

"He's only a messenger for Mr. Farris, J. Fenwick Hatton's man," Dahl said. "Hatton is still shaving close to trouble. I've got to go back out."

"But you're not yet well from your last job for Hatton," Lilly replied. "What does this man expect from you?"

"Chester Goines has robbed three different places that Hatton has interests in," said Dahl.

"Big Chicago?" said Lilly, a dark look coming upon her face.

"Yes," said Dahl. "I've got to go finish things with *Big Chicago*." He considered things and added, "I should have done it before."

"But you said he wasn't one of the men who killed Hatton's daughter," Lilly said.

"I know," said Dahl. "Hatton was specific. He only wanted the killers who were there the day of his daughter's death. But since then, things have changed. I told Hatton I'd get the man. Now I've got to do it."

They stood in silence for a moment, looking out across the land. "We're not even settled in here yet," Lilly said. "What about the cattle you've got Ben Simpson bringing all the way from Las Cruces?"

"Pay Simpson for the cattle," he said. "Tell him and his men to turn them out on the west grassland. They'll be all right out there. I shouldn't be gone long."

"*Shouldn't* be . . . ?" Lilly said.

"I *won't* be gone long," Dahl said, seeing she needed reassurance. "I'm riding to town to meet with Farris and find out more. I'll stop by town on my way and tell Sheriff Tucker to keep an eye on you out here until I get back," he added.

"Farris is in Silver City?" she asked.

"Yes," said Dahl. "That's where I'm headed."

She only nodded, knowing there was nothing to say. This was his life; she wasn't out to change it.

An hour later she stood on the porch with her hand shading her eyes and watched him ride out of sight. "Be careful, Sherman Dahl," she whispered absently, repeating what she'd said only moments earlier as he'd stood with his arms around her.

On the trail, Dahl rode at an easy gait, his bedroll and shotgun tied down behind his saddle, his Winchester repeating rifle resting in its saddle boot. On his hip he wore his tall black-handled Colt. Up under his left arm beneath his black riding duster, he wore a shoulder harness carrying another Colt, this one a smaller-frame double-action with a bird's-eye grip. He had not replaced the bullet vest since he and Lilly had arrived at the hacienda. He hoped that was not something he would regret, he thought, nudging the horse.

He rode on.

Out in front of an adobe saloon in Silver City, he stepped down at a hitch rail, reined his horse, walked inside and looked all around the busy saloon. At a large round table in the far corner, Hatton's assistant, Farris, stood up from a large table and looked toward him. Across from Farris, Sheriff Dan Tucker, aka Dangerous Dan, sat observing patiently. Farris stepped forward as he waved a hand.

"There you are, Mr. Dahl," he said. A whiskey glass sat on the table in front of his empty chair. "Thank goodness, you spared no time in getting here!"

"Not at all, Farris," Dahl said, glancing at the sheriff, seeing what sort of revealing look the seasoned lawman might offer him. "I came straightaway."

Seeing the assistant offer his shaky hand, Dahl took it and shook hands with him. "I regret having to inconvenience you," Farris said. As they stopped shaking hands, Dahl noted dark worry circles lining the man's eyes.

"Not at all. It's my pleasure," Dahl said respectfully. Of course he'd come right away. Hatton had sent him. Farris was the same as talking to Hatton himself. "What may I do for you—or should I say, for Mr. Hatton?"

"I'm afraid it was I, sir, rather than Mr. Hatton, who sent for you," said Farris. He looked worried. "I hope you will forgive me. Please sit down and allow me to explain."

"Of course," said Dahl. As he spoke he looked at the sheriff.

Dan Tucker remained seated but gave Dahl a polite nod. "Mr. Dahl," he said.

"Sheriff Tucker," Dahl said in the same level tone of respect, touching his fingertip to the brim of his hat.

Once seated, Dahl watched Farris seat himself and pick up a bottle of whiskey from the tabletop and say, "May I do the honors, Mr. Dahl?" He held the bottle out over a shot glass standing in front of Dahl's chair.

"Thank you, Farris," Dahl replied. He watched Farris' nervous hand pour the glass full. Then he picked it up and took a sip and set it down. He stared at Farris expectantly.

"Without going into gruesome details," Farris said

to Dahl, "I was just telling the sheriff here what a remarkable service you preformed for Mr. Hatton a short time back. I trust you have recovered well, and are feeling fit?"

Dahl slipped a glance to the sheriff, seeing that the seasoned lawman needed nothing spelled out for him. Tucker knew what Dahl did for a living. He only returned Dahl's gaze without revealing anything he might be thinking.

"Yes, I'm fine, thank you," Dahl replied, the expectant look still on his face.

"Good," said Farris. He paused and looked back and forth between the sheriff and Dahl. "Then allow me to get right to the purpose of my visit." His gaze went to Sheriff Tucker and lingered for just a moment.

"Gentlemen," said the sheriff, taking a hint, cutting a searching glance toward the busy bar, "if you'll excuse me. I need to speak with the owner for a moment."

"Yes, of course," said Farris. He gave a courteous nod.

The two watched Sheriff Tucker stand up from the table and walk away toward the bar. As soon as the lawman was out of sight, Farris leaned forward, needing no more prompting. "It's about Mr. Hatton, sir," he said quickly. "Since his last meeting with you, Chester Goines has robbed three of his business interests."

Dahl just looked at him.

Farris went on. "He and Curly Joe Hobbs' old gang robbed the Cottonwood Territorial Savings Bank, which Mr. Hatton personally had insured through his railroad. He robbed Chase's Hotel in Rocking—another invest-

ment enterprise of Hatton Enterprises—and burned it
to the ground." He paused as if to collect himself before proceeding. "Less than a week ago, he and his men
robbed a stagecoach carrying a sizable amount of Mr.
Hatton's money across the badlands into Arizona Territory."

"A sizable amount?" Dahl asked.

"Yes, two hundred thousand dollars to be exact, sir,"
Farris said, his eyes widening a little at the mention of
such a large mount.

Dahl sat quietly. Two hundred thousand dollars was
indeed an unusually large amount of money to be shipped
by stagecoach across the lawless badlands, especially
for a man who knew the dangers of frontier transporta-
tion the way Hatton did, Dahl thought. But he made no
further comment on the matter.

"As soon as Mr. Hatton received word about the
stagecoach robbery," said Farris, "he went wild. I tried
to reason with him, to make him realize that Big Chicago might have no idea these places he robbed were a
part of Hatton Enterprises."

"He wouldn't listen?" Dahl asked.

"No, not for a moment," said Farris. "Usually Mr.
Hatton understands that with all of his frontier hold-
ings he is bound to cross paths with thieves and murderers like Chester Goines now and then. But this time
he only became morose, inconsolable. I pleaded with
him to contact you, sir, but he would have none of it.
The following day he left, by himself, on his private rail
car. He said he would hunt down Big Chicago himself

and kill him." He paused, then added with finality, "I'm afraid he has quite lost his mind."

"I agree with you, it is probably coincidental that Big Chicago robbed anything belonging to Hatton Enterprises." He considered it further, then asked Farris, "Will he cool down after a while?" Dahl had already begun sensing a dangerous situation in the making, a man like Hatton, a killer like Big Chicago.

"I'm afraid he will not. I have never seen him this way, sir," said Farris. "I would never have come all this way if I thought there was the remotest possibility of him regaining his—"

"Of course you wouldn't, Farris," said Dahl. "Please forgive me." He knew he was being asked to go out to search the badlands for Hatton, to talk sense to him, to stop him or help him. "Go on, finish what you're telling me. Then tell me what can I do for you," he said.

"Yes, sir, thank you." Farris nodded. "I have never seen Mr. Hatton this way. After all that happened, after all the expense, and in spite of how badly he wanted the slayers of his daughter punished . . ." He paused and leaned in closer as if sharing a secret. "After hearing about the stage robbery, he took Curly Joe's head, the string of ears, and he burned them, each and every one."

Dahl studied his worried eyes, then said, "I've had that happen before, Farris. Don't let that by itself concern you."

"You—you have, sir?" Farris asked, piqued with interest.

Dahl offered, "A man like Hatton loses a loved one, often the first thing he thinks of is getting revenge. But afterward, when he realizes that no amount of staring into the pickled face, or at that dried string of trophies, is going to bring back the one he lost, he gets to where he no longer wants the reminders under the same roof with him."

"Oh yes . . . I see," said Farris, rubbing his chin in contemplation. He raised his eyes back to Dahl's, looking a little less worried now, and said, "I daresay, sir, I even recall you told him you wished those grizzly souvenirs might help him. It was as if you already knew they wouldn't."

Dahl only nodded. He sipped the rest of the whiskey from his shot glass and asked, "Any other peculiar behavior you may have noticed before he left?"

"Yes," said Farris. "Ever since employing you to hunt down his daughter's killers, he has become more interested in learning to shoot firearms than he has been in running his many business interests." He raised a finger for emphasis. "I'm not talking about gaming rifles or fowling pieces. He has always been an excellent shot in the fields and on the sporting ranges. I'm talking about those kinds of firearms."

He gestured toward the Colt under Dahl's left arm. "He has been carrying a Colt like the one there on your hip. He not only practices firing it, but drawing it quickly as well. The way men in your line of work must do." He paused again, then added in a lowered voice, "I'm afraid he's gotten quite good at it."

"I see," said Dahl. "It's unusual for a man like Hatton to take an interest in gunfighting—unusual, yet not *unheard of.*"

"From everything you're saying," said Farris, "should I take it you are not in agreement with me on the severity of this matter?"

"No, Farris," said Dahl. "Rest assured that I am with you all the way. I knew before I rode here that I was going to kill Big Chicago if that's what Mr. Hatton, or you in his absence, required of me."

"Oh, I see, sir," said Farris, "and I might add more than just a little relieved." He stopped and said curiously, "But if I may, sir, why are you going so willingly, to answer such an unusual request?"

"I gave him my word," Dahl said flatly.

"I see, sir," said Farris. "That is most commendable of you."

Dahl saw Sheriff Tucker look their way from the corner of the busy bar, and he gestured a nod for the lawman to rejoin them. Once Tucker was back, standing at the table, Dahl stood up himself and said, "Sheriff, will you keep an eye on Lilly and my place while I'm away for a while? I have some cattle coming most any time."

"I'll look after everything," said Tucker. Dahl could see by the gleam in the sheriff's eyes that the lawman would have forfeited a month's pay just to ride along with him. But Tucker knew Dahl worked alone.

"Obliged, Sheriff," said Dahl. He looked at Farris and said, "I brought along my bedroll and my guns. I'm ready to ride."

"Splendid, sir," said Farris. "In anticipation of your

saying yes, I took the liberty of securing myself a horse, a firearm and range clothes. All I need to procure for myself is a bedroll and I'll be—"

"Whoa, hold on," said Dahl. "I always work alone."

"But, sir, I must accompany you," said Farris. "I do so with only the slightest hope that Mr. Hatton will listen to me, as he has on past occasions. I'm afraid if I'm not there, he will be most difficult."

Dahl looked at the sheriff and saw the trace of a wry smile on his face. "I have an extra bedroll, if that's all that's needed," the sheriff said.

"Obliged, Sheriff," Dahl said in a flat tone.

Tucker offered quietly, "I want you to know I'd ride with you at the drop of a hat were it not for how easily Silver City can blow out of control."

"I appreciate that, Sheriff," said Dahl. "But if you rode with me, who could I count on to watch Lilly and my place here?"

"Well spoken, Dahl," said Tucker, with a touch of his fingers to his hat brim.

Part 3

Chapter 15

———

James Earl Coots stared out from the corner of an open window as a lone rider made his way across the stretch of flatlands, leading a pack mule behind him. Shotgun in hand, Coots remained out of sight until the man stepped down from his sweat-streaked horse and hitched it to the rail.

"I'll be hornswoggled," Coots said under his breath, recognizing the man in the new but dirt-coated riding duster. "Mr. J. Fenwick Hatton himself . . . ," he said as if in awe. He uncocked his shotgun and stepped forward, taking his battered hat from a peg beside the door.

At the sound of Coots' boots on the plank porch, Hatton looked up from untying a cargo rope on the mule's back. He saw the attendant looking down at him. Before Hatton could say anything, Coots said, "Howdy, Mr. Hatton. Welcome to the relay station—*your* relay station, that is."

Hatton scrutinized him closely. "Do you work for me, sir?" He held an unlit cigar in the corner of his mouth.

"In a manner of speaking I do," said Coots. "I haul freight to and from here. I'm James Earl Coots. I was a good friend of Norman Beale's . . . and Oscar, of course."

"Yes, I see," said Hatton.

Seeing the rope in Hatton's hand, Coots stepped down from the porch toward him. "Here, allow me to get that for you."

"Thank you, Mr. Coots," Hatton replied. "These are Norman's usual monthly supplies. I decided to bring them out myself since I was headed this way." He stepped aside and let the attendant untie the load of canvas-wrapped supplies from the mule's back.

"Obliged, sir," said Coots, knowing there was more to Hatton being here than delivering supplies. "I suppose you're wondering how come I recognized you?" He loosened the ropes as he spoke. "The fact is, I saw an etching of you in a newspaper a while back." As soon as he said it, he realized the artist's rendering of Hatton had been published along with the story of his daughter's death during a bank robbery, and he dropped the matter.

"I understand," Hatton said. He struck a match on the hitch rail, lit his cigar and looked all around as Coots shouldered the canvas-wrapped bundle of supplies. "I see the company has already taken the attacked coach on across the badlands?"

"A relief driver and guard came out and took it

away yesterday," said Coots. He turned and walked up onto the porch with the supplies.

"I understand a young deputy from Cottonwood killed two of them?" Hatton asked.

"It's a fact he did," said Coots. "I dragged them out back and piled stones over them. I can uncover them if you feel like taking yourself a look-see." His face turned grim in remembrance. "I wish he would've killed every last one of them thieving, murdering dogs. Norman and Oscar didn't deserve this, not to mention those two good stage men, Charlie Stevens and Milton Donahue."

"Yes, tragic," said Hatton, but he seemed to pass over the dead employees with only minimum remorse. "I'm told the young deputy was mistakenly stabbed by a hysterical female passenger."

"Yes, he was," said Coots. "The young woman was full of remorse over it. She left on the relief stage. Deputy Lane didn't blame her for stabbing him."

"I see," Hatton said, considering the matter. "That speaks well for the deputy's character." Then he looked all around and said to Coots, "I should like to shake this young deputy's hand if he is well enough to do so. Where is he convalescing?"

"Convalescing?" Coots swept a hand toward the distant hills west of them. "Out there somewhere, I expect."

"I beg your pardon?" Hatton said curiously.

"What I mean is he didn't do any convalescing here," said Coots. "We got him into the bed. I offered to ride all the way to the Animas Range and bring the doctor from the mine company. But he wouldn't hear of it. Said if anything important had been stuck, he'd be dead before the doctor got here."

"And . . . ?" Hatton stared at him with rapt interest, cigar in hand. Finally he said with a look of stunned disbelief, "Are you telling me he has had no treatment for his wounds?"

"None that I know of." Coots shrugged. "He poured three long drinks from my whiskey jug and had me pull the knife out. The next morning, he was saddled up and gone before I could even think of what it might take to stop him."

"Gone in pursuit of the men who did this, no doubt?" Hatton asked.

"That's what he said," Coots replied. "They killed his sheriff. It sounded like he thought most highly of Sheriff Morgan."

"My goodness," said Hatton, "I'm searching for those same men. . . ." He pondered things for a moment, then said to Coots, "Do you know this country, Mr. Coots?"

"I'm a teamster, Mr. Hatton, I know every trail, road, shortcut and pig path between here and—"

"I would like you to travel with me, Mr. Coots," Hatton said, cutting him off. "I need someone who can help me find this young deputy. Can you track, sir?"

"As well as the next man," Coots said. "But what about these relay horses here? Who'll take care of them? I stuck around to watch them till somebody showed up. To tell the truth, I was headed after them snakes myself once these horses were in good hands."

"The weekly stage will be here this afternoon and

leave first thing in the morning," said Hatton. "I'll leave them a signed message. They will take these relay horses with them."

"A signed message?" Coots asked. "You mean we won't be here this evening? We're leaving today, before the stage arrives and takes on fresh horses?"

"Yes, exactly," said Hatton. "I don't plan on being here an hour from now, not if your horses are watered and grained and trail-worthy. If this wounded young man is already on these killers' trail, can we offer any less of ourselves?"

Coots said, "No, sir, not once you put it that way. As for our horses being trail worthy, Norman Beale took pride in keeping these animals ready to ride at all times."

"Splendid," Hatton said. "I'll quill a message while you go pack your roll. Until we return, this station is officially closed."

Before dark, Hatton and Coots had ridden across the rocky sand flats, following the tracks of the deputy's horse all the way from the hitch rail, until the single set of hooves blended into a collection of hoofprints all headed for the jagged, distant hill line. As the last wreath of fiery sunlight fell behind the western edge of the earth, the two dusty riders stepped down from their saddles midtrail and stared down at the shadowy ground.

Coots took out a short torch, lit it and held it down, casting a circle of flickering light around their feet and their horses' hooves. "It's been a long while since I've tracked anything of a night, Mr. Hatton," he said. "I only hope I still have the knack for it."

"I have the utmost confidence in you, Mr. Coots," Hatton replied.

"I'm proud to hear that, sir," said Coots, examining the belly of the earth as closely as a man prospecting for gold. "I'll do my best not to let you down."

"Thank you," said Hatton. "I must ask, how will you keep the deputy's horse singled out from among these others? I'm most eager to acquire the skills that allow me to track a man by his horse's hoofprints."

Coots gave Hatton a tired but self-assured smile and said, "In this case, Deputy Lane's horse is wearing store-bought American Forge Brand number-seven shoes." He squatted down and guided the torch among the over-lapping prints. "I recognized them as soon as I looked at his tracks out front at the hitch rail." He pointed with the tip of his gloved finger to the thin imprint of a 7 in the corner of a shoe print. "Note also, sir, that this print is always on top of the others," he added studiously.

"Yes, I see . . . a good thing to know," said Hatton, not sounding overly impressed now that he saw the simplicity of Coots' tracking method.

"His tracks will veer away from all these others when the fellow he's after does the same." He gave Hatton a look and pointed out with a raised finger, "Keep in mind that these tracks were not made by men all trav-eling together at the same time. Some of these men were on this trail ahead of the others. A good tracker

has to know how and when to sort them out and dis-
cern them, almost like a Gypsy reading tea leaves."

"Yes, of course, I see what you mean," Hatton said,
sounding a bit more impressed now that he began to
realize how it worked. The two stood and mounted
and rode on, Coots holding the torch low and to the
side, casting a dim glow of light on the shadowy trail
full of hoofprints.

Two miles farther along the rocky trail, Coots stopped
his horse and said, "Hold it, sir." He looked all around
and backed the animal a few steps, Hatton right beside
him.

"What are we doing?" Hatton asked, looking back
and forth in the flickering light.

When Coots held out the torch toward two sets of
prints veering away from the others and out onto a
maze of rocky hillsides, he said almost with a sigh,
"Looks like Deputy Lane managed to single out his
man. There he goes after him." Coots grinned and said
to the ground, "Good job, Deputy."

"Yes. Even with the killer having an overnight start
on him. Outstanding!" Hatton said, sounding more impressed.

"To his credit," said Coots, "Lane knew the man he
was after would veer away from these other tracks
sooner or later. The deputy caught this man when two
of his outlaw pals thought they'd killed him. So it's
likely he's following them for his share of the money,
but staying back until he can get his hands on it without getting himself killed."

"Yes, of course," Hatton repeated, feeling as if he'd just learned one more thing he might need to know about staying alive on this harsh frontier.

The two continued on throughout the night, finding themselves meandering almost aimlessly at times the same way Candles had done, and Deputy Lane behind him. As daylight encroached on the dark western horizon, the two found themselves at the water hole where Candles' hoofprints had been joined by three other sets. Atop some of those prints, the deputy's number 7s appeared to hang back as if to observe and calculate the situation.

"We need to rest here for a while, Mr. Hatton," said Coots, circling the prints so as not to disturb them as he let the horse walk on the water's edge. He swung down from his saddle without waiting for Hatton's reply.

"We must push on, Mr. Coots," said Hatton, "if we're to catch up to this wounded deputy and ride these scoundrels down."

"We'll neither catch up to him nor ride these scoundrels down if we don't rest these animals," Coots said.

"Yes, you're right, Mr. Coots," Hatton relented, worn out from the all-night ride. "But we'll only rest awhile. Whichever one of these scoundrels the deputy is after, I'm confident his trail will take us to the leader eventually. These dogs are constantly splitting up and rejoining."

Coots looked around and said absently, "All in time, sir. Get your horse and yourself watered and rested." As he spoke he looked down in the grainy morning light and saw the broken saddle horn lying at his feet by the water's edge.

"Well now, look what we have here," he said. Stooping, he picked up the severed saddle horn and turned it in his hand. "The saddle horn that the deputy had his prisoner cuffed to."

Hatton looked at the broken saddle horn. Then he looked around at the hoofprints again. "Whoever he met here set him free."

"Yes," said Coots. "It just might be that he made himself some new friends. These water holes almost all have their own cutthroats and thieves lurking about like coyotes. There's no telling what kind of snakes we'll end up having to kill across these badlands." As he spoke, he looked all around the vast, barren lands and gripped his rifle in his gloved hand.

"Then kill them we will, Mr. Coots," said Hatton. "It doesn't matter to me, so long as our bloody trail guides us to Big Chicago."

"Wait, sir," said Coots all of a sudden, raising a hand to silence Hatton.

Seeing the attentive look on Coots' face as the teamster stared outward toward the hills to the west, Hatton asked, "What is it, Mr. Coots?"

"Gunshots, sir," Coots said sharply, answering but wanting Hatton to keep quiet so he could pinpoint the direction of the faint and faraway explosions.

"Yes, gunshots . . . ," said Hatton, listening until he located the sound for himself on the thin, still desert air. "Do you suppose the deputy has caught up to those snakes and needs our help?"

"I don't know, sir," said Coots, standing and dusting the seat of his trousers. "I hope he doesn't need our help." He stood staring off in the direction of rifle shots being exchanged somewhere up in the hills. "I judge those shots to be a day's ride away. At best we'll only get there in time to see who won."

Chapter 16

———

On a wooden balcony above a weathered plank and adobe saloon, Emmen Shay and his brother, Brady, stood looking off in the direction of Saverine Pass, the source of the gunfire they'd heard moments earlier. On the dirt street below them, two of their town guards walked back and forth with shotguns cradled in their arms. The guards gazed off in the same direction as the earlier rifle shots.

"I can send out some riders, Emmen," said Brady Shay.

"Naw, I think not, brother," said Emmen, the decision maker of two. He rolled a thick cigar in his lips beneath a wide black mustache. "Like as not, it's Chester Goines and Curly Joe's old gang. I've been expecting him."

"That was a lot of shooting," Brady said in a warning tone.

"Yes, I know," said Emmen. He stepped over to the

dusty balcony rail and rested a hand on it. "We protect these jakes while they're here in the Roost. Let's not make a practice of protecting them on their journey back and forth." He let out a stream of smoke. "It is a big desert, after all."

"Aye, it is at that," said Brady. "I was only thinking about this *Teacher* fellow, the assassin who killed Curly Joe."

"What about him?" Emmen asked, drawing deeply on the cigar.

"I was wondering if perchance this could be him and some paid railroad gunmen riding our way."

"My information has it that Sherman Dahl always works alone," said Emmen with confidence.

"I hope your information knows when a man might decide to change his mind," said Brady. "The law is getting stronger with each passing day."

"And we should be thankful for it," Emmen said, reaching up a hand and brushing dust from his pin-striped suit coat. "What would our services here be worth if the law became weak and stopped hounding a man?"

"I'm only saying we should be extra careful," Brady cautioned. "Look what's happening to the other Robber's Roost." He gestured a nod toward the northwest. "The Pinkertons and railroad detectives have all but put it out of business this past year."

"Yes," said Emmen, "but tell me, brother, do you find it merely a coincidence that during the same past year our business here has nearly doubled, while the other Robber's Roost has gotten beaten into the ground?

Think about it, b'hoy." He grinned and tapped a finger to his silver-gray temples.

Brady returned Emmen's sly grin. "I'm a worrier—that's for certain," he said.

"I know you are, brother," said Emmen, trying to relax and enjoy his cigar. "Why don't you go find the new redhead and help her sharpen her skills? You sound like a man in need of twirling his rope."

Brady smiled and had turned to walk away when another blast of gunfire resounded from the direction of Saverine Pass. The Shay brothers looked at each other. "All right," said Emmen, "send out Carter and a few men, have them check out the pass."

"That I will," said Brady. He turned and walked away as another rifle shot resounded in the distance. . . .

Eleven miles from the outlaw town, on a steep cliff above Saverine Pass, Bobby Candles and the three desert bandits hurried back along a thin footpath as rifle shots ricocheted off the rocks surrounding them. "Damn them to hell," shouted Lodi, squeezing a bloody graze on his upper arm, "and damn you too, Candles! You said this would be easy pickings!"

Candles, Dad Lodi, Frank Dorsey and Dirty Foot had ambushed the outlaws two days earlier and been engaged in a running gun battle ever since. "I never said they'd walk up and hand the money over to us, did I?" Candles shouted in reply.

"We should have killed him when we had him hanging from his horse's belly," said Dirty Foot, hastily reloading his rifle while Frank Dorsey huddled beside him reloading his big Smith & Wesson revolver.

"No," said Frank, "he's right. There's some big money here." He gestured toward Delbert Garr's dead horse, which was lying stretched out on a narrow trail beneath them. "Some of it's right down there in those saddlebags." He finished reloading and cocked the big revolver. "I've never seen anybody fight this hard over a dead horse!"

"Cover me," said Candles to Dad Lodi. He inched away from beside Lodi and searched back and forth for a place to run to. Having lost his guns when Deputy Lane had taken him prisoner, he carried an older battered Walker Colt that Lodi had lent him when they'd ambushed Big Chicago and his men.

Hearing Candles and watching him begin to slip away, Lodi turned his Colt toward him and demanded, "Where the hell do you think you're going?"

Candles only stopped for a moment. "To get the saddlebags, damn it," he said. "You heard Frank. Do you think these gunmen would be fighting this hard over a dead horse?"

Lodi looked embarrassed. But he remained huddled behind a foot rock. "All right, but don't try anything funny."

"If I could think of something *funny*," said Candles, bullets whistling past them from the rocky hillside on the other side of the trail, "I'd sure as hell try it."

"Get going, Candles," said Dorsey. "We've got you covered. Wait till they reload, then go."

Candles gave a nod toward Dorsey. Then he ducked down for a moment until the firing from the other side reached a lull. *Here goes. . . .*

From the other steep hillside, Big Chicago said guardedly to the five men strewn out behind rocks surrounding him, "Get ready. When he gets to Delbert's horse, pound him, then clear out of here before we all die of thirst."

"I'd like to stay here and skin Candles alive for causing this," said Delbert Garr, who lay beside Chicago, his shirt dirty and torn, his hat missing, his forehead bloody and knotted. He'd been riding the horse at a fast pace along the trail when the rifle knocked the animal out from under him.

"How much money is down there?" Chicago asked, looking down at the dead animal lying in a wide puddle of blood.

"Two stacks of a thousand each," said Garr. He grimaced. "Too damn much money to let a buzzard like Candles get his hands on it." He paused, then said, "To think the sumbitch would shoot at *me*, after we rode together."

"Probably feels like you turned on him when we got so much money among us," said Chicago.

"Well, I did. But damn," said Garr. "I didn't try to kill him. That was your men's doings, none of mine."

"Some folks don't even try to understand things," said Chicago. He shook his head. "You know, this money comes off of your end."

Garr spat and made a sour face. "That figures."

"There he goes!" said Chicago. "Get him!" He threw his rifle up over the rock and began firing repeatedly as Candles appeared on the steep hillside and ran, slid and tumbled toward the narrow trail below. "There,

Bobby!" he shouted through the hail of gunfire. "How do you like *that*, you son of a bitch!"

But Candles didn't hear him as he dived headlong at the dead horse and rolled up against its belly as bullets thumbed into the carcass from the other hillside. "Damn!" Candles said, feeling bullets zip past him and thump into the saddlebags as he reached over to retrieve them.

"Keep him covered, pards," Dad Lodi said to the other two desert bandits. "He's got the bags!" The three fired repeatedly as Candles ducked back down against the dead horse's belly with the saddlebags hugged to his chest.

"I'll be damned, he made it," Garr said bitterly, seeing Candles run five fast steps from the dead horse to the covered edge of the trail, where he stopped to prepare for his run back up the rocky hillside.

"He's still got to make it back," said Chicago. "You, Paul and Buddy are going to pound him before he gets out of sight into the rocks." As he spoke, he began easing back away from Garr. "Thatcher, Russell and I are riding on. We'll be up above you in the rocks so when these snakes follow you in, we'll cut them to pieces."

"Yeah, all right," Garr said absently, still watching Candles, still upset over his share of the money now being in Candles' hands.

Hoping to stall Candles in place a moment longer while Thatcher went and got his horse, Chicago shouted down to him, "Good job, Bobby! You're faster than a damn jackrabbit!"

Candles ducked down quickly at the bottom edge of

the trail and looked in the direction of Chicago's re-sounding voice. "I was there, Chicago," Candles said. "I figure this is my share you were holding for me."

"And right you are, Bobby," said Chicago. "But you could have been more amiable about it. You didn't have to show up with a raging mad-on at everybody." He gave a dark chuckle under his breath.

"I got the mad-on when your *poltroons*, Thatcher and Russell, tried burning me down back at that relay station," said Candles.

"I had no idea they did something like that," said Chicago. "Now I'm upset with them both." He looked up and saw Thatcher standing on a flatter stretch of hill-side, holding the reins to his horse. "Still, wasn't this something we could have squared between us? Did you have to resort to violence?"

"I felt like I did," said Candles, searching the hillside for his best run at it.

"And who are these three jakes you've allied your-self with?" Chicago asked. "Anybody I know?"

"Some pals of mine," said Candles, "I ran into them on my way—"

"I'm Dad Lodi," the dusty bandit called out, prefer-ring to speak for himself. "These two are Frank Dorsey and Pie Sucio."

"It means Dirty Foot," the Mexican cut in on his own behalf.

"I see," said Chicago, easing up the hillside toward Thatcher and his horse as he spoke. "Well, I wish I could say I'm pleased to meet you three, but under these circumstances, you'd know I was just being courteous." He paused for another look toward Thatcher. Then he said as if on second thought, "Hey, wait. I've heard of Dad Lodi, and Frank Dorsey! You two rode with Matt Warner and some other fast-playing gunmen."

"That, we did," said Dad. He and Dorsey gave each other a cool look.

"What about me?" Dirty Foot called out. "Have you heard of me?"

"No, afraid not," said Chicago.

"Maybe you heard of me, but forgot, eh?" Dirty Foot pressed.

"I believe I would remember, Mr. *Foot*," Chicago said, backing up the path as he spoke.

"He's slipping away," Dad Lodi said to Dorsey and Dirty Foot, catching a glimpse of Chicago as he turned and began climbing in earnest the last few yards. Lodi took a close aim and pulled the trigger just as he saw Chicago step out of sight.

Chicago let out a loud yelp and flung himself out of sight behind the large rock where Thatcher stood holding his horse. Shaking his foot like a man with a bee in his boot, Chicago fell to the ground, gripping his ankle with both hands.

"Damn it! Look what they did!" He cursed, seeing where the bullet had sliced the heel off his battered black boot.

"Give me your hand," Thatcher said, hearing the shooting begin again.

"Yes," said Chicago, taking his gloved hand and pulling himself to his feet. "Let's get out of here and get set up for them along the pass. I don't want them hounding us once we get inside the Roost."

Thatcher said, "The kind of money we've got here, you'd think the Shays would take our side, help us kill Candles and his pals."

"I've know the Shays a long time," said Russell. "They won't take sides between gangs like us. The only side they ever take is against a posse or a band of detectives if any shows up." He swung up into his saddle beside Thatcher and Chicago and added, "Which is why none ever shows up."

"I don't give a damn whether or not the Shays take our side, so long as they don't take sides with Candles," said Chicago. "We've got him outgunned and he knows it. If he's smart, he and his saddle tramps will take the two thousand and cut out."

"Yeah, Delbert Garr's two thousand," Thatcher put in with a short laugh. The three hurried along, the rifle and pistol fire resounding heavily behind them. . . .

The firing slowed to a stop almost as soon as Bobby Candles made it back to the safety of the rocks where the three desert bandits awaited him. Flinging the saddlebags to the ground, he opened the flaps and pulled out two bundles of cash and shook them back and forth. The three bandits' grim, weathered faces softened a bit as their eyes widened at the sight of so much money. "Lord God . . . !" Dorsey mumurmured.

"All right, pards! Who was telling you the truth about the strongbox money?" he said. He broke the bands on the stacks of case and fanned the money on the rocky ground.

"*Sí*, you told the truth!" said Dirty Foot. "You are a saint, *mi amigo*, a living saint among men!"

"And I'm telling you the truth when I say there's a hell of a lot more split up among their saddlebags, just waiting for us."

"It's been a long time since I've stolen something you didn't have to skin and eat before the law showed up," said Lodi. He ran his rough hands across the money.

"Was it worth fighting from the saddle the past couple of days?" Candles asked.

"Now that we know there's this kind of money, it's worth from now till next summer if we had to," said Dorsey.

"Yeah, but we're not going to have to," said Candles, feeling bold and in charge now that he'd delivered on the deal the way he'd said he would. "We're going for more."

"They're pulling away," said the Mexican, eying the outlaws across the hillside. "We must follow them!" He jerked his rifle up.

But Candles stopped him, saying, "No, Dirty Foot, let them go. If I know Chicago, he's setting us up for an ambush before we get out of this pass."

Dad Lodi looked at Candles with a whole new attitude now that he'd seen the money. "What is it you want us to do?" he asked.

"We'll circle wide around the pass, from up there,"

Candles said, lifting his eyes to the high ridgeline above them.

"What about us grabbing ourselves some more of this money?" Dorsey asked.

"It's coming, Frank," said Candles with a sly, tight grin. "Trust me—it's coming."

Chapter 17

——

Emmen and Brady Shay stood watching from the balcony of the saloon as Chicago led his men in from the direction of Saverine Pass. "Did you send any riders out like I told you to do?" Emmen asked his brother sidelong as he kept an eye on the dusty, worn-out riders straggling into Robber's Roost.

"Yes," said Brady. "I sent Cree Carter out a couple of hours ago, told him to pick five men to ride with him. Why?"

"Too bad," said Emmen, a fresh cigar clamped between his teeth. "If we had waited awhile, we could have saved them a trip."

"That's Chester Goines, damn his bloody eyes," said Brady, gazing down at the leader and his bedraggled followers. Following the mounted gunmen, Delbert Garr staggering along on foot, like some drunkard searching for home.

"Yes, brother Brady," said Emmen Shay, "it is Big Chicago himself. It appears he's taking up where Curly

Joe left off." He took the cigar from his teeth and gave a halfhearted smile and a short wave toward Chicago. "I understand he is prone to spend his swag as freely as Curly Joe always did," he said. "Let us both hope so, eh?"

"Yes, let's hope so," said Brady. He also lifted a thick hand and waved at Chicago and the rest of the men. A diamond ring sparkled on his fat pinky finger.

Arriving at a town well encircled with a short stone wall, Garr flung himself facedown into the water between two horses and drank. The men only stared at him as they passed around a water gourd and allowed their horses to draw water freely.

"I bet Delbert never was real particular where he drank," Thatcher quipped wryly.

"Nor who he drank with," Russell put in, the two chuckling under their breath.

At a moment when those watching might have wondered if Garr had drowned himself, the gunman finally raised his face from under the water. He threw back his head, slinging back a rooster-tail spray of wet hair. Letting out a deep gasp, he said in a broken voice, "Walking . . . gives a man . . . a powerful thirst."

"That it does," Thatcher said with a flat, bemused grin.

Chicago had stepped down from his saddle beside Thatcher and Russell. "Here," he said gruffly, handing Thatcher his reins. As his horse drank, he dusted off his shoulders, beat his hat against his leg and said to Russell, "Bart, you come with me. Let's pay our respects to the Shays straightaway." He patted the lapel of his dusty coat. "Make them both happy to see us."

At the foot of a tall staircase, Chicago and Russell

were met by two armed town guards who relieved them both of their guns and accompanied them up to the Shays' office. On the way up, Russell stalled for a second and looked at two other guards who sat inside an iron-plated cage that hung from the ceiling above the stairs. Two eight-gauge fluted-barreled deck guns stood mounted on the cage's iron handrail.

Russell looked down onto the saloon below, at three half-naked saloon girls gathered around a twanging piano. Beside the piano stood a guitar, an accordion and a long wooden flute. "Lord God," Russell said with a wide, lusty grin, "all this in broad daylight. Think how it gets in the afternoon." At a long bar three trail-hardened gunmen stood bowed watching the bartender shake a leather dice cup in both hands. "I can't wait!" he laughed.

"Keep moving, pal," said one of the town guards. He gestured Russell on up the stairs without putting a hand on him. "It'll all be waiting for you when you come back down."

"I hope it's not all a dream," Russell said. As he moved onward, he looked back the length of the saloon where green felt-topped tables stood fully seated with players; each player sat with varying amounts of cash, chips and gold pokes sprawled in front of him.

"Jesus, Bart, you've been here before," Chicago said quietly between them as he limped along on his disfigured boot. "Don't act like a hayseed."

"I can't help it," Russell replied, forcing himself to settle down as they rounded the upper landing. "I get like this every time."

"Yeah . . . ," Chicago murmured, taking a quick look back himself. "All the drinking, dope, whores and gambling a man could ever hope for . . . out here under this scorching desert sun. How'd the Shays ever think of something like this?"

"Yeah, and why didn't we think of it first?" Russell whispered as they walked on, passing closed doors where the sound of gasping and groaning and squeaking beds filled the stifling, hot air.

Outside the door to the Shays' office, one town guard waited while the other escorted the two gunmen inside, across the floor and out onto the balcony. At a round table, Emmen and Brady Shay sat with a tall bottle of whiskey uncorked and waiting for Chicago's arrival. Emmen sat with both a fresh cigar and a full shot glass in his fist. Three empty glasses stood in a row like soldiers awaiting orders.

"Gentlemen," Brady said cordially, standing as the two men stopped and stood with their hats in their hands.

Emmen did not stand. "Gentlemen," he also said. He looked the two up and down appraisingly, then nodded them toward chairs as Brady picked up the bottle and began filling the shot glasses. "I have a feeling we heard you out there long before we saw you." He gestured his cigar toward Saverine Pass. "I trust you haven't brought any law down on us, Chester?"

"No," said Chicago. "That was just Bobby Candles and some desert trash he took up with after we gave him the boot. Candles always was a sore loser." He gave a slight shrug and said, "Anyway, I'm not going by *Chester* now. From now on, it's Big Chicago." He looked at Emmen Shay with a tight expression. "I realize you didn't know, not being out there on the trails for a while. Used to be, people called me both. Not anymore."

"Big Chicago it is," Emmen said. "Tell me, then, *Big Chicago*," he said with emphasis, "what have you brought for brother Brady and myself?"

Chicago had picked up the shot glass and swirled it. Now he tossed back the whiskey, set the empty glass down firmly and let out a sharp hiss. Reaching inside his coat, he took out three bound stacks of cash and laid them down in front of Emmen Shay.

"My, my," Emmen said, picking up a stack and riffling the bills. Brady watched intently from where he stood near the table, whiskey bottle suspended, ready to refill Chicago's glass with Emmen's approval. "It's thoughtful of someone, going to all this trouble." He smiled, gave Brady a nod and laid the money back down idly as Brady poured more whiskey.

When Brady had refilled the glasses, he raised his own to Chicago and Russell and drank with them. "Now then, gentlemen," he said as the two gunmen set their shot glasses down. "Let me go over the rules with you and I'll see to it you have the finest rooms, women—"

"We know the rules," said Chicago. "We're neither one of us newcomers, remember?"

Brady looked at his brother for support.

"Be that as it may," said Emmen, "we find it useful to talk about the rules each time you arrive. It avoids any misunderstandings later on."

Chicago relaxed, took a breath and said politely, "All right, we understand. Please continue, Brady."

But before Brady could continue, gunfire resounded once again from the direction of Saverine Pass.

The Shay brothers and the two gunmen gave one another puzzled looks. "Bobby Candles and his desert pals would not be foolish enough to fire on our town guards, would he?" Emmen asked.

"I wish I could say," Chicago replied. "But the fact is, Bobby Candles has been acting awfully peculiar of late. I don't know what he's apt to do. The desert bandits he's riding with . . . ?" Chicago let his words trail. "I think we all know that those sand pirates would do most anything."

"Yes, we all know . . . ," Emmen said studiously, gazing off toward Saverine Pass.

From a high and well-covered point above Saverine Pass, Deputy Eddie Lane had looked down through his telescope an hour earlier and watched Candle and his desert bandits maneuver up around the canyon wall. When he'd seen they had missed the trap Chicago had prepared for them, he'd started to get back on Candles' trail, put a bullet in him and end the chase. But before he'd collapsed the telescope, he scanned the trail below in the other direction and saw two riders come out of a stand of rock and cactus.

"What the . . . ?" Adjusting the telescope, he recognized one of the men to be James Earl Coots, the teamster who'd saved his life the day the young woman had stabbed him. J. Fenwick Hatton, he only recognized after studying him closely and recalling the etching he'd seen of him in a recent Denver newspaper. Lowering the telescope an inch, Lane said quietly, "Damn it, Coots. Neither of you has any business out here."

Raising the telescope again, he swung it in the direction of Robber's Roost in time to see the six town guards riding down onto the canyon floor, headed unknowingly toward Coots and Hatton. Collapsing the telescope, he gave a quick gaze toward the rise of dust standing in the air behind Candles and the bandits.

Killing Candles would have to wait, he told himself, reaching back and stuffing the telescope down into his saddlebags. He couldn't let Coots and Hatton ride into six riflemen on the narrow canyon floor. "Let's go," he said, batting his heels to his horse's sides, sending it down a long, steep, rocky path, halfway between the two men and the six town guards.

On the canyon floor, the leader of the town guards, a gunman named Cree Carter, was the first to notice the rise of dust billowing along the hillside to their right. He said over his shoulder to two other riflemen, "Fisher, Brody, both of you ride a head a ways, make sure we're not riding into somebody's trap."

"Like whose, Apache?" Dee Fisher asked, seeing the dust himself now that he'd taken a closer look up the steep hillside standing before them.

"Apache don't make dust," said Leon Brody, "unless it suits their purpose to do so." He jerked his horse's reins sidelong and booted it forward around Carter and the others. "Let's ride," he said to Fisher.

Cree Carter watched the two men ride ahead at a

fast pace. After a moment he booted his horse into a quicker pace himself and said to the others behind him, "Let's stay close behind them. Keep your ears open. If this *is* a trap, we'll hear them ride into it."

As soon as Deputy Lane's horse stepped down to the trail, he turned it toward the two riders and put it into a run. When he rounded a turn and faced Coots and Hatton from less than thirty yards, he saw them throw their rifles to their shoulders in surprise.

"Don't shoot!" he shouted.

"Wait, Hatton, it's Lane!" said Coots, recognizing the young deputy in time to lower his rifle and keep from firing.

"Deputy Lane? Good heavens, Deputy!" said Hatton, lowering his rifle and steadying his horse while Lane's animal pounded closer along the dusty trail. "I might have shot you, young man."

"I've come to warn you, Coots. There's armed riders coming from Robber's Roost," Lane said, sliding his horse quarterwise to a halt.

"Uh-oh," said Coots, "how close are they?" He stared along the rocky trail.

"Too close," said Lane. "You've got to get off this trail."

Hatton started to say something, but Coots grabbed his horse by its bridle and said, "Come on, sir, you heard him. Get off the trail!" Even as they spoke, Coots heard the pounding of the two horses' hooves coming around the same turn in the trail.

The three wasted no time turning their mounts and booting them off the trail. Just as they put the horses

onto a thin path running into a steep slope of rock and
cactus, a shot rang out behind them and a bullet whined
and ricocheted off a rock. "How many are there?" Coots
called back to Lane, who brought up the rear, keeping
Hatton between the two of them.

"Two, right now," said Lane. "But there are four more
coming along the trail behind them."

Another shot rang out, then another.

The three rode on quickly even as the path beneath
them turned narrower, pressing them to a wall of jagged, creviced rock. Shots continued to follow them for
another hundred yards until suddenly their path stopped
and all that lay ahead for them was a hand-over-hand
climb up to the next switchback trail.

"What're we going to do, Deputy?" Coots asked,
looking worried, the three of them dropping from their
saddles and taking slim cover against the rock wall.

Lane looked both men up and down, judging their
odds at climbing the rocks to the trail without getting shot. Finally he said, "Wait here. Hold them off
while I get above them. From up there I can either push
them back or get them chasing me. When you see your
chance, hightail it out of here." He gestured a nod down
a two-hundred-foot slide of rock and dirt and low, cling-
ing cactus. "Either that or slide down and take your
chances."

Hatton looked down, then all around, his eyes wide.
"My God, Deputy. Hold them off—"

Coots cut Hatton off, saying to Lane, "What about
you?"

Grabbing a bandolier of ammunition from his saddle horn, Lane said, "Don't worry about me. I'll get out on foot, from up there. Now get ready to do it."

Hatton stood frozen for a second. Shots exploded.

Bullets whined and thumped against rock. "You heard him, sir," Coots said, grabbing Hatton by his forearm and pulling him back against the rock wall for cover. "Start shooting!"

As the two fired almost blindly at the sound of the rifle shots coming from the turn in the narrow path, Lane hurried up the crevice's hand- and toeholds until he reached a rock perch that stood half hidden from the trail below. From there he could not clearly see the two riflemen, but at least he could catch a glimpse of their hats, and see smoke from their rifles rise from among the rocks.

Lane began levering rounds and firing, first at one position, then the other. "Pour it on them, Deputy!" Coots shouted, already feeling the intensity of the gunfire lessen now that Lane was firing down on them from a good position.

"*Arghhh!*" shouted one of the riflemen, feeling a bullet slice down the back of his shoulder. He fell and scrambled back against a rock for cover, dropping his rifle in pain.

"Are you hit, Leon?" Fisher called out, also ducking back against rock to keep out of the gunfire raining down on them.

"Yeah, damn it, I'm hit," Brody replied in a pained voice. "Can you see him up there?"

Dee Fisher leaned out and looked up among the rock above them. Before he could duck back, a shot from

Lane's Winchester bored down, punched through his collarbone and sent him sprawling in the dirt.

Go, Lane demanded silently, staring down toward the spot where he'd left Coots and Hatton.

As if they'd heard him, the two mounted quickly and raced away along the narrow path, lying low in their saddles, while Lane continued a heavy steady fire down at the two wounded riflemen. But just as Coots and Hatton had gotten past the two riflemen, Coots leading Lane's horse by its reins, Lane saw them appear on a stretch of trail and ride right into the four other town guards who had taken position on either side of the wider trail.

"No!" Lane shouted as rifles exploded all around Hatton and Coots at close range. Coots turned loose of Lane's horse and managed to get a shot off at one of the advancing riflemen. But then he went down, horse and all, in a hail of bullets. The town guard had struck so fast that Hatton wasn't even able to return fire before his horse fell out from under him and sent him spilling headfirst onto the rocky ground.

Thinking that Coots was done for, Lane swung his rifle at the men gathering around Hatton and dragging him across the trail. But realizing the danger of shooting into them from this distance and taking a chance on hitting Hatton, he let out a breath of resignation and let the rifle slump at his shoulder.

Chapter 18

———

More than an hour had passed by the time Lane had reached the trail on foot. Coots had crawled a few agonizing feet and lay reaching for his dead horse's stirrup. When Lane stooped down and turned him over, Coots looked up at him and said in a choked voice, "Help me . . . get mounted. I can still ride."

"Shhh, take it easy, Coots," said Lane, seeing that the teamster was talking out of his head. "I'll get you some water."

Coots grabbed his forearm, his grip tighter than Lane expected. "No, Deputy . . . I want to ride."

"No, Coots, you can't ride. You don't even have a horse," Lane said bluntly. "I'm going to get you bandaged up best I can. Then I've got to leave you here. I have to get on their trail."

"I'm . . . going too," Coots said with iron determination.

But Lane ignored him. He knew what he had to do. When he'd dragged the wounded teamster off the trail and prodded him against a rock, he stooped down and laid a canteen beside him, then said, "Lie here and get some rest. I'll be coming back for you, Coots. You've got my word."

As Lane took a step back, he heard a quiet voice say behind him, "Turn around slow, Deputy. Make sure the rifle isn't pointed in my direction."

Lane froze. "Who's asking?" he replied before making a move.

"I'm not *asking*," said the voice. Lane heard a hammer cock. "I heard the man call you 'Deputy,'" the voice continued. "You've got one second to turn around and tell me who you are."

Lane considered it, then let the barrel of the Winchester slump toward the ground. He turned and stood, his feet shoulder width apart.

Sherman Dahl took a step forward, noting the dark imprint of a star on the chest of Lane's otherwise frayed and faded shirt. "Are you Sheriff Morgan's deputy, Eddie Lane?"

"I am," said Lane, already beginning to realize this was none of the riffraff from Robber's Roost, or any of the outlaws who frequented the trails back and forth to the thieves' haven. "Again, who's asking?" he insisted.

"It's him, Mr. Dahl. I feel certain of it," said Farris, standing back a few feet, holding the reins to their horses as well as Lane's, a cocked rifle in his hands.

Dahl looked the young man up and down, noting the Colt stuck behind his belt, another Colt in a holster on his hip. "We've been seeing your tracks here and there all the way from the relay station."

"So now you've found me," Lane said, not giving an inch. "Who are you?"

"I'm Sherman Dahl. This is Farris. We're searching for J. Fenwick Hatton."

"I am Mr. Hatton's personal assistant," Farris offered proudly.

"The Teacher . . . ," Lane said, scrutinizing Dahl closely. Turning to Farris, he said, "Hatton could have used your *assistance* a while ago." He gave a jerk of his head in the direction of the trail. "But you're too late now. He's gone."

"I know," said Dahl. "We saw it from too far away to do anything about it." He gestured toward the ground and asked, "Is that James Earl Coots, the teamster from the stage depot?"

"Yeah," said Lane with regret. "Coots is a good man. He saved my life. Now it looks like I've gotten him killed—Hatton too, for that matter. I led them down into a dead end. I tried to get them out, and this is the outcome."

"We saw it," Dahl said quietly. "You did the best you could."

Lane stared at him. "I don't need anybody telling me I did the best I could," he said. "Are you going to stop pointing your gun at me?"

Dahl lowered his rifle and uncocked its hammer, now that he saw Lane realized they were on the same side. "I suppose you're going after them?" he said to the young deputy.

"Yes," Lane said in a short, clipped tone. He stepped forward and held out his hand toward Farris. "If you've been watching, you know that's my horse. I'll be taking it back now, much obliged," he added courteously, yet in a firm voice that offered no further discussion on the matter.

Farris gave Dahl a look for approval and, upon getting it, handed the horse's reins over to Lane. "I'm afraid the animal has taken a bullet graze," he said.

Lane looked at the bloody streak across the horse's rump. "I'll attend to it," he said. "It's high enough up that it won't hurt to ride him."

"We're going after him too," Dahl said.

"I figured as much," said Lane.

"We'd all have a better chance if we stuck together up here," Dahl said.

"I work alone," Lane said bluntly.

"So do I," said Dahl. "But we're going to be shooting at each other if neither of us knows what the other is doing."

"If you know what happened at the stage depot," said Lane, "you'll know that my only interest was to get the men who killed my sheriff. Now I've got to make things right for Coots here. Now that this Hatton fellow is captured, I feel like I owe him something too."

Coots called out in a weak voice from where he lay leaning against the rock, "Nobody owes me anything. . . . I came for Norman and Oscar."

"For who?" Farris ask with a puzzled look.

"Never mind." Lane shook his head. "Norman was his pal. Oscar was Norman's dog. I expect we all fight for our own reasons." Lane paused, then looked at Dahl as if stricken by an idea. "Here's a deal for you,

Teacher," he said. "You and I will ride together provided Farris here stays behind and looks after Coots."

"I don't need . . . anybody looking after me," Coots said, almost rising to his feet. "I'm after the men who killed Norman and Oscar."

"Please, take it easy, Mr. Coots," said Farris, stepping forward and stooping down over the wounded teamster. Farris looked up at Dahl in agreement. "I'll stay here, if this is what it's going to take to get Mr. Hatton back alive."

"You heard him, Deputy," said Dahl. "We're all after the same men. You've got yourself a deal."

Lane nodded, but he looked at Dahl and asked, "What are you getting out of this, Teacher? Is Hatton paying you?"

"He paid me for killing Curly Joe Hobbs and his men after they killed Hatton's daughter," said Dahl. "But that was a while back. I'm doing this because I told Hatton I would."

"Oh . . . ?" Lane considered it.

"It's true, Deputy Lane," said Farris. "Mr. Dahl isn't paid for being here. He's here because I told him Mr. Hatton needed his help."

Lane looked skeptical, checked his horse closer, then checked the saddle cinch and tacking, thinking as he went about his task. Finally he turned to Dahl and said with resolve, "Newton is mine as soon as we get him in our sights."

"Who?" Dahl asked.

"Bobby Candles," said Lane. "He went by the name

Newton. He's the one who killed Sheriff Morgan. When the time comes, I want you to leave him to me."

"He's all yours," said Dahl. "Let's ride, while we've still got daylight." He gave Farris and Coots a look.

"You needn't worry about us, Mr. Dahl," said Farris. "We're going to be just fine here. If Mr. Coots improves, who knows, we may even venture forward."

"Don't do anything foolish, Farris," said Dahl, he and Lane ready to turn their horses to the trail.

"Something *foolish* . . . ? Oh no, sir, not I," said Farris.

Coots and Farris watched as the two rode away along the dusty trail. When they were out of sight, Farris said to Coots, "How badly are you wounded, Mr. Coots?"

"I'm not wounded," said Coots. "I'm nicked, scraped, burned and battered. But I told you, *I can ride.*" He scooted upright against the rock, drew a big Colt and jiggled it in his hand. "I didn't come all this way to kill these snakes just to let a few bullet grazes set me down."

Farris smiled and said, "Nor did I, sir." He arched a bushy gray eyebrow and said in an almost guarded tone, "The fact is, I only came to find Mr. Hatton. But now that he's in these scoundrels' hands, I'm ready to make a fight of it."

Coots looked him up and down and asked, "Have you ever been in a gunfight?"

"Oh no, sir, never," said Farris.

"Good," said Coots. "It's about time you were."

Emmen and Brady Shay stopped their horses at the edge of Robber's Roost and watched as Bobby Candles and the three desert bandits rode into sight from beneath a steep hillside of cactus and standing rock. As the four riders drew nearer, Emmen turned to four town guards sitting atop their horses behind him.

To the man nearest him, he said, "Zero, back these three up, give us some breathing room."

Brady added, "Keep your eyes open. Candles is quicker than a cat."

"Yes, sir," said Zero Paige, the town guard Candles had approached an hour earlier and told he needed to see the Shays.

When Candles rode closer he said over his shoulder to the three bandits, "You men stop here. Keep an eye on the town guards while I talk to Emmen."

As Candles' horse stepped even closer, Emmen Shay said, "Before you even start, Bobby, let me warn you, Big Chicago and his men are in town. It sounded to me like there's bad blood between yas."

"There is?" Candles gave a shrug. "Then it's news to me, Emmen. I did some work with Big Chicago and his men, and then we all split up." He gestured a nod toward the three men behind him. "I've been working with these three ever since."

Emmen and Brady both eyed Candles suspiciously. "You know how it works here, Bobby," Emmen said. "Brady and I rule the Roost. If you start any trouble here, you're dead. We take no sides."

"I understand that," said Candles. "I'm not here looking to start any trouble," he lied. "Me and my men are looking to lie low, hide out, same as everybody else who comes here."

"Hiding out is an expensive thing to do, Bobby," said Emmen. "Not everybody can afford it."

"We can," said Candles. He took out the three stacks of money from inside his coat and flashed them long enough to prove his solvency. Then he put the money away, smiled and said, "Of course if you think it's best we move on, that's what we'll do."

"We won't hear of it, Bobby," Emmen said. He gave an oily grin. "What kind of men would me and brother Brady be if we let you ride away from here without first spending all that money?" He jerked a nod toward the three bandits and asked, "Who's your pards here?"

"It so happens these men are neighbors of yours, Emmen," said Candles. "This is Dad Lodi, Frank Dorsey and Pie Sucio."

The Shays stared at the three.

"I've heard of Dad Lodi and Frank Dorsey," said Emmens. "These two used to charge folks for drinking at a water hole the other side of Saverine Pass."

"We still do," Dad Lodi said proudly, touching the brim of his faded, battered hat.

"Sometimes double," said Dorsey, with a flat, serious expression. "I don't call it selling water. I like to think we sell peace of mind. Once folks pay us, they can drink with no fear of getting shot in the head."

"I understand." Emmen nodded.

"Perhaps you have also heard of me, eh?" the Mexican cut in. "In English, *Pie Sucio* means—"

"I know what it means," said Emmen Shay, cutting him off. To Candles he said, "How long are you and these men planning on visiting the Roost?" He reached out and rubbed his thick fingers and thumb together toward Candles.

Candles grinned and relaxed. Nudging his horse forward, he pulled a stack of the money from inside his coat and held it out to Emmen Shay. "Long enough to win all your money, nail all your whores and drink all your whiskey," he said.

Satisfied with the money, Emmen passed it on to Brady, who riffled it himself and put it away. "You'll find rooms at the Embassy Hotel," Brady said. "I'll have them stick a whore and a bottle of rye in each of your rooms—first bottle's on the house. If you wear the whore out, send her down. We'll send up a fresh one."

"Obliged, Emmen," Candles said with a touch of his hat brim.

"Don't mention it," said Emmen. "Just get in there and show us how fast you can spend your money."

"Oh, wait. . . ." Candles hesitated and took on a troubled countenance.

"What is it, Bobby?" asked Emmen.

"I told you there's no bad blood between me and Big Chicago, far as *I'm* concerned." He paused, then said, "Is it safe to say he feels the same?"

"Chicago knows the rules here, same as everybody else," said Emmen.

"Sure, he knows the rules," said Candles. "My question is, will he abide by them?"

"He'd better," said Emmen, "else he'll find himself on a mighty hard spot." He turned his horse and added,

"I told you, Bobby, brother Brady and I rule the Roost. Anybody who doesn't like it, they'd be well advised to pass us by and keep headed north."

"That's good enough for us," Candles said with a faint smile and a tip of his hat.

Chapter 19

No sooner had the Shays arrived back at their office above the saloon than Brady looked down from the side window and saw Cree Carter and three dust-streaked town guards step down from their saddles. "Jesus, what now?" he said, watching Carter jerk Hatton to the ground and give him a kick. The three guards helped the two badly wounded riflemen across an alley and through the back door of a doctor's office.

Stepping over beside his brother and looking down, Emmen called out through the open window, "Carter, what the hell went on out there?" He eyed the hatless man lying curled on the ground as he spoke. "It sounded like Bull Run all over again."

Carter nudged Hatton with his boot toe and replied up to the Shays, "He's no *bull*, but he was damn sure on the *run*—till we stopped him, that is." He paused and pulled Hatton to his feet. "You're not going to believe who I've got here."

"Don't even think you're going to have me guess, Cree," Emmen said in a warning tone of voice.

"Sorry," said Carter. He shook Hatton by his shoulder and said, "This is none other than J. Fenwick—"

"I'm J. Fenwick Hatton," said Hatton, cutting short the introduction.

The Shays looked at each other in rapt silence for a moment until Brady whispered, "My God . . ."

Carter said, "Did you hear me up there?"

"Yes, we heard you, Cree," Emmen cut in. "Bring him up here. Let's take a better look at him. Use the private stairs," he added in afterthought.

"Holy Moses, brother," Brady said to Emmen as Carter gave Hatton a push toward a small private door that opened to a hidden stairwell up the rear of the building. "Do you suppose that could actually be J. Fenwick Hatton?"

"If it's not, you will never have seen a man die so quickly in your life," said Emmen. He glared at his brother. "And I'm talking about Cree Carter, not the sumbitch he has in tow."

Moments later the two heard boots in the hall. When Brady opened the office door, Carter gave Hatton a hard shove forward, then stepped in behind him, accompanied by Zero Paige, who had joined Carter at the bottom of the stairs.

"Here he is, Emmen," said Carter, "Mr. J. Fenwick Hatton, unless the sumbitch is lying."

"Is he wounded?" Brady asked, looking Hatton up and down.

"Naw," said Cree, shoving Hatton again, this time

even harder. "He's a little battered from the trail and carrying a few bullet nicks, but otherwise he's fit as a French fiddle."

"Damn, Cree, take it easy," said Brady Shay, catching Hatton to keep him from falling to the floor.

Emmen stood up from behind his desk and picked up a copy of the *Denver Star*. Studying the newspaper as he stepped around his desk, he gave Hatton a close look and said, "It's him, sure as hell."

"Yes, it is I," said Hatton. "Wouldn't I be quite the fool to impersonate myself?"

Emmen and Brady gave each other a puzzled look. Then Emmen took control by jabbing a finger in Hatton's chest and saying, "Look, Mr. J. Fenwick-*by-God*-Hatton. In this office, you speak when you're spoken to."

Even with his wrists tied together in front of him, Hatton made a lunge at Emmen. But Carter and Paige caught him from behind.

"He's been hateful and belligerent ever since we caught him," said Carter. "Say the word and Zero and I will scatter his teeth for him."

"You need to settle yourself down, Hatton," said Emmen Shay. "It looks like you and us are going to be spending some time together."

"I don't get it, brother Emmen," said Brady. "What do you have in mind?"

Emmen stepped over to his brother and looped an arm around his broad shoulder. "If there was one thing I have learned over the years, it is this." He raised his fingers and his cigar for emphasis and continued. "When you are fortunate enough to get your hands around a rich man's throat, do not turn it loose until he has spit forth a fountain of gold."

"You will rot in hell, sir," Hatton said, his fists balled tightly, "before you ever see a dollar of *Hatton* gold."

"Aye, you say that now and it's understandable," said Emmen with a dark chuckle. "But let's see how you feel when we've cleaved off a couple of your fingers and ask you again, real nice-like."

"We're going to hold him for ransom?" Carter asked, he and Zero Paige grinning at each other.

"Hell, yes," Carter said, speaking out of turn in his excitement. "That's the only natural thing to do with a rich bastard like this."

Emmen walked over to Carter and Paige with a dark expression and said, "Both of yas, get out of here. My brother and I have things to talk about."

Carter knew he'd made a mistake, yet he hesitated and said, "But, Emmen, I brought him to you. That's got to be worth something in all this."

"You're right, Cree," said Emmen, with a second of consideration. "Stay where you are." He walked behind his desk, picked up a big Army Colt from an open desk drawer, walked back and shot Carter in the forehead.

"Lord God!" Zero Paige stood stunned.

Emmen swung the pistol toward Paige from only four feet away. "Whoa, wait, Emmen!" Paige said, talking fast, his eyes wide in terror. "I didn't catch him. I didn't bring him here. I had nothing to do with it. I've got nothing coming!"

Emmen lowered the big Colt and uncocked the hammer. "I'm so happy to hear you say that, Zero," he said. "Now go get a bucket of water and a scrub brush." He grinned. "My brother and I would *still* like to talk."

"Yes, sir," said Paige. He turned and hurried out the door.

Hatton stood staring down at the body on the floor at his feet. Brady walked over with a long boot knife in his fist and a strange smile on his face. "Hold out your wrists, Hatton."

Hatton did as he was told and watched the knife blade slash through the hemp rope, freeing his hands. "Now sit down over there," said Brady, pointing the knife toward a large, straight-back chair.

As soon as Hatton sat down, Emmen stepped over, slapped one handcuff around his wrist and cuffed its mate to the chair arm. "Just so you don't turn rabbit on us, Mr. Hatton," he said.

Hatton stared up at him with no sign of fear in his eyes.

"Now, let me ask you," Emmen said to Hatton, taking the knife from Brady's hand. "If you were to pen a letter to the person most likely to send us, say . . . two hundred thousand dollars, rather than have us cut you into strips and feed you to coyotes, who would that person be?"

"Go to hell, sir," Hatton replied stubbornly.

"My goodness, brother Emmen," said Brady, "two hundred thousand dollars? That is a powerful lot of money."

"Yes, it is," said Emmen. "But how many times do you suppose an opportunity like this will come our

way, brother Brady? It's two hundred thousand or nothing. We either turn this into our biggest deal *ever* or
we forget it. We spend the rest of our lives serving up
whores, drink and dope to every hard case who makes
it here ahead of the law."

"I will die, sir, before I see a dollar of my money in
the hands of a rat like you," said Hatton.

"Then die you surely will," said Emmen Shay, gripping the knife in his fist, "but not before you beg me to
kill you."

Inside the Gold Poke Saloon, Big Chicago stood at a
long ornate bar, each arm slung around the naked shoulders of a young prostitute. "My, my," Chicago laughed.
"I haven't been here two hours. Look at all the friends
I've made." Along the bar the rest of the men stood with
women of their own. In front of the men stood bottles of
rye, mescal and tequila, along with open leather pouches
of Mexican-grown cocaine, marijuana and dried peyote
cactus buttons. A whole roasted goat had been brought
in, still sizzling, and set atop the bar, a big carving knife
stuck in its ribs.

"I was never treated this well upon returning home
from the war," Baldhead Paul remarked morosely to a
bare-breasted young woman who stood stroking the
top of his shiny head as she fed him peyote buttons.

"You poor thing," she cooed sympathetically. "Here,
have another. This will make up for it." She reached
out, picked up a third peyote button and popped it into
Paul's mouth. He swallowed it with a drunken cross-
eyed leer and washed it down with a swig of mescal.

In a corner of the busy saloon, a guitar, an accordion and a wooden flute played happy fiesta music. On the dirt and tile floor an elderly Mexican showman danced with a scruffy, toothless black bear. The sow bear stood on her hind legs, her thick paws embracing the old man, swaying to the music. A short, ragged striped skirt girthed the cumbersome animal; a string of saliva swung from her rubbery lips, a circle of gnats and flies danced in the air above her bristly ears.

But the music suddenly stopped. The laughter and the gaiety followed, waning to a halt when Bobby Candles and his three bandits filed through the batwing doors and stopped and looked all around. Even the big sow bear turned her dance partner loose and stood swaying deftly, staring at the four newcomers.

"My goodness, men, look who's here," Chicago said, peeling the whores from his sides in order to have his hands near the guns in his waist sash.

Candles' first impulse was to raise his Colt and start shooting. But upon seeing two men in the iron birdcage suspended from the ceiling atop the stairs, he whispered over his shoulder to Dad Lodi, "Easy, now. We're on neutral ground."

Lodi and the other two desert bandits eyed the eight-gauge deck guns mounted on the rail of the iron-plated birdcage. "You heard him, fellows," Lodi whispered in turn to Dorsey and Dirty Foot. "Let's keep this cordial and polite."

Chicago's tight stare eased into a laugh once he realized Candles wasn't going to make a move under the watchful eyes from the birdcage. "I swear, Bobby Candles, you are a puzzle to me. We waited and waited for you and your sand bandits to show up in Saverine Pass. But you never did!"

"Show up, why would we, *Chester*?" said Candles. "So you and your men could ambush us?"

"Well, *yes*," Chicago said with a bemused shrug. "That was one possibility. The other was, we might have felt bad about all that's happened and wanted to square things with you." He shook a finger and grinned. "You seem to always go around thinking the worst of everybody. That'll ruin a friendship quicker than anything."

Baldhead Paul, his brain starting to churn from the peyote buttons, said with his crossed eyes a-swirl, "It's not *Chester* anymore. It's Big Chicago."

"Quiet, Baldhead, eat your buttons," said Big Chicago. "Bobby is only calling me *Chester* to aggravate things." He gestured up toward the birdcage, seeing the two guards staring down intently. "But I'm going to suggest, Bobby, that this is a poor time for us to go drawing guns and shooting one another."

"I agree." Candles let out a tense breath and stepped closer, saying between them, "I can put off killing you for the time being." He patted his lapel. "My men and I are going to relax here, spend Garr's share of the strongbox money . . ." Garr bristled and almost reached for his gun, but Buddy Short stopped him as Candles continued. "And decide the best time and place to stake you down and skin you like a buck elk."

"Bobby, Bobby, Bobby." Chicago grinned and shook his head, undisturbed by Candles' harsh talk. "I know there'll be a time when one of us has to kill the other.

It's a natural thing between friends." He shrugged. "But until that time, let me buy you a drink. I know how thirsty it can get out there, eating my dust day in, day out."

"No, *Chester*," said Candles, pulling a wad of money from inside his coat. He gave Delbert Garr a smug look and said, "Let's let my *former pardner*, Delbert, buy us all a drink."

A bartender wearing sleeve garters strung out a line of clean shot glasses along the bar. He uncorked a bottle of rye as the men gathered closer around Chicago and Candles.

As the bartender filled the shot glasses, suddenly Baldhead Paul let out a loud scream and charged across the floor, his arms spread, his shiny head lowered like that of a charging bull. "I'll kill that sow!" he shouted. "She never treated me right!"

The two guards in the birdcage stared intently, the big eight-gauge deck guns poised and ready on the cage's handrail.

"What do you suppose he means by that?" Chicago asked Candles.

"I don't know," said Candles, glancing up at the birdcage. "You better give him room."

Behind the bar the big bartender with the gartered shirtsleeves grabbed a rope hanging from a large brass bell. He jerked the rope vigorously. "Hurry, hurry!" he shouted above the clanging bell, the bawling, snarling bear and its cursing, wild-eyed challenger. "Get your money down! We've got ourselves a bear fight!"

Chapter 20

On the floor of the Gold Poke Saloon, the three musicians grabbed their instruments and took shelter behind the piano. The frightened piano player did not retreat. Instead he stood with his back to his keyboard, his arms spread as if to protect the helpless piano from a rolling, thrashing, bouncing mountain of fur, human limbs, discarded boots and ripped clothing.

At one point the big snarling sow, her ripped skirt hanging from one leg, slung Baldhead Paul high into the air, leaving him pinned for a moment on a rack of antlers. The trembling piano player screamed as the enraged sow turned to him, her arms outstretched as if requesting him to accompany her. Along the bar and in a cautious circle, the drinkers cheered and goaded and shook fists full of money, each shouting his support for both Baldhead Paul and his opponent.

"I am not through with you!" Baldhead Paul shouted as soon as the antlers turned him loose and he hit the tile floor.

The piano player let out a sob of relief as the big sow turned toward Paul and caught him in midair as he hurled himself at her.

"Jesus," said Candles, turning away in disgust, "he can't leave that damn bear alone."

"I know," said Chicago beneath the din of the crowd, the bawl of the bear and the screams of Baldhead Paul, now being mauled on the bloody floor. "Not to speak ill of the man, but it's hard to conduct serious business with somebody when you can't even tell who he's talking to, let alone what he's apt to do next."

Candles gave him a look; then his eyes took on a hard glare. "Whatever you're about to propose, I'm not going for it, *Chester*," he said. "I would not trust you with a she-baboon."

"That's only prudent of you," Chicago said with a thin smile. He raised his shot glass and grinned as the bear jumped up and down on Baldhead Paul, using its big paws like fists, batting his head back and forth with each swing. "But you have to admit, you make more money in one week with me than you will your whole short life with those three scrubs."

"I don't know about that," Candles said smugly. "We're not doing so bad." He patted the money in his lapel and gave a toss of his eyes around the large saloon. "We're both frequenting the same fine places."

"Right, we both are for now," Chicago said cynically. "But if you're counting on Garr's cut holding you over till your next score, you're as stupid as I think you are."

Candles grinned and threw back his drink. "My next score might be closer at hand than you think, *Chester*," he said. On the bloody floor behind them, Baldhead Paul let out a muffled scream as the big snarling sow held him up, his head squeezed between her paws. Burying his face in her wet, toothless mouth, she bawled loud and long and slung him back and forth violently by his head.

When the bartender first rang the big brass bell, Brady Shay had stepped over, opened the office door a crack and looked down upon the spectacle. "Another nimrod who thinks he can whip anything female," he said over his shoulder to his brother, Emmen. "We've got to tell these whores to quit feeding peyote—else we need to get rid of the bear altogether."

"Get rid of Old Louise?" said Emmen. "I don't think so."

Still cuffed to the chair arm where Emmen had left him, Hatton lay slumped to one side, a long welt from a gun barrel running the length of his jaw. "Maybe we need to think about how Old Louise can help us get our distinguished guest here believing we'll kill him if he doesn't do as he's told."

"Yeah, how's that?" said Brady.

"Simple." Emmen smiled. Holding his cigar scissor-style between his fingers, he blew a reflective stream of smoke. "Instead of us wearing ourselves out, chopping off fingers and making threats, let's have Old Louise do our work for us."

"Are you saying that flea-bitten old bear will scare a rich like Hatton getting into up off of his gold?" Brady asked.

"I'm saying it's worth a try," said Emmen, "to keep me from bloodying our office again."

"There's nothing harder than getting a rich man to turn loose of his money, brother Emmen," Brady said. "That's how they become rich to begin with, not turning loose of it."

"We'll see," said Emmen. He opened the office door, stepped out onto the balcony and looked down at the bloody tile floor where the big sow bear stood holding Baldhead Paul upside down, using his face as if it were a mop. Among the hooting and catcalls, Shay called down to the old Mexican, "Edwardo, stop the fight."

All eyes turned upward to the landing where Emmen stood, cigar in hand. Some of the men started to complain, but a look from Emmen stopped them cold as he pulled back his swallow-tailed coat and let them see the handle of a big Colt at his waist.

"*Sí, Senor Shay,*" the old man replied. He rushed in with a short quirt and soundly slapped the big sow on her broad rump.

The bear turned in his face and let out a loud bawl. But she shied back from him, dropped onto all four and ambled away a few feet and sat down.

Emmen stared down at the bloody bear and said to the old Mexican, "When she settles down, put her collar on her and bring her up here."

"Up there, senor?" Edwardo asked, as if not to believe his own ears.

"Would you hear me better if I stick my foot in your face?"

"*Por favor!* Forgive my stupidity, senor! I will bring her right away!" Edwardo replied hastily. "As soon as I have cleaned the blood off her."

"Naw, leave all the blood on her," said Emmen with a grin. "I want to introduce her to a friend of mine."

Emmen walked back inside and shut the office door. As soon as he was out of sight, the men in the saloon began to argue and curse over the outcome of the halted fight. When one man reached across the bar and grabbed the bartender by his forearm, the bartender gave an upward glance at the two men in the birdcage.

"Stand away from him!" one of the guards shouted down at the crowded bar. On either side of the man, the other customers cleared the way quickly. Jerking free from the man's grip, the bartender ducked straight down and crawled quickly along the catwalk behind the bar.

"Oh my God!" the lone man cried, looking up at the two eight-gauge deck guns aimed down at him. "Don't shoot. I meant no harm. I wasn't going to hurt him. I'm drunk, see? I'm drunker than a damn dog!"

At the end of the bar, the bartender sprang back into sight and called up to the birdcage, "No harm done, Victor. No harm, Ulan. He's just drunk, like he said."

"Then get him out of here," one of the guards called down in a harsh tone.

The bartender ran back along behind the bar, snatched up a billy club and laid a whack across the man's bare head, sending him crumbling to the floor. "You asked for it, you damn fool," he shouted down at the knocked-out customer. "You can't be manhandling a bartender!"

The guards in the birdcage sat down and shoved their swivel-mounted guns away from the bar. Customers sighed with relief and moved back to their places along the bar. A Chinese swamper appeared and dragged the knocked-out man away to the rear door. Two more swampers hurried forward, pulled Baldhead Paul to his limp feet, helped him to the open rear door and gave him a shove into the late evening air, toward a line of rickety plank privies whose rancid odors permeated the night.

One of the Chinese men ran forward with Baldhead Paul's gun, which had fallen from his holster during the trouncing he'd taken. As he reached out to slide the gun into the holster, Frank Dorsey's hand wrapped around the gun handle. He said, "I'll take my pal's weapon, lest he hurt himself." He gave a tight grin.

The Chinaman gave him a curious look and rattled something in his own tongue.

Behind the unsuspecting Chinaman, Dad Lodi yanked his long braid up and down roughly and said, "Hey! Get out of here—go boil a dog."

The two Chinese swampers walked back inside, grumbling in their native language, stepping around the struggling half-conscious drinker the bartender had hit with the billy club.

Leaning back on a stack of wooden shipping crates, Baldhead Paul said through bloody, swollen lips, "I—I licked that bear, eh?" His crossed eyes danced wildly in every direction, the pupils large and shiny in a flicker of light from an overhead lantern.

"Yeah, you beat the hell out of the bear," said Dad

as his fingers riffled through Paul's ripped and ragged clothes and found one stack of dollars, then another.

"Hey, what are you doing?" Paul asked from within a swirling peyote stupor, his brain badly jarred and addled from the beating.

"We're taking all your money, Baldhead Paul," said Lodi. He handed the money over to Dorsey, who stuffed it down into his waist. Dirty Foot stood back, keeping an eye toward the rear door.

"On your feet," Lodi said to the bloody, bruised, incapacitated gunman. "Take a little walk to the jakes with us." The two jerked Baldhead Paul to his feet and half guided, half dragged him along the alleyway to the line of privies, farther out of the lantern light.

"What the hell is this?" Paul asked in a dreamy, trancelike voice. "You took all my money . . . ?"

"That's right. Now we're going to cut your throat, Baldhead," Dorsey said close to Paul's mangled ear. "Then we're going to leave you back here, let you bleed to death."

"Oh, I see," said the hallucinating gunman, offering no further questions on the matter.

Inside the Gold Poke, the drinkers and gamblers had settled back into their vices along the bar and at many green felt–topped gaming tables strewn about the place. As the old Mexican bear handler led the big sow up the stairs to the Shays' office, a man and a half-naked whore on their way down leaped over the banister to avoid passing the big animal.

"Where the hell is Baldhead?" Buddy Short asked, looking all around the crowded saloon.

Chicago said, "Last I saw him, two Chinks were dragging him out back. They'll probably throw a bucket of water on him and send him away."

"Uh-uh," said the wary outlaw, having none of it. "Baldhead never leaves a place until the drinking's all done."

"Maybe all the peyote and mescal have altered his thinking," said Chicago.

"Yeah," Candles added, standing beside him, "not to mention getting the hell pounded out of him by a bear." He laughed and threw back a long shot of tequila from a bottle.

But Buddy Short only gave Bobby Candles a sharp, suspicious stare.

"Relax, Buddy," said Chicago, seeing the look on Short's face. He leaned in closer to him and said, "I don't trust this sumbitch any more than you do. But the fact is, he's been standing here beside me all along."

"Yeah, and where's those ragged-assed sand bandits he's got riding with him?" Short asked. "You never want to turn your back on them rattlesnakes."

"That I can't tell you, Buddy," said Chicago, glancing around the crowded bar. "I'll send Russell and Thatcher to take a look for them."

"Never mind," said Short, seeing Russell and Thatcher busily drinking and pawing at two half-naked young women at the far end of the bar. "I'll go look for myself."

"What's got your pal Buddy Short stoked up?" Candles asked, liking this position he found himself in. He wondered idly just how many of Chicago's men his bandits could rob and kill without fear of reprisal.

Chicago stared at him, then said bluntly, "He thinks Baldhead Paul Crane might have run afoul of you and your desert snakes."

Candles sighed into his tequila bottle and shook his head. "It's disheartening, how little faith some of us have in our fellow man."

Chicago stared at him longer, closer. "You know, I might have misjudged you, Bobby. You might be the only sumbitch as low-down evil as myself." He tipped his glass slightly toward Candles as if in a toast.

At the rear door of the crowded saloon, Buddy Short grabbed one of the Chinese bar swampers by his long braid and spun him around. "Hey, you. Did you and another fellow lead my friend out back?"

"You betcha, you betcha." The Chinaman didn't understand a word, but he stared and nodded nervously with a fearful smile on his face.

"Bear fight, damn it," Short said, trying to explain. "Big man, fight bear." He crossed his eyes in an attempt to describe Baldhead Paul.

"Ah, he!" said the Chinaman, a light seeming to have come on in his head. He pointed to the rear door and said in broken English, "Wit frens, wit frens!"

"*With friends*, my ass," Short growled. "Come on. You're going with me." He grabbed the frightened man by the nape of his thin neck and stomped away toward the rear door, his free hand clamped on his gun butt.

In the birdcage above the milling drinkers, whores and gamblers, one guard turned and said to the other, "Did you see that? One of Chester Goines' men just grabbed a Chink and dragged him out the back door toward the privies."

"These sick-minded bastards." The other guard let out a sigh and shook his head in disgust. "Nothing they do surprises me."

"No, that's not what I meant," said the guard. "It's Buddy Short. He had his hand on his gun. He looked awfully mad. What if he kills the little Chinaman?"

"That's the risk one takes, working abroad," said the guard. He settled into a straight wooden chair. "We get paid to keep them in line between these walls. What they do in the jakes out back is no concern of mine."

Moments later, the three bandits stepped through the batwing doors, having walked all the way around the large building to wash Baldhead Paul's blood from their hands at a public well. Leading the three, Dad Lodi gave Bobby Candles a faint, telling smile as they sauntered through the milling crowd over to the bar.

"How's the evening going, Dad?" Candles asked, Chicago busily watching a topless whore twirl her breasts in opposite directions.

"Couldn't be better." Lodi grinned and patted the stacks of money in his waist.

"Drink up then, my *campañeros*," Candles urged.

But as the three lined up along the bar and inspected their hands and shirtsleeves for any traces of blood, the rear door slung open wide and an enraged Buddy

Short ran inside. Whores screamed, customers leaped out of his way as Short swung his cocked Colt in the direction of the crowded bar and bellowed like a man possessed, "Bobby Candles, you rotten, murdering sumbitch!" He stood with his breath heaving in his chest, both arms covered with Baldhead Paul's blood up to his elbows.

"Whoa!" Candles threw his arms in the air, making sure the two men in the birdcage saw him make no move for his gun. Alongside him the bandits did the same.

Even Chicago, seeing what was going on, threw his hands up. "Buddy! Drop it! Don't be a foo—"

But Chicago's words were swallowed up by the explosion of both the big deck guns from inside the birdcage.

In a split second Buddy Short turned from an enraged gunfighter into a large roiling spray of dark blood, chunks of flesh, bone matter and shards of shattered tile lifted from the floor.

"Lord God!" a customer cried out as Short's ghastly remnants splattered all over the wall like some exploding star, and showered down all over the cowering crowd. "Look at his foot!"

On the floor where the tile had exploded, Buddy Short's left leg, boot and all, stood rocking back and forth, covered with blood. "Jesus," said Candles, keeping himself from smiling as the severed leg finally toppled over onto the floor. "Talk about leaving a place in a hurry."

"You're behind this, Candles, I know you are," Chicago growled, making sure to keep his temper in check, having just seen the guards reload the two deck guns. He kept his hands high as the Shay brothers stepped out onto the upper landing, guns in hand, and looked down on the blood-spattered crowd.

Chapter 21

As Emmen and Brady Shay walked down the blood-splattered stairs, Emmen looked up at the birdcage with disgust, wiping his palms on a handkerchief after using the stair banister. "Both guns, at once, Ulan?" he asked one of the guards with a sour and skeptic expression.

The guard said, "Better safe than sorry, Emmen, is what you always say. I had no idea Victor here was going to shoot too."

"There was no time to talk about it," the other guard said. "He came in and threw down on Candles. Candles didn't even go for his gun. It was all Buddy Short's doings."

Emmen turned a stiff gaze to Bobby Candles, who gave a grin and a shrug. "That's me right enough, peaceful to a fault," Candles said. He wiggled his fingers, his hands still raised chest high.

"Same with us," said Dad Lodi, wiggling his fingers,

giving Dirty Foot and Frank Dorsey a look, coaxing them to follow suit.

"All of you get your hands down," Emmen said. He called out to the Chinese swampers, "Get some buckets and scrape Buddy Short off the furniture." He studied the lone severed leg still in its boot and said, "One of yas bring Short's leg up to the office." He said to Brady, "Maybe we'll get some use of it, after all this mess."

The man who had earlier been billy clubbed staggered in through the rear door, the welt still on his head. He pointed in the direction of the privies and said in a shaken voice, "There's one sitting back there with his throat cut ear to ear."

"Damn it, what next?" said Emmen. He stomped on down the stairs, his brother, Brady, right behind him, and walked out the open back door.

At the bar, Chicago gave Russell, Thatcher and Garr a nod. "Go see who it is out there."

Russell grumbled under his breath. But he clamped a whore to his side and said, "Come on, honey, you're going with me." He looked at Thatcher and Garr as they joined the other customers streaming out behind the Shays. "I've got ten dollars says it's Baldhead Paul Crane."

"Do I look stupid enough to take that bet?" Thatcher said, his half-naked whore walking at his side, his arm around her. Delbert Garr walked along alone, still boiling over having lost his money to Candles and his bandits. The bandits sauntered along behind him, three abreast, smug grins on their weathered faces.

In a moment Bobby Candles and Chicago stood at

an empty bar. The two guards still sat above them in their iron cage, but the bartender and the rest of the patrons had all trampled across the bloody floor and spilled out around the privies like a herd of cattle.

"It's quiet moments like this when a man takes stock of himself and begins to ponder his life," Chicago said quietly.

Candles stared at him, lifted a shot of tequila and said bluntly, "You're down to three men, *Chester*." He cut a glance toward the rear door, having watched the way his three bandits had closed up behind Russell, Thatcher and Garr. "Things being as they are, you could lose another one any minute."

"Why, you . . ." Chicago straightened and instinctively laid his hand on the butt of the big Colt in his waist sash. But the sound of a deck gun turning on its swivel caused his hand to freeze, open wide and then rise away quickly.

"Easy, Chester." Candles grinned, wagging a finger back and forth. "You don't want to leave here the way Buddy Short did."

"All right, Bobby," Chicago said, "I'm ready to reconcile all our differences."

"I'm not," Candles said with the same sly little grin. He backed away from the bar, keeping his hands in plain sight of the two guards above them.

"I'll get new men, Bobby," Chicago said.

"And I'll kill them," Candles returned. He backed farther away toward the front door.

"This is foolish," said Chicago. "You've got law on your tail, you've got three men you can't trust as far as you can spit. I'm offering to set things right with you, Bobby, and get back where we both ought to be."

Before turning and walking out the door, Candles called up to the guards in the iron birdcage, "You fellows keep an eye on *Chester* here. He looks like a man all set to blow up any minute."

Chicago stood at the bar, staring with killing rage, knowing there was nothing he could do with the big deck guns standing over him. . . .

Upstairs, on the floor of a small dark room off the Shays' office, Hatton came to, feeling something hot, coarse and wet swabbing the length of his face. His eyes flew open, then shut tight; he lay as still as stone. He heard the bear snort, felt a blast of strong foul-smelling breath on his saliva-lathered cheek. *Oh my God!*

The big bear stood over him, a heavy front paw pressing down on his chest. The animal's wet nose poked and probed his face, his neck, his closed eyes. *Oh my God! Oh my God!* He felt its toothless mouth close around his ear and twist and yank as if to rip the helpless appendage from the side of his face.

Then the bear turned loose of his ear, as if bored with it. Hatton's head dropped back to the plank floor. He opened his eyes in time to see the wide black mouth close down, only an inch from his face, and let out a long, loud bawl that shook the very bones inside his chest. *Easy, fellow . . . Easy, fellow . . .* Hatton repeated the words over and over to himself, as if reciting a chant.

The big bear stepped back and began raking a powerful claw down his chest as if to open him for a curious look-see inside. Yet, bracing himself for the feel of his flesh being sliced by a fistful of daggers, Hatton felt a sense of relief when he realized the bear's sharp fore-claws had been filed down to hard, stubby buttons.

His sense of relief heightened as the bear turned in the grainy darkness, ambled across the plank floor and dropped onto its belly. *All right, James*, he thought to himself, *you've made it this far. Hold out—win this game!*

Keeping close watch on the resting bear, he crawled an inch farther away, then another, slowly, until he felt the bite of a leg iron around his left ankle. He lay staring up at the ceiling, the only light in the room coming from a window where a flickering glow shone in dimly from oil pots lining the streets below.

What is going on here . . . ? Hatton looked down at the leg iron, the length of chain bolted to the floor. It didn't take him long to answer himself. This was a place the Shays used to frighten, coerce and torture—a place where they forced men to submit to their will. This was the place where debts, both real and alleged, were collected. This was the place where gold claims changed hands, land titles, cattle, anything of value that the two thugs and their henchmen made men forfeit in order to save their lives.

Well, not him, Hatton decided with a firm set to his wet, grimy jaw. His was a fortune made the hard way, a life hewn from the hardest of matter, the most unfor-giving of substance. He could give it up with no less effort, he thought, staring hard through the darkness at the big panting bear.

It went through Hatton's mind that his wealth and

his existence had somehow been related to the death of his daughter—not that he had caused such tragedy, simply that the loss of those he'd loved had been a part of what fate had bequeathed him. He had caught a brief, ugly glance of Curly Joe's head in the small briny tomb before he released it and burned it to ashes.

His success had always carried with it a price, and whatever that price had been he had paid it. *As well all men must,* Hatton reminded himself. For even one more touch of his wife's and daughter's hand he would gladly offer up all he owned. But to those who would rob him, those who had offered nothing, neither in sweat nor in blood: *Not one damn dime,* he told himself.

Staring at the bear, he let out a loud bawl of his own, his fists clenched at his sides, as if daring the big animal to devour him. But the big sow only stopped panting for a moment. She stared at him, cocking her head curiously to one side. Then she lowered her big head, dismissing him, and began licking her forepaws.

Standing on a plank walkway out in front of a wooden privy where Baldhead Paul Crane's body sat slumped to one side, Emmen Shay and his brother, Brady, both looked down at their blood-soaked boots. "Damn it to hell," Emmen cursed in disgust. In a lowered tone, he said to Brady, "Do you see what I mean about cashing in, getting out of this blasted business?" He held a glowing oil lantern at shoulder height.

"Yes, brother Emmen, I couldn't agree more," Brady replied, raising a boot and slinging it back and forth.

When the customer had found Baldhead Paul's body,

he had slammed the privy door and run back inside the saloon. All the blood had poured down Paul's chest; most of it lay in a thick puddle inside the closed door. When Emmen opened the door, a pool of blood had spilled out over his and his brother's boots.

"All right, Hu, get him out of there," said Emmen to the leader of the Chinese swampers who had gathered around the open privy door.

"And send out a bucket of water to throw over our feet," Brady called out in afterthought.

Standing in the crowd behind the Shays, Russell, Thatcher and Delbert Garr heard a dark chuckle and looked to their left where the three desert bandits stood staring back at them. Knowing they had the eye of Chicago's men, Dad Lodi pulled out a stack of money they'd taken from Baldhead Paul. In full view of the three, he licked his thumb, rifled the money and put it away.

"These sonsabitches," said Garr, taking a step toward the bandits.

But Russell turned loose of his whore and grabbed Garr. "Let it go," he said. "You heard Chicago. All these tramps are doing is trying to set us up. Look what happened to Short."

"What are we supposed to do, let them walk all over us, kill one of us any damn time they want to?" Garr asked Russell, staring hard at the three taunting bandits.

Dirty Foot crossed his eyes and grasped himself by the throat, mocking Baldhead Paul.

"Damn this!" Thatcher growled. "I can't take it anymore. Let's kill them," he said to Garr.

"No!" Russell grabbed him by the arm too. "We'll do what Chicago told us to do," he said in a stern tone, still holding Garr's arm. "He said 'no trouble here!' That's how it's going to be."

Three guards with shotguns stepped forward out of the crowd and eyed all of the gunmen equally until both sides settled down. "See this?" Emmen said sidelong to his brother. "This is a sign from hell that we need to get all we can off of this J. Fenwick Hatton fellow while the getting's good."

"I back your play, brother Emmen," said Brady. "Tell me what you want to do."

"It'll be daylight before long," Emmen said, looking off toward a thin, pale light mantling the horizon. "We've got to get Hatton to write that message and tell us who to deliver it to." He looked down at the blood on their tall boots.

Seeing his brother's state of mind, Brady said to the gathered customers, "All right, folks, get back inside. Enjoy yourselves! Let Hu and his Chinks get this all cleaned up."

As the crowd disbursed itself and moved back inside the saloon, the Shay brothers walked all the way around the large building and climbed the private wooden stairs to their rear office door. Once inside, Emmen slammed the door loud enough to awaken the old bear handler, who lay asleep in a big wooden chair. On one side of the chair, the big bear rose and stared blankly at the Shays.

"What's the bear doing out here?" Emmen asked the bleary-eyed Mexican. On the other side of the chair sat a small bucket of rocks; beside the bucket lay a short prospector's pick. "Have you been chipping rocks instead of doing like I told you?"

"No, Senor Shay," said Edwardo. "I put Louise in there to scare him. But then I took her outside to relieve herself," the old Mexican said. "When I brought her back, she lay down beside this chair and would not get up."

"You're her handler, Edwardo. You should be able to make her do what you tell her to do," said Brady, his hands on his hips.

"*Sí*, it is true," said the old Mexican. "But I am an old handler and she is an old bear. Sometimes it is easier to let an old sow do as she pleases." He gestured a hand up and down the bear. "But as you can see, most of the dried blood is still on her. If I made her stay in the room, she would have licked herself clean, out of spite."

"All right," Emmen conceded.

Brady toed the bucket of rocks with his wet boot and shook his head. "What is it you're always chipping for, Edwardo, gold, silver . . . diamonds?"

"Who knows?" The old Mexican shrugged. "I have chipped rocks ever since I was a *niño*. I have never found anything."

"Jesus," said Brady, "then why don't you stop?"

"I chip for a purpose that I do not yet know," he said with a sad expression. "But someday I will see what my chipping has led to." He shrugged. "Anyway, it is not easy to stop chipping when one has chipped as long as I have, even when one's father and his father before him have chipped rocks without knowing wh—"

"Enough of this," said Emmen, cutting the old Mexican off. He looked around the dim-lit office and asked, "Where did Hu's man put Buddy Short's leg?"

Edwardo pointed at a blood-smeared roll of canvas stuck under the edge of Emmen's desk. Emmen stepped over, dragged out the canvas and unrolled it on the floor. He looked at Short's leg, seeing where the loads of scrap iron and nail heads in the deck guns had chewed it off just below the knee. "Perfect," he said, standing and dusting his hands together.

"It's getting near daylight," Brady said, gesturing toward the encroaching sunlight on the eastern horizon.

"Yes, I see it is," said Emmen. He stooped and picked up Short's leg by the boot. "Let's get started, then, shall we?"

Chapter 22

On a steep hillside beneath a guard outpost two miles from Robber's Roost, Sherman Dahl and Eddie Lane hugged themselves against a large embedded boulder. They listened quietly, making sure they had not been heard by the two guards above as they'd climbed upward. Their horses stood waiting, out of sight, hitched among the rock and scrub cedar alongside the meandering trail below.

After a moment of tense silence, satisfied that their presence had not been detected, the two nodded at each other in the grainy morning light. Then they slipped away quietly in opposite directions, each headed up the rocky hillside on his belly, as if some strange reptile.

In the guard camp atop a cliff overhang, a young gunman named Curtis Stroud picked up his rifle from against a rock and walked to an edge overlooking the trail to Saverine Pass. "I could have sworn I heard a horse down there a while ago," he said to an older gunman named Toby Myers.

"Relax, kid. You'll live longer," said Myers, leaning back against his saddle beside a low campfire.

"Living longer is no concern of mine," Stroud said, gazing out and down across the trail below.

"Mine neither," said Myers. "It's just something to say." He finished rolling himself a smoke and ran the thin cigarette in and out of his mouth to wet it and firm it up. "The only reason we're out here is because Emmen Shay got nervous, all the new blood drifting into the Roost." He struck a match in his cupped hands, lit the cigarette and blew out a stream of smoke. "This is the first time this lookout post has been used in nearly a year."

"Yeah, I heard," said Stroud, still probing the purple morning light, restless, bored. "I'm starting to wonder if coming here to work for the Shays was a bad idea."

"It's a guard job. What did you expect it to be?" Myers asked, leaning back, making himself more comfortable against his saddle.

"I don't know what I expected, but it sure as hell wasn't this," said Stroud. "I was better off working for the Mexes, scalping 'Pache for a living. At least I got to see lots of country."

"You'll get used to it here," Myers said. "I liken this job to being a prison guard. Only difference is our killers and thieves are running loose, with money to spend. Instead of us protecting society from them, we protect them from society." He grinned. "It's sort of the way hell would have it."

"I don't believe in hell," Stroud said flatly. Looking back down, he said, "I could've sworn I heard a horse. . . ."

"You might have," said Myers, standing, blowing out a stream of smoke and dusting the seat of his trousers. "There's some prospectors and hermits travel these trails of a night." He walked over beside the young gunman and looked down. "There's even a small tribe of Utes who come to the Roost now and then selling cactus buttons, loco weed and whatnot—"

No sooner had Myers spoken than he crumbled forward as Stroud heard the smack of a rifle butt and looked around at him. "Damn!" said Stroud, seeing Dahl standing behind the knocked-out older gunman. But no sooner had Stroud himself spoken than he also crumbled to the ground.

Lane looked at Dahl in the grainy morning light and said, "So far so good." He stooped and dragged Stroud back from where he'd landed dangerously close to the edge of the cliff. "I'm glad we didn't have to kill them."

"No need," said Dahl. "We'll tie them around a tree and take their horses and boots. By the time they get loose and walk back to the Roost, we should have freed Hatton and be gone."

"If he's still alive," said Lane.

"He's still alive," said Dahl. "The Shay brothers aren't going to kill a man like J. Fenwick Hatton unless they have to. They're going to want to make some money off him."

"You sound mighty sure of yourself, Teacher," said Lane. .

"I don't mean to sound arrogant," Dahl said. "But I know men like the Shays, and I know men like Hatton. They are a lot alike in a lot of ways. In a test of wills, they better not underestimate J. Fenwick Hatton. He didn't get rich by being weak or stupid." He stooped and dragged Myers back from the cliff edge and across the campsite to a tall cedar. "I'll wager that by now he's working on a plan for freeing himself."

"I hope you're right," said Lane.

When the two had seated the knocked-out gunmen back to back on either side of the thick cedar trunk, they tied them with a coil of rope Stroud carried around his saddle horn. While Lane pulled the two men's bandanas up over their mouths and tightened them, Dahl stepped over and poured the remnants of a pot of coffee onto the low campfire and stamped out the remaining embers.

Mounting the two men's horses, they rode the switch-back trail down to where their own horses stood waiting in the new morning light. They dropped the saddles and bridles from the gunmen's horses and shooed the animals away. Then they stepped atop their horses and rode away toward Robber's Roost.

The bear was back. In the hours before, Hatton had heard the door creak open, and he'd heard the heavy footsteps of the animal as it walked out of the darkened room. But moments ago he'd awakened from a guarded sleep as once again he'd heard the door creak open and close. He'd heard words whispered in Spanish; he'd heard the rattle of the chain fastened to the bear's thick leather collar.

Now, lying back against the wall, his eyes closed, feigning sleep, Hatton smelled the bear. He heard the large animal breathing, licking, lapping, sucking and grunting. Without moving he opened his eyes slowly when he heard the door close and heard boots walk away.

In the early light he saw the bear down on its belly, its lowered head busily gnawing with its bare gums. This time, unlike earlier, the bear was also chained to the floor. Straining for a closer look, Hatton saw the shredded boot lying beside the bear's bobbing, twisting head. Then he swallowed a tight knot in his throat when he recognized the human foot in the bear's bloody, slobbering mouth, its paws holding the calf of the leg as it ripped off the smallest toe and crunched it in its toothless jaws.

All right . . . This was what the Shays thought it would take to break him . . . ?

Hatton held his head over to one side and closed his eyes. He tried not to hear the bear going at its gruesome breakfast, gnawing the stub of the leg on the plank floor. But these were not sounds and smells that he could easily block out. He took a deep breath and waited for a moment, collecting himself, before he let out a long, gut-wrenching scream, and watched and listened for boots and voices on the other side of the door.

Behind his desk, Emmen Shay grinned wisely and stood up before Hatton's first scream ended. When the old Mexican and Brady Shay started toward the door to the small room, he stopped them with a raised hand.

"Hold it," Emmen said in a lowered voice. To the

Mexican he said, "Edwardo, you chained the bear down when you gave her the leg, didn't you?"

"*Sí*, just like you told me to do," the bear handler replied, standing, his small rock-chipping pick in his hand. "Always it is better to chain Louise when she is chewing something. Or she will let no one near her but me." As he spoke he pitched his small pick and a broken rock back into the bucket.

"Then what's our hurry?" Emmen asked smugly, looking at Brady. "Let's let Mr. J. Fenwick Hatton know how it feels to stare death in the face."

"Hatton is not a young man, brother Emmen," said Brady. "What if this scares him to death? Then we'll get nothing out of this . . . no letter, no money."

From the other room, Hatton screamed again, this time longer.

"I believe you worry too much, brother Brady," said Emmen. "Listen to that. Hatton has the lungs of a buffalo."

"Help me! Help me!" Hatton screamed from the other room. "I'll write the letter, I'll tell you who to send it to! For God's sakes, *please*! Get me *out of here*!" His scream was followed by a long, loud bawl of protest from the big sow.

"There," said Emmen with a dark grin, grasping the door handle. "I do believe he's coming right around."

When a few more screams had resounded and a few more tense moments had passed, Emmen finally relented and chuckled and reached out for the door handle.

Hearing the door handle turn, Hatton, who had been

leaning against the wall screaming, hurriedly rolled himself into a ball on the plank floor and lay trembling and sobbing as the door opened and the Shays and the old Mexican bear handler walked in.

"Do I hear you correctly, Hatton?" Emmen asked in a taunting voice. "You've had a change of heart? You want to write the letter we discussed?"

"Any-anything you want!" Hatton sobbed, his face buried in his arms on the floor. "I'll write the letter. I'll pay you anything you want. Keep that bear away from me. I don't want to die this way. . . ." His words trailed away in a long, terrified sob.

"There, there, Hatton, calm yourself down," Emmen Shay said, consoling him with a pat on his sobbing back as he grinned and winked at his brother. "We're not going to feed you to this bear. Not so long as you do everything we tell you to do."

"Yeah," Brady said, getting in on it. "Don't be like that hardheaded sumbitch the bear was just finishing off. He thought he could double-cross us Shays and do as he damned well pleased. But just look at what it got him."

Edwardo walked over to the bear, unfastened the chain from the floor and grabbed the wet, bloody leg from her mouth with a sucking sound. He led her grumbling and growling out of the room into the office. "All right, now," said Emmen, "the bear is gone. You sit up and pull yourself together."

Hatton rolled up from a ball and leaned back, his face in his hands. "Just tell me what it is you want me to say."

"First things first," said Emmen. He and Brady helped Hatton to his feet and led him out to the office. "Who is the person we need to contact?"

"That—that would be my assistant, Mr. Carlton Farris," Hatton said. "But I'm afraid he's a long way from here."

"Oh, we won't let that bother us" Emmen said. "We'll just have to remind him that you'll be awaiting a response, while we keep you chained to the bear."

Brady Shay stepped in with a smile and set pen and ink on the desk. "Have a seat, Mr. Hatton. We'll help you choose your words just right."

Turning to the old Mexican who stood holding the bear's chain, Emmen said, "Take that stinking bear out and wash her down. Mr. Hatton here is going to be chained to her. We certainly want him to see our hospitable side, don't we, Edwardo?"

"*Sí*, of course," said the old bear handler. He jerked on the bear's chain and led her toward the rear stairs. As he left by the rear door, a guard hurried up the stairs and knocked on the front office door.

"Yeah, what is it?" Emmen asked, throwing the door open.

"There's a rider out front, Mr. Shay," said the guard, a shotgun cradled in his arm. "He managed to slip in here right under the trail guards' noses."

"Oh, really?" said Emmen Shay. Instead of going down the stairs right away, he first walked to a front window, grabbing Hatton on his way. Peeping down at the lone figure sitting atop the big chestnut bay, he said to Hatton, "Does this one belong to you?"

The sight of Sherman Dahl surrounded in a half circle by the armed town guards stunned Hatton for a
moment, causing him to hesitate. When he did speak
he wasn't certain what to say. "Why, no, he doesn't work
for me—"

"Sure he does," Emmen concluded, cutting him off.
"You stalled too long." He gave a short grin and shoved
Hatton back to Brady, who quickly seated him and held
him down in his chair with a big hand on his shoulder.

"One word from you, Emmen," the guard said, "we'll
blast this jake into the next territory."

"No, not just yet, Charlie," said Emmen. "I want to
hear what this man has to say." He adjusted his Colt in
his holster and walked toward the stairs.

Chapter 23

Sherman Dahl sat on his horse facing a gathering of armed town guards. His rifle stood from his lap, its butt resting on his thigh. As soon as Emmen and the guard accompanying him stepped out onto the board-walk, the other town guards cleared a path for them and stood with shotguns and rifles in hand. A few feet away stood Bobby Candles and his three desert ban-dits. A few feet from them stood Big Chicago and his three remaining men.

"Who the hell are you, and how'd you get past my guards at Saverine Pass?" Emmen asked. On the bal-cony overhead, Brady Shay watched through the barely opened door.

"I'm Sherman Dahl. I work for J. Fenwick Hatton, the man you're holding here."

"The Teacher . . . ," Shay said as if in reflection. "I've heard of you."

"I've heard of you too," Dahl said. "You're one of the Shay brothers."

"Aye, I'm Emmen Shay," he said, giving a touch to the brim of his derby hat. "Now, what about my guards up in the pass?"

Sherman gave a nod in the direction of Saverine Pass. "We didn't kill your guards. We tied them to a tree to keep any rifle shots from tipping you off."

Emmen gave a stiff, mirthless grin. "You did neither them nor me a favor by sparing their lives." His expression turned curious. "When you said 'we,' how many men are you talking about?"

Rather than give Emmen Shay a number, Dahl let the question pass. He gave a glance toward Big Chicago and his men and said to Shay, "Enough to take down what's left of the Curly Joe Hobbs Gang, Chester Goines and all."

The cage guard, Ulan Hayes, whispered to another guard beside him, "Hear that? There's a posse out there. They followed Big Chicago here." He inched away until he stepped inside the saloon.

Big Chicago cut in and said to Dahl, "I don't go by Chester Goines anymore, Teacher." As he spoke he grew bold enough to step forward and lay a hand on the big Colt in his waist sash.

Dahl did not let the gesture go unanswered. He lowered his rifle barrel halfway toward Chicago until the testy gunman lifted his hand away from his gun butt and let it fall to his side.

"Easy, now, the both of yas. I'll stand for no trouble in the Roost," Emmen said firmly, "unless it's trouble of my own making. I offer sanctuary here, for any man on the run who can afford it. I won't have that sanctuary violated. If you've any bark on toward Big Chicago, take it up with him after he leaves here, but not before."

"I understand your situation," Dahl said. "That's why I didn't ride in here shooting."

"What did you hope to accomplice riding in here, Teacher?" Emmen asked.

"I told you," said Dahl, "I work for J. Fenwick Hatton. I know your men brought him here. I came to take him home."

Emmen gave a dark chuckle. "I hate to disappoint you, Teacher," he replied. "But your Mr. Hatton is not leaving the Roost—not just yet anyway. He's too busy to leave right now." He grinned again, took his cigar from his mouth and blew out a stream of smoke. "He's in the midst of writing a letter."

"A ransom letter . . . ," Dahl said without having to be told.

"Good guess, Teacher," said Emmen Shay. He gave a sweep of his hand toward the inside of the saloon. "You are welcome to come inside, accept our hospitality while he writes the letter. I'll even have a man grain and water your horse." He raised a finger for emphasis. "Of course, as soon as he has the letter composed, you're going to deliver it to his man, Carlton Farris, and see to it my demand is met. Deal?"

Dahl only stared at him.

Emmen shrugged and said, "I'm certain Mr. Hatton's people will want to give me what I ask for. Hatton himself has decided to be most generous."

"I want to see him," Dahl said in a mild but firm

tone. "I want to see that he's all right." He still made
the offer of cooperating with the Shays.

Emmen took a step out off the boardwalk, looked up
at the balcony and called out, "Brother Brady, bring out
Mr. Hatton, allow this man to see him."

The office door opened. Onto the balcony stepped
Brady Shay, pistol in hand. Following him came the
bear handler. Behind the handler came Hatton and the
big bear. Hatton walked along barefoot, a chain linking
his ankle to the collar of the bear.

"I see why he's being generous," Dahl said to Emmen Shay. He saw the dried blood on the bear's muzzle and around its wet, shaggy flews.

"Yes," said Emmen, "and rest assured, if I don't get
what I want, I'll slit his gullet and let the bear eat him
from the inside out." He gave his short, tight grin. "You
will *not* want to test me on this, Teacher. The animal is
a man-eater." As if to prove himself, he called out to
Hatton and said, "Mr. Hatton, tell your man here what
the bear had for breakfast."

"She—she ate a man's leg," Hatton said. "Mr. Dahl, I
implore you. Please do as they say, and please be quick
about it." He gestured a hand toward the big bear, who
stood rocking back and forth on her thick paws. "This
bear could turn on me at any time—"

"All right, Hatton, enough said," Emmen Shay cut
in with a sharp tone. "Take our guest back inside, brother
Brady."

Dahl had listened closely to Hatton. He'd heard the
fear in Hatton's voice. Yet there was something in the

voice that told him the fear was not real. Hatton was concerned for his life, of that Dahl had no doubt. But Dahl had a feeling Hatton knew he had more to fear from the Shays and their men than he did from the bear he was chained to.

Dahl had judged J. Fenwick Hatton to be a man who would not frighten easily. What he'd just seen and heard only strengthened his opinion. Besides, he told himself, Hatton was worth nothing to the Shays *dead*. What kind of fool would the Shays have to be to chain something as valuable to them as J. Fenwick Hatton to a bear, unless they knew the bear was no great risk?

"So, what's it going to be, Teacher?" Emmen asked, sounding impatient. "Do you cooperate with me, or do I feed your man Hatton to the bear?"

"I'm not your delivery boy, Shay," Dahl said. "I told you I came here to get him—no ransom, no reward."

"What?" said Emmen. "You came here thinking I'd turn him over to you and get nothing in return? You must be crazy."

"You get something," said Dahl. Out the corner of his eye, he saw Brady Shay, the old Mexican, the bear and Hatton all file back inside. The balcony door closed.

"Oh? And what might that be?" Emmen asked, his gun hanging from his hand.

"My word that I won't kill you," Dahl said. His rifle barrel came down slowly until it pointed toward Emmen Shay from a distance of fifteen feet.

Uh-oh. . . . Upon hearing Dahl, Big Chicago took a quick look around the streets, doorways, rooflines, alleyways as he took a slow step back from between Delbert Garr and Bart Russell. He'd seen Dahl in action before. Dahl didn't bluff.

"Easy, men," said Emmen Shay, seeing all of his town guards tensed, poised and crouched, their guns ready, aimed at Sherman Dahl. "The Teacher's bluffing." He raised a hand to keep his men in check. "He knows he's dead if he pulls that trigger."

Seeing the look on Dahl's face, Bobby Candles sidestepped, putting the three desert bandits between himself and Dahl. Like Big Chicago, he also took a quick look around the street.

"Say the word, Emmen, and I've got him!" Zero Paige blurted out. As he spoke he raised his rifle to his shoulder.

Seeing him, Emmen Shay bellowed loudly, "No, Zero, you idiot!"

Upstairs, Brady Shay had just closed the balcony door when he heard his brother Emmen's voice, followed by the sound of a distant rifle shot. "What the hell?" He hurriedly backed around the big desk to where the Mexican, the bear and J. Fenwick Hatton stood. While Brady and the Mexican stared out in the direction of the rifle shot, Hatton stooped down to the bucket of rocks and stood up with the small pick in his hand.

"Look out, senor!" the old Mexican called out to Brady.

But the Mexican's warning didn't help; it only caused Brady to turn quickly, facing Hatton. The last sound Brady Shay heard was the hard sharp clunk of the pick, as Hatton buried its four-inch spiked tip deep in the center of his forehead.

"Madre Santa de Dios!" Edwardo cried out, seeing Brady turn in an aimless half circle and stagger head-long through the balcony door. As Brady turned away from Hatton, his hand went instinctively to the Colt on his hip. But he found only an empty holster.

Having snatched the Colt, Hatton turned with it pointed at Edwardo and the bear, who had taken in the commotion and stood up deftly on her hind paws in a fighting stance. "Get her back or I'll shoot her!" Hatton warned.

"No, please, senor, I beg of you!" said Edwardo, already reaching into his pocket for the keys to the leg iron.

On the street, Emmen and his town guards were doubly stunned. The rifle shot that had reached in as if from out of nowhere had just splattered Zero Paige's blood all over them. But before they could even take cover or retaliate in any manner, they heard the crash of the balcony door and looked up in time to see Brady Shay stagger forward, the handle of the pick hanging perfectly down his nose as if being worn as some sort of bizarre carnival ornament.

"Jesus!" said one of the town guards as Brady me-andered forward, his big arms spread, and crashed through the handrail and off the edge of the balcony.

"No! Brother Brady!" Emmen Shay shouted, seeing the big man slap facedown onto the street in a large puff of dust. He stared to run out to his fallen brother, but before he could take a step, Dahl's rifle bucked in his hand. The shot sent Emmen Shay flying backward through the door of the saloon.

A blast of buckshot exploded wildly in the air when one of the town guards stepped forward from among the chaos and fired on Dahl. But as he'd pulled the trigger, another shot whined in from out of nowhere and nailed him in the chest. He flew backward in a spray of blood.

Dahl felt a shot graze his thigh as he jerked the bay around, but instead of levering up another round, he let the rifle fall from his hands and jerked a Colt from his holster.

Another shot came from Lane's hidden position out on the rough terrain surrounding the town; another town guard fell in a red mist of blood. The Shays were both dead, but their men were still fighting. Dahl saw no way to stay alive on the street, and he wasn't about to leave without Hatton. Ducking low in his saddle, he booted the bay forward, onto the boardwalk and inside the saloon.

"Here he comes, Victor!" Ulan Hayes cried out. Seeing the bay pound onto the boardwalk toward the door, Hayes had already begun to race up the stairs. At the top, he pulled the cage over to the landing by a rope and jumped inside. He stepped over beside Victor Andre and grabbed one of the deck guns.

"I got him, Ulan!" Victor yelled, swinging his deck gun toward Dahl and pulling the trigger as Hayes hurriedly swung the second big gun around.

Dahl heard the blast; in a long mirror he caught a glimpse of a six-foot length of bar lift in an explosion of wood splinters, brass rail and broken shot glasses. But he stayed low in the saddle, reining the bay onto the staircase and upward, knowing there were more shots coming from the big guns at any second.

Behind the pounding hooves of the bay, the next blast, this one from Hayes' big gun, took out a four-foot section of stairs and left an ugly hole trimmed in chewed and jagged edging above the plank floor. In a rear corner two half-naked whores had ducked beneath a table. They screamed and grasped each other as debris settled on the tabletop above them.

"In here!" Hatton shouted at Dahl, swinging the office door open and firing at the iron birdcage. Ulan, wielding the big deck gun, fell back with a bullet in his upper shoulder, but he threw himself forward and grabbed the big gun and swung it toward Dahl again.

Inside the office, the bear handler had taken the chain from Hatton's ankle and led the big bear over into a far corner. He gripped the chain tightly and the bear stood on its hind legs and let out a loud bawl at the sudden entrance of horse and rider. Dahl's bay reared slightly at the sight and sound of the bear, but Dahl settled it, reached down and grabbed Hatton by his outreached arm.

"Jump on!" he shouted. He jerked Hatton up onto the saddle behind him.

"There's a rear stairs," Hatton said, gesturing the Colt toward the other side of the office. The door to the rear stairs stood ajar. Behind them a blast from a deck gun blew away the office door and a large part of the wall beside it. From the street, rifle fire streaked in; bullets screamed upward through the open balcony door, into the office ceiling.

"Please, senors! Go! Ride quickly!" the old Mexican cried out. "Flee before they kill us all!" Beside him the big bear stood with its paws spread, threatening them.

"Hang on," said Dahl to Hatton. He booted the bay across the office floor, through the partially open door and down the rear stairs.

"Who is firing out there?" Hatton asked as the bay leaped out of the rear door and pounded along the dirt alley without any of the town guards risking themselves to run around the building and fire at them.

"It's Lane," said Dahl.

"Yes, of course, I should have known," said Hatton.

Dahl heard the steadiness in Hatton's voice now that he was free and able to fend for himself. "Are you wounded, Mr. Hatton?" he asked over his shoulder.

"Nothing worth mentioning," Hatton replied, hanging on to Dahl with one hand, his other hand holding the Colt from Brady Shay's holster. "To be honest, I've never been better, sir," Hatton added.

"Good," said Dahl, the two sitting straighter, the bay slowing its pace a little on the rocky ground. The firing from Robber's Roost had waned gradually until it finally halted altogether.

"What are you doing up here, if I may inquire?" Hatton asked, letting the Colt slump at his side. Beneath them the chestnut bay ran at a quick but easy pace.

"Farris came to me," Dahl said. "He's waiting back along the trail with Coots."

"A good man, that Farris," said Hatton. "Coots is alive, then?"

"Yes, he's alive," said Dahl. As they spoke they looked over at the trail of dust rising behind the hooves of eight horses, Chicago's, Candles' and the rest of their men's, pounding away toward the main trail into Saverine Pass. The outlaws had gathered their horses and left Robber's Roost, convinced that Teacher, Lane and whoever else was out there would be right on their trail.

"Another good man, that Coots," Hatton said, taking a canteen that Dahl had lifted from his saddle horn and handed back to him.

"Yes, it seems so," said Dahl. Looking out at the rising dust headed toward the high trail that led to the rocky hillsides, he said, "I'll get you somewhere safe, and then Lane and I are going to settle accounts with Big Chicago and Bobby Candles."

"Somewhere *safe*?" Hatton said indignantly. "I should say not, sir."

"No offense intended, Mr. Hatton," said Dahl. "I only meant that Deputy Lane and I will travel a lot faster on our own."

"I will not slow you and Deputy Lane down, Mr. Dahl," Hatton said firmly. "If I do, you may feel free to leave me behind."

"I don't leave a man behind, Mr. Hatton," said Dahl. "That's why I'm careful of who rides with me." He looked down at Hatton's bare feet. "You don't have a horse. You don't even have boots."

"Boots, ha!" said Hatton, dismissing the matter out of hand. "What good are boots and a horse if a man has no purpose, no direction in which to dispatch himself?"

Dahl didn't answer. Instead he gazed ahead to where he saw Deputy Eddie Lane ride into sight and rein his horse toward them across the rocky ground.

Chapter 24

No sooner had Dahl and Hatton ridden down the rear stairs and made their getaway than Ulan Hayes climbed down from the swaying birdcage, loosened the keeper on a long chain and lowered the heavy cage to the floor. Jerking a bar towel from atop the bar, he quickly stuffed it inside his shirt over his bleeding shoulder wound and started loosening the deck guns from the iron handrail.

"What the hell are you doing?" asked Victor Andre, who jumped from the iron cage and ran out front, where he'd seen Emmen and Brady Shay lying dead in the street. "It's over. The Shay brothers are dead."

"Yeah, that's what I figured," said Ulan, still working feverishly on taking the deck guns off the iron handrail. "I figure that's why everybody out there stopped fighting."

"What's the use?" said Victor. "I told you, they're dead."

"*They* are, but I'm not," said Hayes. "Neither is all

the sonsabitches who ride here from as far off as El Paso City just to spend their plunder with us." As he talked he gave a jerk and a grunt and stood holding one of the big eight-gauge deck guns in his hands. "Far as I'm concerned, we're still open for business. There's still a Roost, and I'm going to be the man who rules it." He gave the gunman a serious look. "If you want to work for me, grab that other deck gun. I'll pay you twice what the Shay brothers paid you."

"Hey, I'm with you, pard," said Victor. "What's our plan?"

"Big Chicago and his men have hightailed," said Hayes. "But whoever is out there has already gotten onto their trail, I figure. We're going to fall in behind them and chop them into dog meat. They can't get away from us without running right smack into Big Chicago's gunmen."

"But what if we accidentally kill Chicago's men?" Victor asked.

"Between you and me," said Hayes, lowering his voice in secrecy, "if I kill some of Chicago's men, it won't be accidental, not after all this trouble they brought down on us. Do you get my drift?"

"Oh, yes, I get it," said Victor. "I was hoping you'd say that." He reached out and jerked the other deck gun from its swivel. "We're not going to fire these heavy bastards from our saddles, are we?"

"No way," said Hayes, "not with this hole in my shoulder. Besides, we're going to need a keg of powder and some scrap iron to load them with. There's a buckboard down behind the livery barn. I'll meet you there."

He turned and headed toward the rear door. "Go out there and round up anybody who wants to ride with us. Get them over to the barn and let's get rolling. Once we bring back a few heads on some sticks, the word will get around who's running the Roost."

"You got it, pard!" said Victor Andre. He turned and ran back out the front door, the big, stubby deck gun in his hands.

Out in front of the Gold Poke Saloon, several town guards had dragged the Shays' bodies out of the street and lined them up beside four dead town guards. "What are we going to do now, Charlie?" a gunman asked a burly guard named Charlie Prine.

"Do I look like I know?" Prine asked, scratching his beard as he appeared to consider things. Surrounding him, the men stood staring down at the bodies, their shotguns and rifles hanging from their hands.

"The first thing Ulan Hayes and I are going to do is kill Teacher and the men he's got waiting out there, make it clear that nobody rides in and shoots up Robber's Roost," Victor said, walking up into their midst with the big deck gun.

"What are you talking about, *you and Hayes*?" said Prine. "Who put you two in charge, Victor?"

"We're putting ourselves in charge," said Victor Andre. "Anybody wants to ride with us, get your horses and follow me." With no more on the matter, he turned and hurried away toward the livery barn.

"What the hell is he going to do with the deck guns?" a town guard asked, staring after Andre.

"Damned if I know," said Charlie Prine, already walking away toward the livery barn. "But if there's to be a fight with the men who did all this, I don't want to miss my share of it."

"What? You must be crazy, wanting to ride into another gun battle after getting out of this one alive!" a town guard called out to him. "Think of all the whores and whiskey we'll have, until it all runs dry."

"You think of it," said Prine, over his shoulder. "I hired on here as a fighting man."

"But the men who hired you are dead. There's no one ordering you to go out there looking for a fight," the man called out.

"I don't need to be ordered to fight," said Prine, hurrying his pace. "I can smell a good fight from a mile away."

Most of the town guards only shook their heads and looked back down at the bodies in the dirt. "I don't want to end up like these poor sonsabitches," said one. He spat and wiped a hand across his lips.

"Hell no," another gunman put in. "The Shays are dead. I've got better things to do than get myself killed for no reason."

But two guards named Donald Shumate and Bill Albertson gave each other a questioning look. "What do you think, Don?" Albertson finally asked.

"Hell *yes*, is what I think," Shumate replied. They turned and walked away behind Charlie Prine. As the two left, a third man named Colorado John Young called out to them, "Wait up. I'm coming along." He passed a smug half grin to the remaining guards. "They'll need me to keep Ulan Hayes on the right track."

Behind the livery barn, Hayes had already mounted the deck gun, swivel and all, onto one of the wooden-slat sides of the buckboard. He led two horses from the barn as Victor and the four men walked up to him. "I brought some help," Victor said, walking over and starting to mount the deck gun on the other side of the buckboard without being told.

"Good to see you're riding with us, Charlie," said Hayes.

"I never turned down a good dance or a fight in my life," Prine said. He eyed the bloody bullet hole in Hayes' shirt. "Here, I'll hitch these horses if you want to get your shoulder looked at."

"It's been looked at," said Hayes, but he let Prine take the horses anyway. Turning to the other men, he raised a Colt from his holster and checked it one-handed as he said to the other three, "Good to have you, Shumate, Young, Albertson. I'll tell you the same thing I told Victor. I'll pay you twice what the Shays paid you."

"Whoa, hold on, Hayes," said Young. "Who gave you the say-so over who gets paid what?"

Hayes shrugged his good shoulder. "I saw the opening, I sort of took it upon myself. Why?"

"Because I've been here a hell of a lot longer than you have, that's why," Young said sharply. "Not to be a prick about it, but I think I know a little more about these hills and passes than somebody who's spent the past year looking down from a birdcage."

"All right," said Hayes. "Anything else? Now's the time to speak your mind, before we get out there and find ourselves on hard ground." He looked from one man to the next, then back at Young.

"Yeah, I got something else," Young said, growing bolder now that he felt he had Hayes knuckled down. "To hell with what the Shays paid us. I figure from here on out, we split whatever the Roost makes right down the middle. What say the rest of yas?" He looked back and forth with satisfaction.

"Anything else?" Hayes asked.

"Not just this minute . . . but I'll let you know when something comes up," said Young. Again he gave a smug grin. "Fair enough?"

"Fair enough," said Hayes. He shot him.

"Jesus!" said Albertson, seeing the effortless manner in which Hayes raised only the tip of his gun barrel, holding the Colt at his waist after checking it and turning the cylinder.

"Damn . . . you, Hayes," said Young, staggering backward and falling to his knees, both hands grasping the spreading blood on his lower belly.

"Get his gun," Hayes said quietly. He watched to see which of the two men was quicker to follow his order.

"Got it," said Shumate, stepping over, bending and snatching the Colt from Young's holster. Albertson made the same move, but he was a second behind Shumate.

"Shumate . . . you . . . turd," said Young in a strained voice.

"Shut up, Colorado John, you had your say," said Shumate.

Out front on the street, the town guards heard the gunshot. But when one of them turned to run toward the livery barn, another grabbed his forearm and stopped him, saying, "Leave it alone," in a knowing voice.

At the barn, when Shumate handed Hayes the Colt, Hayes stuck it down behind his gun belt, looked at the two and said, "Anything else?"

"Hell no, I'm good with it," said Shumate.

"Me too," said Albertson. "No problem here. I'm glad to still be working."

"Get our horses, Albertson," said Hayes. To Shumate he said, "Help Victor get this buckboard ready for the trail."

"Right away," said Shumate, seeing Albertson head inside the barn at a trot.

Out on the dusty flatlands, Dahl stopped his bay as Eddie Lane rode up and slid his horse to a halt, his battered telescope in his hand. "Good to see you alive, Mr. Hatton," Lane said.

"All thanks be to you two gentlemen," Hatton replied with a grateful nod. Now that the horse had stopped, he swung down from behind Dahl and stood barefoot on the hot, rocky ground.

Lane gestured his telescope toward the dust in the wake of Chicago, Candles and the others and said, "It's no secret which way they're headed. They figure once they're up inside the pass, they can set up a surprise for us any time they feel like it."

Dahl said, "Then the closer we dog them, the less they'll *feel* like it. It'll be hard for them to set up an ambush when we're shooting bullets up the backs of their shirts."

"That's true," said Lane, seeing Dahl ready to pound away in pursuit of the fleeing outlaws. "But we've got something else to figure in. Shay's town guards." He gestured in the direction of Robber's Roost. "There are three riders and a buckboard headed out across the flats right now."

"A buckboard?" Dahl asked, gazing out through the drifting trail dust.

"Yep," said Lane. He handed Dahl the telescope. "You won't see them without this. I caught sight of them leaving town. They're headed out right behind the outlaws."

Dahl raised the telescope to his eyes and looked out across the rocky flatlands. He watched the three men on horseback and the two men in the buckboard ride in and out of sight through the dust. "They've brought along the two eight-gauge guns from above the saloon," he said. "Those things are man-eaters."

Cutting in, feeling a part of things, Hatton said, "My goodness yes, we've seen what those guns can do. They'll be hounding us from behind."

"Not if we don't let them get behind us," Dahl said as he swung the telescope off the buckboard to see farther out along the trail to where Chicago and the outlaws were disappearing onto the rocky trail that headed up into the pass.

Lane said to Hatton, "They figure we're already on the same trail following behind Chicago and Candles. That's where they'd like to get us."

"Yes, I see," Hatton said, pondering the idea of being pressed between the two bands of gunmen. "But I take it you're not going to allow that to happen."

"No, sir, we're not," said Dahl without looking around from the telescope. "We'll let these town guards get between us and Chicago and Candles. In all that rising dust, they won't see who they're following. Let them chew one another up while we lie back and follow them through the pass."

Lane threw in, "We'll ride over whatever's left of the town guards and the deck guns when we reach the other end of Saverine Pass."

"What about Carlton Farris and Mr. Coots?" Hatton asked, sounding concerned.

"We left them a good ways back in the pass," said Dahl. "If they're watching and listening, they'll know what's coming."

"I certainly hope so," said Hatton, considering the matter.

"We all hope so," said Dahl. He reached a hand down to Hatton and helped him back up behind his saddle.

Lane gestured toward a lower end of the hills to their left. "While the dust has us hidden from them, let's get out of here. I spotted a trail over there. Before the dust settles we can be on it and find our way over to the pass."

"Lead the way," said Dahl. He gave a light tap of his heels to the bay's sides.

Chapter 25

James Earl Coots sat slumped in the saddle at the edge of the cliff where Farris stood holding the horse by its reins. Farris had helped Coots to his feet and onto the horse within minutes of Lane's and Dahl's leaving them along the trail to rest and recuperate. Riding double most of the way, the two had made good time along the trail.

But upon reaching their present position, the two had stopped when they'd heard all the gunfire. Instead of riding down onto the stretch of flatlands surrounding Robber's Roost and taking a chance on jeopardizing any plans Dahl and the deputy might have made, they waited out of sight high atop the trail to Saverine Pass.

"It appears the miscreants we're after are headed this way, Mr. Coots," said Farris, staring hard, holding his hand above his eyes as a visor. "But I'm afraid I see no sign of Mr. Hatton."

In spite of the pain in all of his bullet nicks and

grazes, Coots had forced himself upright in the saddle, also looking out at the riders. Beyond Big Chicago, Bobby Candles and the others stood a long, drifting rise of dust. Farther in the distance behind them, he watched the buckboard and the other set of riders pound along the trail, leaving a dusty wake of their own.

"It's best to face facts, Mr. Farris," Coots said solemnly. "He might be dead. But whether he's dead or alive, we won't know until we put these men down and meet up with Lane and Dahl." He turned his eyes to Farris and added, "At this point whether he's dead or alive won't change anything either. I came here for my friend and his dog. Do you understand?"

"Yes, I understand," said Farris. "Do not doubt me, sir. Regardless of Mr. Hatton, I am here until it's finished, whatever it takes."

On the trail below, Big Chicago turned to Bobby Candles, who rode beside him, and said above the sound of their horses' hooves, "I hope you know enough not to turn your back on those water-hole bandits of yours."

"I know enough not to turn my back on any sumbitch I've ever met," Candles replied, letting Chicago know where they stood. "You'll do well to always bear that in mind, *Chester.*"

"It troubles me to see you take this kind of attitude," said Chicago, "here at a time we all need one another's help to stay alive."

"Help . . . ?" Candles looked at him as they rode on. "I don't need your help, Chicago. The truth is, the best thing could've happened to you was Teacher and the deputy arriving and shooting holes in everybody. Another day or two, my bandits would've had your boys picked clean."

Chicago felt his temper starting to boil. He slowed his horse a little and started to say something to Candles. But Russell rode up beside him and said, "Chicago! We've got somebody on our tails."

"Is it Teacher?" Chicago asked.

"Is it the deputy?" Candles cut in.

"No, it's neither," said Russell. "It's three riders and a couple of men in a buckboard. I can't make them out for all the blasted dust, but I think it's some of the Shays' town guards."

"The town guards?" Chicago looked back over his shoulder, but like Russell he couldn't see anything on the dusty back trail. "Why the hell would the guards be chasing us?"

Candles said with sarcasm, "Maybe they want to give us our money back, for having to leave town so fast."

"Russell," said Chicago, "take one of the desert bandits with you, ride back and see who it is."

"Right away," said Russell, cutting his horse sharply and circling back to the others.

"Why one of my men?" Candles asked Chicago, the two still riding along at a fast clip.

"Because that's how it's going to be, Bobby," said Chicago. "One of my men goes, one of your men goes with him. I'm not going to get caught short by you until I see you've had a change of attitude." He spurred his horse ahead on the rocky, dusty trail.

A few yards back, Bart Russell circled his horse back

among the men and sidled up among the three desert bandits. Before he said a word, Dad Lodi shouted to him above the horses' hooves, "Who is that back there?" He jerked his head back toward the three riders and the buckboard obscured by the billowing dust.

"That's what we want to know," Russell shouted in reply. "Candles and Chicago told me to take one of yas, ride back and check them out."

"Damn it to hell," said Dad Lodi, not liking the sound of it. He looked back and forth from Dorsey to Dirty Foot, and said, "Sucio, go with him."

"What, because I am Mexican?" Dirty Foot asked, anger flaring in his eyes.

"That's right, now get going!" said Lodi. He turned back to Russell and said, "If this is a trick you and Candles are pulling, I'll nut you like a spring pig."

"Keep running your mouth, *sand bandit*, you won't get the chance to do any *nutting*," said Russell, pulling his horse away, Dirty Foot right beside him.

Circling back inside the dust behind the others, both Russell and Dirty Foot pulled their wide bandanas up over the bridge of their noses. "Stick on the trail," Russell said behind his bandana. "We'll see them better than they see us."

"This is not the first time I have back-trailed someone," Dirty Foot said sharply.

"That's a good thing to know, Dirty Foot," said Russell. "I expect I won't have to hear any excuses if you screw things up."

Staring through the dust as they rode back along the trail, both Russell and the Mexican made out the buckboard at the same time the band of riders drew closer. "I was right," said Russell. "It's not Teacher and the deputy. It's the Shays' town guards."

"Why are the town guards chasing us?" Dirty Foot asked.

"I don't know why," said Russell. "Did you slip out without paying them whores for oiling your belly?" ·

"You are a real funny man," said Dirty Foot. He stared with hatred in his dark eyes.

Russell chuckled at his own little joke. Staring harder back through the dust, he said, "Nothing says they're chasing us. Maybe they're just *following* us."

"I don't think so," Dirty Foot said, recognizing the deck guns mounted on either side of the bouncing, swaying buckboard. "When I look back and see two eight-gauge deck guns pointed at me, I must think that those people are not my friends."

"Ordinarily I would agree with you, Mex," said Russell, "but today, I'm thinking these men are out to tree the wrong coons." He rode back closer to where the trail dust was much more settled.

"What are you doing, you fool?" Dirty Foot called out to him, holding his horse back in the thicker dust.

"I'm going to let these jakes know who we are," said Russell. "We'll find out quick enough if they're wanting to be friend or enemies. . . ."

Back along the trail, Ulan Hayes half stood from the buckboard seat at the sight of the riders in the tail end of the trail dust, the nearer one staring hard from behind his bandana, a rifle hanging in his hand. "There's two of them! They've spotted us, Victor," Hayes said, also with a bandana over his mouth.

Driving the buckboard, Victor Andre asked, "What do you want me to do?"

"Swing wide and cut across them," said Hayes. "Don't let them ride ahead and warn the others!" Looking at the three town guards on horseback, Hayes waved his good arm at them and said, "Spread out, get around them! Stop the sonsabitches!"

Inside the trail dust, Russell lost sight of the buckboard for a moment. "Where the hell did it go?" he shouted at Dirty Foot, fanning his hat back and forth as if it might help him see through the dust.

"I don't know where it went!" Dirty Foot shouted in reply, hearing hooves pound along on either side of the trail behind them.

Suddenly Russell heard the buckboard driver let out a loud "*Yihii*" to the team of horses. Then he saw the buckboard emerge from out of the dust, cutting straight across the trail between him and the Mexican. Without a second to spare, he dived from his saddle and hugged the rocky ground.

"Holy mother of—" Dirty Foot's voice fell beneath the roar of the two big deck guns firing as one.

One shot picked up the Mexican bandit, horse and all, off the ground and blew them backward fifteen feet. When they landed, the two mangled bodies rolled another ten feet and came to a blood-smeared halt in the dirt.

The other shot had missed both Bart Russell and his

horse, the frightened animal having bolted away when
Russell dived from its back. But the blast of scrap iron
picked up a large scoop of rock and dirt and rained it
down the cowering gunman's back.

"Damn it!" Russell said, his face pressed to the hardened trail. He lay still as stone listening to the buckboard roll on across the trail, out of the dust, and swing
forward toward the rest of the outlaws.

Far ahead of the buckboard and the three guards on
horseback, Chicago and the others had heard the loud
blast of the deck guns as they rounded up off the flatlands and into the cover of rock. "Good Lord, Bobby,
was that what I think it was?" said Chicago to Candles
as they stopped up on the trail, out of the dust, and
looked back on the flatlands.

He jerked the bandana down from across his face.

"If you think it was the two deck guns from the
Gold Poke Saloon, you're damn right it is," said Candles, also jerking down his bandana.

"But why the hell are they shooting at us?" Chicago
asked, staring back, puzzled, seeing the buckboard and
horsemen racing in and out of sight through the broken
patches of remaining trail dust.

"Damned if I know," said Candles. "Why don't you
stay here and ask them?" He turned his horse and
pounded a few yards farther up the trail, then stopped
and looked back out across the flatlands, seeing the
bloody smear of Dirty Foot and his horse. Farther to
the right he saw Russell running in a crouch, chasing
his spooked horse.

"Jesus!" Candles said aloud.

"What do you see?" Chicago asked, booting his horse forward to catch up to Candles, the other men right behind him.

"I see we're going to have to pick some high ground for cover, and fight these men," said Candles. "They're acting like they've lost their minds!

"They think they're shooting at Teacher and the deputy," Candles said. "They can't see it's us."

"Oh, I think they know it's us all right," said Chicago. "I think they're running amok, like a pack of dogs with no leader. They're out to kill whoever happens to get in their sights."

Chapter 26

On a ridge overlooking the trail, James Earl Coots said to Farris, "Here they come, Mr. Farris. Wait until they get right under us. Then let them have it."

"Right, sir," Farris said, shaking, nervous, but determined. "Right under us . . . let them have it," he said, repeating the teamster's instructions as if to commit them to memory.

Coots nodded. "You'll be all right," he said.

On the trail below, Chicago pushed his horse forward and joined Candles. The rest of the men crowded up around the two and looked back toward the buckboard as it slipped out of sight and onto the trail. "Spread out, all of you," Chicago shouted. "Take position higher up, in the rocks, where it won't be so easy to aim those big guns—"

His words were cut short as a bullet from Coots' rifle slammed down into his shoulder and sent him flying from his saddle. "That's for Norman and Oscar," Coots yelled from a rocky perch.

"We're trapped! Take cover!" Candles shouted, his spooked horse racing back and forth aimlessly as he scanned the rugged hillsides above them.

Thatcher jumped down from his saddle as more shots exploded from Coots' and Farris' guns and thumped and ricocheted all around him. He grabbed the wounded Big Chicago by his riding duster and pulled him into the safety of rocks.

"Higher, climb higher!" Candles shouted, hearing the buckboard and the pounding hooves of the horses running fast along the trail toward them. For a moment, Candles rode back and forth like some captain preparing his troops. But as gunfire came whining along from down the trail, and raining down from above, the gunman gave up his bold-looking stance and raced away, leaving the rest of the men scattered among the rocks to fend for themselves.

"The sumbitch has run off," Dad Lodi said to Frank Dorsey as the buckboard rolled up into sight flanked by the three town guards.

Manning one of the deck guns as the buckboard slowed down enough to fire, Ulan Hayes aimed toward the spot only ten yards away where Delbert Garr sat behind a rock firing rounds as quickly as he could lever a fresh one into his rifle chamber. Just as Garr stood up and took aim, Hayes pulled the trigger on the big gun.

"Oh my goodness!" Farris remarked, seeing the blast from where he and Coots lay thirty feet above the melee.

Garr seemed to disappear from the waist up in a red-pink mist of blood, meat and bone matter. The rock wall behind him stood splattered with a blood-dripping imprint. Also seeing the blast, Coots replied to Farris above the roar of heavy gunfire, "I've got to get that gun before it gets us."

"You don't intend to go down there?" Farris asked in disbelief.

"Cover me," said Coots, and he was up and gone, running in a crouch along the jagged ledge above the buckboard.

In the buckboard, Hayes jumped over to the other deck gun and fired it toward Dad Lodi and Dorsey's position. But Lodi and Dorsey had anticipated the big guns coming and scrambled away, farther up the hillside, as Hayes pulled the trigger. "Damn it, I missed," Hayes shouted, hurriedly reloading the big gun as the buckboard slid around in a complete turn and headed back, Victor slapping a whip to the horses' backs.

Back along the trail, Shumate, Prine and Albertson raced their horses back and forth, keeping a heavy barrage of fire on the steep, rugged hillside. When they saw the buckboard rolling back toward them, Prine shouted, "Here comes Hayes, give him room!"

"Pour it on them, Hayes!" shouted Shumate, firing wildly at the men in the rocks.

But as the buckboard gained speed and Hayes busily reloaded the second deck gun, Coots had run down over rock after rock until he'd reached a place ten feet above the rolling buckboard, where he leaped out like a cat. He landed with a loud thump on both feet and caught on to a side rail with one hand and steadied himself. Hayes turned, facing him in time to catch a pistol barrel across his jaw and a shove off the buck-board and down the steep side of the trail.

"Pour it on—!" Shumate had started to call out again, not seeing what had just happened. But when Coots swung the reloaded gun around and pulled the trigger, Shumate lifted from his saddle amid the loud blast and disappeared in a red cloud of flesh, bone and saddle fragments. His horse, catching a nonlethal peppering of sharp iron fragments, ran away whinnying.

Hearing the loud blast streak past him, Victor had jerked around and looked over his shoulder. When he saw Coots standing at the other gun, swinging it around for another forward shot, he let out a scream and leaped from the speeding wagon.

"Good Lord, that ain't Hayes!" said Albertson to Prine, the two of them seeing Coots leap into the driver's seat, take the traces and brake the speed of the buck-board down.

Seeing Coots from another position, Big Chicago said to Thatcher, "Get ready to go as soon as he's fired this next shot and has to stop and reload."

"I'm already *ready to go*," said Thatcher, shaking his head, seeing blood seeping down from under the ban-dana Big Chicago held to his wounded shoulder. "I never seen anything get so screwed up in my life."

Chicago said bitterly, "This damned *Teacher* and his deputy pal. They knew that losing the Shays would be like cutting the head off of a snake. The rest of the body could still wiggle around, but it didn't know what to do."

On the buckboard, Coots stood braced behind the

second big gun. He held his fire even as Albertson and Prine bored down on him, riding low in their saddles, firing repeatedly. Coots knew that the closer he let them get, the better his chances of blasting them both with one shot. *Wait . . .* , he told himself. He heard bullets zip past him. *Wait . . .* A bullet thumped into the front of the buckboard. *Now!*

"All right," Chicago said to Thatcher as the blast from the big gun resounded along the trail, "let's get going. Candles has already gotten out of here. I will not allow him to be the only one coming out of this mess alive."

When Dahl, Lane and Hatton had ridden up off the flatlands on a less-traveled trail, they'd followed the sound of gunfire toward the start of Saverine Pass.

Atop a cliff overhang, gazing out through his telescope, Lane rose in his saddle at the sight of Bobby Candles racing up off the trail and turning his horse onto a narrow path that wended its way below them. "It's him," he said sidelong to Dahl, who sat with Hatton seated behind his saddle. "The murderer I've been searching for this whole time."

"Tell me, then, will you shoot him from up here when he passes below us?" Hatton asked.

"No," said Lane. "This is something I have to do one-on-one." He closed the telescope and put it away. He looked at Dahl and said, "I'm sure you understand."

Dahl only gave a shrug and nodded toward the trail below. "I'll circle around and stay out of sight. If Big

Chicago is still alive, I'll catch him when he sticks his head up above the pass."

"Obliged," Lane said to Dahl, touching his hat brim. "See you soon." He turned his horse and rode off on a thin path leading down to the trail.

"Obliged," Dahl said in reply. He touched his hat brim in return.

Hatton remarked to Dahl, "He sounds as if he's not coming back."

"Were you expecting him to?" Dahl asked, watching Lane ride out of sight. "He's found the man he's been after."

"But what about the others still down there?" Hatton asked. "What about Chester Goines?"

"Big Chicago is our man. He always was, remember?" said Dahl. He turned his bay back onto the trail behind them.

"Yes, of course," said Hatton, "although to be honest, in all the excitement, his death became of less and less importance to me."

"That's how it is, sometimes, when you go off to kill a man like Chester Goines," said Dahl. "Killing him becomes the léast of your problems."

A silence followed as the bay carried them onto the trail leading over toward Saverine Pass, where the big guns had fallen silent, and where the rest of the gunfire had all but stopped. "I—I did a foolish thing, coming up here, thinking I would reap vengeance for myself," Hatton said quietly, "and that doing so I would rid myself of all sadness and regret that have overtaken me."

"Nothing helps rid our pain in the loss of a loved one," Dahl replied over his shoulder, as if he had close and personal knowledge of such matters. "The only thing we can take from loss is what it teaches us, and the strength it instills in us."

Hatton thought about it, and said, "I must've thought that becoming a fighting man would make a difference, change my sorrow somehow—help me forget my loss."

"All men are fighting men," Dahl said, nudging the bay onward. "It is only a matter of *for what*, or for *how much*." He smiled to himself. "I'm certain you found that out when the Shays chained you to a bear."

"Ha! Yes, indeed I did," said Hatton, his spirits seeming to lift all of a sudden. "In studying that horrid creature, a realization came to me, that I have been chained to some sort of bear my whole life. This bear, like all my other bears, had no teeth or claws. All that frightened me was that it was *a bear.*" He managed to chuckle.

"Even a toothless, clawless bear could have killed you," said Dahl.

"Yes, but I decided it was better to die fighting the bear than to be imprisoned by my fear of it."

"And there you have it. . . ." Dahl smiled again to himself as the two rode on in silence.

When they reached a stretch of flatlands leading over to a long ledge above Saverine Pass, they watched Big Chicago and Dick Thatcher top the crest on horseback, stop suddenly and stare toward them from a distance of two hundred yards. "There's the son of a bitch I want to see spitting up blood," Big Chicago said to Hatcher. He dropped the bandana he held against his wounded shoulder and drew the big Colt from his waist sash.

"Wait, Chicago," said Thatcher. "We can get away from him."

"No, we can't," said Chicago with resolve. "We've tried that, remember?" He stared at Dahl as he checked the Colt and held it in his bloody hand. "Anyway, there comes a time when enough is enough. Either I kill him or he kills me. If you want out of it, get in the wind. I'll take it from here." He jerked the reins to his horse, his Colt and reins in the same hand. His wounded shoulder kept his other arm hanging limp down at his side.

Chapter 27

Staring back at Big Chicago, Dahl said over his shoulder to Hatton, "It looks like Chester Goines has finally decided to settle up." He slipped his rifle into his saddle, swung his leg over his saddle horn and slid down to the ground, the bandana tied around the bullet graze on his thigh crusted over with dried blood. "Take the bay and find you both some cover."

"No, sir," said Hatton with determination. "I will have my say with this scoundrel, after all the trouble he has caused me. Anyway, there are two of them. You will need my help."

"Ride away, Hatton," Dahl said firmly, drawing his Colt and letting it hang down at his side. "If you see I need help with the other gunman, drop him with the rifle. That's all you get."

Hatton did as he was told. Slipping forward into the saddle, his bare feet inside the stirrups, he turned the bay and rode a few yards away. When he stopped, he drew the rifle from the saddle boot, checked it, cocked it and held it ready. As he watched Dahl walk limping toward the mounted advancing gunman, he failed to see Bart Russell ease his horse up over a ledge eighty yards to his right and stop abruptly.

Dust-covered, ragged and bloody from diving to the trail earlier to keep from getting shot by the deck gun, Russell saw the gunfight about to take place before him. He wiped a dirty hand across his sweat-streaked eyes and slipped his big Remington from his holster. "By God, Teacher . . . ," he whispered at Dahl, easing his horse forward a step. "You *will* die today. . . ."

Dahl walked on, watching Big Chicago boot his horse up into a run, barreling straight toward him. He saw Chicago firing wildly at him, both the rise and fall of the running horse and the reins in his gun hand affecting his aim. A bullet thumped into the ground in front of Dahl's feet. As Chicago let out a loud yell, Dahl stopped cold, raised his black-handled Colt to arm's length and took careful aim as another of Chicago's bullets streaked past his head.

"Damn it!" Big Chicago bellowed, his hammer finally falling with an impotent click. He tossed the Colt away and reached to pull a rifle from its boot. But Dahl's Colt bucked in his hand, the sound of the shot echoing off across Saverine Pass.

Big Chicago tumbled backward from his saddle, a long ribbon of blood uncoiling in the air as the bullet punched through his heart. He hit the ground head-first, at an odd angle, his big head pointing in one direction, his whole body pointing in another.

Dahl only stared warily toward him for a moment,

realizing that the outlaw wasn't going to get up. But as he let the Colt slump down at his side, he heard Hatton cry out, "Mr. Dahl, watch out!"

As Dahl swung around, raising his gun, he heard two rifle shots resound almost as one. The first bullet sliced across his shoulder, spinning him backward to the ground. As soon as he hit the dirt, his instincts made him roll over and stop on his belly, his Colt stretched out in both hands.

He looked quickly in Hatton's direction and saw the smoking rifle come down from his shoulder. Fifty yards away, he saw Russell roll from his saddle, his rifle flying from his hand. The dead gunman bounced along the hard ground behind the running horse, his right foot stuck tight in his stirrup.

"Got him, Teacher, sir!" Hatton called out excitedly.

"That you did," Dahl said quietly to himself, rising to his feet and slapping dirt from the bib of his shirt.

Hatton rode forward to him quickly, looked down and said, "You're bleeding! Are you hit bad?"

"It's only a graze," Dahl said. "What's one more graze more or less?"

Hatton looked relieved. Then he considered what Dahl said, and chuckled and replied, "Yes, indeed, what is one more graze?"

Three miles away, Deputy Lane rode across a long bed of spindly wild grass and barrel cactus, toward the spot where he knew Bobby Candles would be riding into sight. But over the edge of a small rocky rise, Candles had already spotted him and dropped down from his saddle and taken a well-covered position. *It's about time you come to me, you idiot stable hand. . . .*

Candles smiled to himself, easing up enough to peep out through some dry brush and see Lane step down from his saddle a hundred yards away and slip his rifle into its boot—a bad mistake, Candles thought. *All right, Deputy. This time I'm the one with the rifle. Let's see how it goes. . . .*

Lane walked forward through the bracken and roughage until he stopped fifty yards away. He looked back and forth as if he hadn't come prepared for a fight, but rather to get his bearings. His Colt remained in his holster.

"Dumb fool is lost," Candles chuckled to himself under his breath. He continued to watch Lane look all around. Finally he said to himself, *All right, it's time I put you out of your misery. . . .* Without hesitation he cocked the rifle, jumped to his feet, took quick aim and pulled the trigger. The shot resounded out across the pass.

Three hundred yards down the trail up from the pass, Coots and Farris stopped their horses and sat in silence for a moment. It had been a while since they heard any shooting close to them. Neither of them said a word, but they nudged their horses forward warily, each with a rifle in hand.

Standing now, relaxing, with a grin on his face, Candles levered another round into his rifle chamber in case he needed it, which it now appeared he would not, he told himself. He watched Lane stand wobbling, bowed at the waist, his hand clamped to his belly.

"Bet that hurts like hell," Candles called out, walking forward, no hurry, no problem. He'd seen gut shots before. This one, coming from a rifle, would buckle the deputy's knees any minute. Lane would rock there for a few seconds, then pitch face-first in the dirt. *Pretty predictable*, Candles told himself. This poor, dumb bastard had no business ever wearing a badge. . . .

Lane stared at him through flat, blank eyes. When Candles stopped, the deputy dropped to his knees, as predicted. "Oops." Candles chuckled. He walked closer now that he saw it all going his way. "What's happening, stable hand, is that your belly is filling up with blood," he said casually. "You can hold it in awhile, but it just makes it worse—best if you just let it bleed on out." He grinned. "But don't let me tell you what to do."

Lane rocked back and forth as Candles propped his rifle back over his shoulder like a hunter returning from a long day in the field. He stopped twenty feet away and pushed his hat up and said, "What was you thinking, walking down here without your rifle? Letting me get that close? Giving me a shot like that? That was stupid. *Stupid, stupid, stupid!*" he ranted. "You gave me a damn near perfect shot!"

With his forearms across his lower belly, Lane said in a strained voice, "Guess, what, Newton?"

Newton, this fool still called him. . . . "Okay, what?" Candles grinned smugly.

Lane stopped rocking suddenly. "You missed," he said, the strain gone from his voice. His left forearm uncovered his right. His right hand swung forward from across his belly, a big Colt coming around cocked, firing round after round into Bobby Candles' chest. On the fifth shot, Lane stopped. He stood and walked forward. He cocked the Colt on its last shot and aimed it down between Candles' fading eyes. "I bet my life you couldn't hit a damn thing," he said, and he pulled the trigger.

When Coots and Farris topped the rise, leading their horses, rifles in hand, Lane saw them. But he stood with his hand chest high and said, "It's me, Eddie Lane. Don't shoot."

The two looked relieved and walked forward. They stopped and looked at Bobby Candles' bullet-riddled body and the bullet hole between his partially open eyes. "I bet he's deader than he ever thought he'd be," said Coots.

Lane nodded. "Yes, I got the one I was after," he said with relief. "What about you, did you get the man who shot your friend and his dog?"

"I put a bullet in him," said Coots. "Whether or not I killed him, I don't know." He nodded at Farris and said, "We got so busy keeping each other alive, I had to give up on my vengeance, let things run their course."

Lane nodded. "I understand. If you didn't kill Chester Goines, I've got a feeling Teacher did." He gave a nod in the direction where he'd left Dahl and Hatton. "Him and Hatton are up there a couple of miles back. I heard some shooting."

"What?" said Farris, looking surprised. "My employer is still alive?"

"Yes, I'm certain of it," said Lane. "Turns out you and he are both most capable men when it comes to taking care of ourselves."

"I have always liked to think I could stand the test if it were ever put upon me to do so," Farris said proudly.

"Let's go," said Coots. "Now that it's over, if we stand around too long we'll start talking too much about it."

"Yes, you're right, Mr. Coots," said Farris. "We must keep moving, in case any of these scoundrels are still alive and lurking about."

"Oh, I'm sure some got away," Coots said, swinging up easily into his saddle in spite of his many cuts, nicks and bullet grazes. "But they won't be wanting to tangle with us, I'll wager."

Farris swung up into his saddle as well and turned his horse in the direction Lane had pointed. Seeing Lane still standing on the ground, reins in hand, he said, "Deputy, will you be leading the way?"

"No," Lane replied, "you two go on. Teacher's not expecting me. He knew I was gone after this one." He nodded at Candles' body lying sprawled in the dirt. "Tell him it's done. Tell him adios for me," he said.

The two watched in respect as the deputy stepped into his saddle and rode away. Finally Carlton Farris said with a sigh, "Well, *that's that*, as they say." He took a deep breath and said, "Mr. Coots, will you think me terribly *odd* if I tell you I will miss all this?"

The teamster only stared at him for a moment; then he gave a faint grin as the two turned their horses and rode away.

Arizona Ranger Sam Burrack makes a roaring return—with his own special brand of justice! Don't miss a page of action from America's most exciting Western author, Ralph Cotton.

HANGING IN WILD WIND

Coming from Signet in August 2010

Vientos Salvajes, New Mexico Badlands

The first shot from the ranger's big Colt sent outlaw Morris Wheeler flying backward through the open door of the Belleza Grande Cantina. The sound of the gunshot sent people scrambling in every direction, emptying the busy dirt street. Even as Wheeler crashed down across a table filled with empty bottles, shot glasses and wooden cups, the ranger had already turned around, his smoking Colt poised and ready. He searched the street warily for his next target.

He saw no one, but he knew there were three others. He'd seen them before he'd even ridden into Vientos Salvajes. He had lain atop a rocky trail and watched the outlaws through his battered army telescope. He'd counted four of Silva "the Snake" Ceran's gang riding toward the bustling badlands town, each of them wearing a long tan riding duster and a broad-brimmed black hat. One of the four he'd recognized as the woman, Kitty Dellaros. The other three were Andy Weeks, Delbert Trueblood and Morris Wheeler. The men were noted thieves and murderers to the man.

He'd seen no sign of Silva Ceran himself, but he had an idea that the gang leader was somewhere nearby, lying low, letting his posse take all the heat that had been on their trail for more than two weeks, ever since the payroll robbery near the mining town of Poindexter.

The ranger stepped toward an alleyway that ran alongside the large cantina. From inside the alley a flock of frightened chickens burst forth in a flurry of batting wings, squawking above the pounding of hooves. Silva "the Snake" Ceran wasn't here, but in this deadly business, the young ranger had learned quickly to take what he could get.

These were Silva Ceran's people; there was no questioning that—a few of his people anyway, he thought. Riding with Ceran had become a popular pursuit among the swell of saddle trash who preyed on the citizens along both sides of the border.

The ranger knew very little about Kitty Dellaros other than her name and the reports that she'd been riding with Silva Ceran of late. As for the three gunmen, he knew them well enough. He'd been carrying around posters of their grim faces in his saddlebags for weeks. The three were desert outlaws from the old Sugar Blanton Gang. He also carried each man's name written down on a list that he carried in his vest pocket along with the battered stub of a lead pencil. He'd hoped to put his pencil to good use today.

As he turned to gather Black Pot, his Appaloosa stallion, he heard a voice call out from in front of the cantina, "Ranger, you must come quickly, *por favor*. This one is still alive." An elderly man jumped up and down in place, waving his long, bony arms to get the ranger's attention.

Still alive . . . ? The ranger looked surprised. But no sooner than the old man had spoken, a gunshot accompanied by a string of cursing and a crash of breaking glass erupted from inside the cantina. "Stay out here," the ranger said, giving the old man a quick once-over, making sure this was not a trick of some sort.

"Yes, of course. I will wait out here," the old man said.

Inside the darkened cantina, Morris Wheeler had dragged himself to his feet and managed to snag a young woman by her long black hair as she stood stunned, staring wide-eyed at him. He stood slumped against the bar, his bloody left hand entangled in the woman's hair, holding her against him. "You moved too slow, little *chick-chick*. Look what it got you. . . ."

"Please don't hurt me," the young woman said in a trembling voice.

"We'll see," Wheeler said, his voice strained and weakened. "You're taking me out of here, little missy. I die, you die. . . ."

"Turn the woman loose, Wheeler," the ranger called from inside the door.

Wheeler turned to face him, his Remington in his bloody right hand. "Or what, Ranger?" he growled. "You going to shoot me again?"

"Most likely," the ranger replied, his Colt leveled as he took a step forward.

"Getting shot don't matter much to me now," Wheeler said, gesturing with his gun down the front of his bloody shirt. "I'm shot to hell already."

"I can get you some help," the ranger said.

"Shit, you can," said Wheeler. "Look at me—I'm dead. You did this, you sonsabitch."

"It needed doing, Wheeler," said the ranger. "If it wasn't me, it would've been somebody else soon enough. We both know that."

The dying man considered it. "Yeah, I guess so." He gave a chuckle and shook his head. "Get out of here, darling," he said to the young woman, turning loose her hair and giving her a shove. "Next time ... don't stand around so long."

The young woman bolted away like a frightened deer.

"Now, as for you, Ranger ... ," Wheeler said. He cocked the Remington with his bloody thumb.

The ranger's Colt bucked once in his hand. The shot hit Wheeler an inch to the left of the bloody wound in his abdomen. The impact flung him in a full circle along the bar. He caught himself. "Gawddamn it," he said in a pained and outraged voice. "You did it again." He stood bowed at the waist.

"Drop the gun or I'll keep doing it," the ranger said with no remorse.

"Jesus, Ranger . . . you can't just shoot a man who's already—"

The ranger cocked his Colt. The sound caused the outlaw to stop and say, "Wait, damn it." His Remington slipped from his hand and landed with a hard thud on the floor. "There. Satisfied?"

"What about that help?" the ranger asked. He stepped forward, keeping an eye on the bowed outlaw's hand, which dangled near the top of his boot well.

"Don't do me no favors . . . ," Wheeler moaned.

"Suit yourself," said the ranger. He took a bottle of whiskey from the bar, uncorked it and held it out to the outlaw.

Wheeler gave him a curious look, but took the bottle from his hand. "Figure a little kindness will get me . . . to tell you where the Snake is?"

"I know where he is," said the ranger, keeping an eye on Wheeler's poised bloody hand. "He's at the end of whatever trail those three are on." He gave a gesture in the direction the other three outlaws had taken out of town.

"Smart sonsabitch," the dying outlaw growled under his breath. He managed to take a swig of whiskey without straightening. "You're that ranger they're all talking about—the one who killed Junior Lake and his gang." He looked up at the ranger's dusty silver-gray sombrero and added, "Sam something-or-other."

"Arizona Ranger Sam Burrack," the ranger said. "Yes, that's me."

"That figures." Wheeler gave a sneer of contempt. "I just wish I could see you once Trueblood and Weeks get done with you. . . ." His voice had grown weaker and had started to slur from the steady loss of blood.

"Are you going to die or what?" the ranger said coolly.

"Why, are you going to shoot me again?" Wheeler asked angrily.

"Might," said the ranger. "I want to get on your pals' trail." He watched the hand that was near the boot well.

"You want to get ahold of Kitty . . . like every other man does," said Wheeler. "I know what you want."

Since Wheeler brought up the woman, the ranger pursued the matter. "Is she the Snake's woman?"

"Ha—he thinks she is . . . ," Wheeler said. It sounded as if it was growing difficult for him to form his words. "She'll throw open her knees for . . . anything that's got a pecker. . . ."

The ranger nodded. "I've heard that.

Wheeler said with a suggestive tone, "I just bet you have."

"Are you going to die or what?" the ranger asked again.

"I'm going to. . . . Just shut up." Wheeler's bloody fingertips lowered inside the edge of the boot well. *Any second now*, the ranger told himself.

Wheeler's hand came up quickly, for a dying man. But the ranger was ready. *A knife . . . ?* He saw the bloody hand to raise up as Wheeler tried to stab the blade toward him. But in Wheeler's condition, the big knife slipped from his hand and fell to the floor.

Sam's boot stamped down onto the blade as Wheeler fumbled to try to grab it. "The shape you're in, you pull a knife?" Sam said. He pulled Wheeler up by his shirt and leaned him back against the bar.

"It's all . . . I had left," Wheeler said, sounding weaker, his eyes looking more and more distant. "You didn't leave me no choice . . . Arizona Ranger Sam *fucking* Burrack."

"I didn't come here bringing choices," said the ranger.

The three riders did not slow down until they topped a high ridge five miles from town. "Whoever it was, he ain't riding alone," Delbert Trueblood said, he and Weeks looking back across the flat stretch of land below. Tagging behind them, Kitty Dellaros nudged her limping horse up beside them.

"That's what I'm thinking too," Andy Weeks said to Trueblood, sounding winded, looking worried. "We're lucky we didn't run into them on our way out of town."

"Damn lucky," Trueblood agreed.

"It's one man," Kitty Dellaros said with disgust. She edged her horse a few feet away from them and stepped down from her saddle.

"Yeah?" The two gunmen looked at each other. "How the hell do you know that?" said Trueblood.

"I looked back," said Kitty. "You two sods could have looked back too, if you wasn't in such a hurry to run out on Wheeler."

"Watch your mouth," Weeks warned.

"We did look back," said Trueblood. "There's others waiting to trap us back there. Ain't you been listening to us?"

"I'm listening, but I'm not hearing anything," said the woman, pushing her hat brim up on her forehead. "I don't know how you sods ever made it this far."

"Call me that one more time," said Weeks, "and see if I don't kick your ass, same as I would a man."

"That goes for me too," said Trueblood.

The woman didn't answer, but she didn't take their threats too seriously. They didn't want her going to Ceran with complaints against them. Instead of replying she shook her head, raised her horse's front hoof and ran a gloved hand along its foreleg with a critical eye. "Easy . . . ," she purred when the horse resisted her touch.

The two outlaws nudged their horses over closer to her. "Is that horse going to make it?" Trueblood asked as he and Weeks stared at her from behind, taking pleasure in the sight of her even in the loose, ill-fitting riding duster.

"No," said Kitty. She lowered the horse's foreleg and patted the animal's hot muzzle. "This is as far as he goes." She raised a short-barreled Colt Thunderer from a holster beneath her duster. She held the shiny nickel-plated gun out at arm's length toward the horse's sweaty head.

"Don't even think about firing that gun," Weeks said quickly. "It's a dead giveaway where we are up here."

"What else can I do?" Kitty said with resolve, staring at the lame horse as if speaking to it instead of the outlaw.

"You can leave him," said Trueblood. "The critters

will make fast work of him tonight once they catch his scent."

"Yeah, right," Kitty said without turning her eyes from the horse. What he'd suggested was unthinkable. She took a deep breath.

Weeks shouted, "If you fire that damned gun, I swear to God I'll—"

She squeezed the trigger. The sound of her shot rolled out across land and sky. The big horse's knees buckled beneath him. He collapsed dead onto the rocky ground.

"Damn it to hell!" Weeks shouted, being cut short in the midst of his threat. "You are the most hardheaded bitch I have ever come across!"

"Shut up, Weeks," Kitty said. She swung the Thunderer toward him, not needing to cock the short double-action Colt. "I just killed a horse that I *liked*. Think what I'd do to a sonsabitch I can't stand."

Weeks' hand started to go toward the gun on his hip. But he stopped himself, seeing she had him cold.

"Both of yas settle down," said Trueblood. He raised his rifle from across his lap and held it loosely covering the two of them. "We're being dogged by somebody back there, whether it's one man or a dozen. This is no time for us to start falling apart."

"It's one man," Kitty insisted. "It's that ranger, Burrack, who killed Junior Lake and his gang." Her eyes and gun remained locked on Weeks.

"Burrack, huh?" said Trueblood. "How the hell do you know that?"

"Because I saw him riding in," Kitty said. "You two

wouldn't stop humping your whores long enough to look out the window when I told you too, else you would've seen him yourselves."

"How do you know Burrack?" Trueblood asked, looking suspicious.

"Jesus . . ." Kitty lowered the nickel-plated Thunderer and shook her head. She looked back along the trail that led across the flat desert land below. "I don't *know* Burrack. I saw him once in Yuma. He always wears that gray sombrero and rides that big Appaloosa. The horse belonged to Outrider Sazes until one of Junior Lake's boys stopped the Outrider's clock."

Trueblood and Weeks looked at each other questioningly. "You sure know a hell of a lot about the man for not knowing him."

"I want to know all I can about any sonsabitch who's out to kill me," Kitty said. As she spoke she let the Thunderer slump down along her side. "Anyway, we've got a problem," she added, gesturing the gun barrel toward the dead horse.

Weeks grinned. "The way I see it, you're the one with the problem. We've got saddles beneath us, ready to ride."

Kitty didn't answer. "Which one of you am I riding with?"

They both grinned. "What's in it for us?" asked Weeks.

"What's in it for you?" She pushed up her hat brim again. "How about this? I won't tell Silva that neither of you offered me a ride out of this hellhole after I lost my horse."

"The thing is," Weeks said, grinning, "if we leave

you afoot out here, we don't have to worry about what you tell the Snake—not ever again."

Kitty looked at the rifle in Trueblood's grip. Then she looked away for a moment, knowing he was right. When she looked back at the two outlaws her countenance had changed. She gave them both a coy smile. "All right, fellows, I think we all *know* what's in it for you. The question is, when and where?"

"It can't be soon enough for me," said Trueblood. "I got cut short back there with my whore."

"Yeah, me too," Weeks said with a hungry look in his eyes. "There's a water hole up ahead." He nudged his horse over, reached a hand down and helped her swing up behind his saddle. "I've been craving a piece of you for the longest time."

"Silva can't hear about us doing this," said Kitty, sitting behind him.

"Hear that, Weeks?" said Trueblood in a mocking tone. "Don't you ever tell the Snake what we're about to do." He nudged his horse forward on the narrow trail.

"What? Tell Silva Ceran we both crawled into his warm spot?" said Weeks. "Do I look that crazy to you?"

"A writer in the tradition of Louis L'Amour and Zane Grey!"
—*Huntsville Times*

National Bestselling Author
RALPH COMPTON

Available wherever books are sold or at penguin.com

S543

No other series packs this much heat!

THE TRAILSMAN

**Follow the trail of the gun-slinging heroes of
Penguin's Action Westerns at
penguin.com/actionwesterns**